Advance Praise for *The Marriage Bed*

"In *The Marriage Bed*, truths long hidden are revealed, not only in Asa, the grieving husband, but others affected by the tragedy at the novel's center. All are fully human in their flaws and strengths, including characters a lesser writer would depict as mere stereotypes. *The Marriage Bed* is an exceptional novel—perfectly paced, riveting, unrelentingly honest and wise in its depiction of what William Faulkner called 'the human heart in conflict with itself.' A remarkable achievement."

—Ron Rash, author of *Serena* and *The Caretaker*

"What a terrific novel this is. With scrupulous and warm honesty, it traces the intricacies of loyalty and betrayal in a long and loving marriage—and the shocks of life in a mortal body. A beautifully accurate book, with its own astute surprises."

—Joan Silber, author of *Improvement*,
Winner of the National Book Critics Circle Award

"Tommy Hays has long been one of my favorite writers working today, and *The Marriage Bed* only deepens my love for his fiction. No one can tell the stories of old love and young love and the inherent complications of both as well as Hays, and there's certainly no one who can tell them more poignantly."

—Wiley Cash, author of *A Land More Kind Than Home* and *The Last Ballad*

"Tommy Hays draws you into his fictional worlds like no other writer I know. In *The Marriage Bed*, Hays's most powerful novel yet, a freak accident shatters lives in all directions, exposing hidden fault lines. But the miracle of Hays's writing lies not in his description of the disaster—though the description is heart-stopping—but in the way he unearths a longing for connection from its ruins. Tommy Hays looks at our world with all its sense of shame and betrayal and wild hope and shows us how to love it. *The Marriage Bed* is a triumph."

—Abigail DeWitt, author of *News of Our Loved Ones*

"Tommy Hays has crafted a thoughtful novel that takes on troubling matters with his characteristic warmth and wit. *The Marriage Bed* is both heart-rending and life-affirming and treats all its characters with TLC. And it's a page-turner, too! This story is quality fiction from a quality author, and a true pleasure to read."

—Therese Fowler, author of *Z: A Novel of Zelda Fitzgerald*

"Tommy Hays's beautiful novel slyly leads us down circular tunnels and interstices of a family private life, where secrets lie waiting to erupt after tragedy hits. Asa Flowers has lost his wife in a freak accident, and in his struggle to escape marital betrayal, personal failures, and misgivings as a parent, finds himself drifting down a kind of modern River Styx—where Asa's adult son and daughter—at turns fierce and tender in their own grief—intercept and steer their father and themselves back toward the light."

—Jessica Keener, author of *Strangers in Budapest*

"Happy families are all alike—until misfortune strikes, things fall apart, and a story gets going. And what a story this is! Beautifully written, *The Marriage Bed* engages the reader's interest on every page as this once-happy family navigates toward a new order."

—Josephine Humphreys, author of
Rich in Love and *Nowhere Else on Earth*

THE MARRIAGE BED

THE MARRIAGE BED

Tommy Hays

— BLAIR —

Printed in Canada
Cover design by Laura Williams
Interior design by April Leidig

Blair is an imprint of Carolina Wren Press.

The mission of Blair/Carolina Wren Press is to seek out, nurture, and promote literary work by new and underrepresented writers.

We gratefully acknowledge the ongoing support of general operations by the Durham Arts Council's United Arts Fund and the North Carolina Arts Council.

This novel is a work of fiction. As in all fiction, the literary perceptions and insights are based on experience; however, all names, characters, places, and incidents are either products of the author's imagination or are used fictitiously. No reference to any real person is intended or should be inferred.

Library of Congress Cataloging-in-Publication Data
Names: Hays, Tommy author
Title: The marriage bed : a novel / by Tommy Hays.
Description: Durham : Blair, 2026.
Identifiers: LCCN 2025034302 (print) | LCCN 2025034303 (ebook) |
ISBN 9781958888636 hardcover | ISBN 9781958888704 ebook
Subjects: LCSH: Marriage—Fiction | LCGFT: Fiction | Novels
Classification: LCC PS3558.A875 M37 2026 (print) | LCC PS3558.A875 (ebook)
LC record available at https://lccn.loc.gov/2025034302
LC ebook record available at https://lccn.loc.gov/2025034303

To the memory of my friend Steve Baker,
beloved psychiatrist and lover of nature,
who knew trees and people like nobody's business.
And whose first question to me was always,
"How's the book going?"

I have so much of you in my heart.

—JOHN KEATS

These are the days that must happen to you.

—WALT WHITMAN

• • •

THE MARRIAGE BED

CHAPTER 1

Asa, Tuesday Evening

If Asa Flowers had known the mood he would find his wife in, he would have stayed at school and graded papers. Instead, he was on his way home, listening to the weather forecast on the radio. A system bringing rain and occasional wind gusts was moving up through Georgia and South Carolina and would arrive in the western North Carolina mountains by nightfall.

Asa pulled into the drive and well past the great shaggy hemlock that stood in the middle of the yard. The tree, under assault by aphids, had gotten bad about dropping limbs. He moved Betsy's Prius from under the tree and rolled up the windows.

As he came up the front walk, he noted the October air had turned unsettlingly balmy. Dark clouds drifted in, and the sky, although he couldn't say exactly how, looked unlike itself.

He found the front door ajar. Not a good sign. When Betsy was stressed, she left doors unclosed, tops unscrewed, and pretty much everything she came in contact with undone. Over the years he had learned it was a barometer of her mental state. He spent half his married life closing, locking, and putting things back. Inside, he'd set down his satchel that bulged with papers on Toni Morrison's *The Bluest Eye* and hung his jacket in the foyer when he heard Betsy out in the kitchen talking on the phone.

"How will I tell him?" Probably on the phone with Alice Stromquist, her longtime friend and fellow high school English teacher. When he walked into the kitchen, his wife wasn't on the phone. She sat at the table, reading what looked like a letter. Luna, their seventy-pound, gray-muzzled chow mix, greeted him and then returned to her bed in the corner of the kitchen.

"What's that?" Had his wife received one of the dreaded termination letters? He'd thought Betsy safe from cuts, having taught in the system for more than twenty years.

Looking distraught, she set the letter down. Damn. What would they do without her salary with two kids in college? He slid the letter over and began to read it—a form letter from AARP inviting Betsy to join.

"That's what this is about?" He slid it back across the table. "They send it to everybody who turns fifty. It's not the draft. You don't have to join."

His wife wasn't a hysterical person, but she'd gotten sensitive about her age. She was a striking woman, with high cheekbones and China blue eyes. People compared her to Joni Mitchell. Her long hair had streaked gray over the years and the crow's feet around her eyes deepened, but if you asked him, this made her beauty more substantial. Although he would have written *cliché* in the margin if it had appeared in one of his students' papers, he thought of her as a fine wine that had come into its own. Lately she'd been working out and taking more pains with her makeup.

The other night she'd lingered in front of her dresser mirror, tracing her finger around her mouth. "Think I should have a little work done?" She climbed into bed beside him.

"Are you kidding?" he said, surprised his wife would even consider such a thing. "You're beautiful the way you are."

"You're sweet." She smiled and kissed him.

"Besides, I doubt if our insurance covers it," he said. She frowned and turned off the lamp.

Now as he stood in the kitchen, watching his wife, he knew he'd wandered into treacherous territory. He could remind her that he'd joined AARP eight years ago. He could remind her that it was a sound organization. They did all kinds of important lobbying. He'd gotten $60 off their hotel room last month when they had gone to visit their daughter, Sarah, who was a junior at Chapel Hill.

Or he could distract her with an update on the latest installment of what he and Betsy had come to refer to as "The Misadventures of Quentin," Quentin being a former student of Betsy's at Asheville High who had made his wife's life miserable for the two years she taught him. Undaunted by low grades and stiff criticism in high school, Quentin was now an English major plaguing Asa's American Lit class. Quentin was convinced he could outwrite the entire American literary canon, and nothing anyone said or did could disabuse him of this notion. Today in class he'd dismissed Whitman as *Master of the Masturbatory*, a moniker the Bard himself might have gotten a kick out of.

One look at his wife's face and he knew he shouldn't say anything. How many times over the years had she said to him, "All I need is for you to listen."

He fished a beer out of the refrigerator and sat down across from her. She would talk at some length, consider all the angles, plumb all the depths. He'd sit tight, nod, and resist rushing in with answers. He noticed the dusty wine bottle on the kitchen counter. It usually sat on top of the kitchen cabinets, on a high shelf over the stove. The empty bottle, its dingy label mottled and half worn away, was an artifact from his proposal twenty-five years ago. Asa always forgot about the bottle until Thanksgiving or Christmas when he'd climb up on a stool to fetch down the big serving platter, the bottle sitting beside it. But now Asa couldn't help studying the bottle. What was it doing down from its perch?

He watched his wife. Women felt age more acutely. That wasn't to say that Asa hadn't noticed changes in his own aging reflection. His ears had reddened and veined, his nose grown bulbous, and his thinning hair migrated to his ears and eyebrows. He noted these changes with an almost scientific curiosity.

He remembered all the papers waiting for him. Then he wondered if Betsy had had a chance to read his new poems yet. He thought they were some of his strongest. What was she planning for supper? Hadn't she said something about salmon? He hoped she would make it the way she prepared it lately, searing it on high heat in the frying pan. But he noted there were no signs of her making dinner. She was usually well into cooking by the time he got home from work.

Betsy turned to him, looked him in the eye, and smiled a smile whose tenderness caught him off guard. What day was it? Only Tuesday, but who was he to protest weekday sex?

With an expression somewhere between regret and relief, she said, "I haven't been feeling like myself."

"Maybe the dosage is off again," he said. For some time, she'd applied a drop of estrogen cream to the inside of her wrist. Her doctor was forever adjusting the dosage.

"It's not menopause." She rubbed her hand along the table edge. "It's us."

"Us?"

She looked up. "I've found myself attracted to someone else."

He looked at her for a minute: *Found yourself?* He drank a long swig of beer. Outside the wind scratched a quince branch against the kitchen door, an animal clawing to get in.

"Someone else," he said finally. In third grade his friend Bill Parks had walked up to him and without warning and without any reason Asa ever learned, socked him so hard in the stomach he couldn't breathe.

"Listen," Asa said, pressing down on the kitchen table as if it was about to fly away. "Listen," he repeated, but couldn't think of anything to say. "All couples go through this empty nest syndrome." Yes, those were the words people used. Weren't they?

"Asa . . ."

"I don't think it's all that unusual, being attracted to someone else," he went on. "When it comes down to it, everybody's attracted to everybody. Right?" Hearing himself, he knew he'd made absolutely no sense.

"I'm talking deep down in my bones attracted," she said.

Asa noticed his wife's ears. How had he never really seen them before? Surely, he must've. They were so delicate looking, shiny crescents of shell canted just enough so that they peaked out from beneath her long hair. The more he looked at them, the stranger they appeared, fragile yet self-contained pieces of his wife.

Asa took another swig of the beer and tried to refocus. He felt shaken, the tectonic plates of their marriage shifting. Out of the corner of his eye, he saw something dart across the kitchen floor, and Luna went over and sniffed around the oven.

"What does this mean, Betsy?" How strange to speak her name, as if she were a student he'd called on in class.

A gust rattled the windows.

"Who is he?" Asa tried to keep his voice steady.

Betsy reached across the table as if to hold his hand, but instead grabbed his beer, took a sip, and slid the bottle back. "It's not a he."

A siren started up somewhere in the distance.

He sat up in his chair. "You're attracted to women? I mean . . . Really? Women?" He shook his head in disbelief. It was strange enough that his wife was interested in someone else, but the fact that it was a woman took it to a second level of strange.

"You're such a Four," she said. Ever since she had gone on that Enneagram retreat, Betsy talked about everyone, including him, in a shorthand of numbers. He learned that a Four meant, among other things, overly dramatic. *This was overly dramatic?* he thought. Suddenly he felt perfectly calm, as if none of this had anything to do with him.

"I've been having feelings," she said.

"For women?" he asked quietly.

"One woman."

"Alice?" he asked. It had slipped out, but it made sense. Alice and Betsy had been friends for as long as Asa could remember.

She shook her head.

"But still a teacher?" He kept an even tone, feeling like a therapist with his client.

"What is this helping, Asa?" she said.

"So, it is a teacher," he persisted, but gently.

The windows rattled again.

"How long have you been having these feelings?" He tapped his fingers together.

"We've been friends for years, but this past year it began to be more than that."

His calm vanished; he could feel the pulse in his neck. "When we've been making love, have you been thinking about whoever she is?"

"Of course not."

"When we have sex," he said, "have you been faking all that?"

"No more than usual," she said.

He let his head drop. He could feel the bile rise in his throat.

"I enjoy the physical closeness with you," she said. "But I'm not aroused."

"What about the other night on the couch?" He gestured toward the living room.

"A change of venue is not what I need." She narrowed her eyes at him.

"If this is about the facelift, I can always pick up an extra class or two."

She looked at him with what felt like pity.

Then it hit him. "You want a divorce! That's it, isn't it?"

Tears sprung to her eyes. "Why would you say that?"

A vague thought formed in a dim corner of his mind. "You're having an affair."

She paled.

"You had to think about it," he said.

"I'm not having an affair." She looked away.

"You didn't say that with conviction."

"Nothing's really happened." She cleared her throat.

"An emotional affair, an affair of the heart," he said.

So, he thought, *this is what it feels like to step off a cliff.* Never had Asa imagined he would have a conversation like this with Betsy. Their marriage seemed solid, and while, like many couples, they had rough patches, especially during Mitchell's roiling high school years, nothing had ever risen to the level of threat.

"I'm not giving you my permission if that's what you're asking." He crossed his arms.

"I don't need your permission," she snapped.

Out the window, the sky had gotten darker still. Nothing made sense. He was tired, but so much more than that. Bone-weary. Exhaustion like a fast-moving infection inhabited every fiber of his being.

It had only been a few minutes, but already he was nostalgic for his old life, the life of last night and all the nights before when he would come home to dinner, talking over their day as they ate, she putting away leftovers and he doing the dishes, afterwards them on the couch grading papers or preparing their classes, then she leaning back against him as they watched an episode of *Doc Martin* or *Endeavor*.

"I couldn't not tell you," she said.

He thought about their kids. Sarah, the college junior, and Mitchell, a year younger and a sophomore at a small liberal arts college down in South Carolina. It was Mitchell, their volatile, depressive boy, this news could derail.

"What'll we tell the kids?"

"Why tell them anything?" she said. "This is between us."

"At some point we'll have to tell them, and family and friends." He felt that old calm again, as if the tide had just gone out.

"Stop it," she said. "You're doing what you always do."

"Which is?" he asked.

"Catastrophizing."

How could she say this was catastrophizing, he thought? *It's not catastrophizing if it's a catastrophe.* "Do you intend to act on your feelings?"

"We don't need to tell anybody anything, and if eventually we need to talk to the kids, we'll cross that bridge when we come to it." She looked up at him.

It made him feel sick that she'd already thought about what they would do.

"Do you intend to act on your feelings?" he asked.

"This is something I need to explore," she said.

"You sound like you're setting off on an expedition," he said.

"Fuck you, Asa. I'm trying to talk to you." The phone rang in the hall. Betsy started to answer it, but he took her hand.

"Let it ring, for God's sake." He despised his pleading tone.

"It might be someone about the apartment," she said. "We've had a few calls already. One student said he read a lot of graphic novels and but wasn't sure that qualified as being well read. Did you put that in the ad again?"

What difference could that possibly make? But he answered her: "It raises the quality of applicants."

"It discourages potential tenants." She sat back down but kept looking in the direction of the ringing phone. "You don't want to rent it."

Asa started to answer the phone, but blessedly it stopped ringing.

"Asa," she said.

"Yes?"

The phone began to ring again. Betsy looked off in its direction. Asa knew their talk would go no further till he answered it. When he picked up the receiver, he heard operator chatter in the background.

Finally, a man's voice came on the line, "Mr. Flowers?"

"Yes?"

"This is the North Carolina Democratic party."

"No."

"You've been so generous in the past."

He slammed down the receiver and started back into the dining room, but then the phone rang again. He snatched up the receiver. "I wouldn't give you a dime if they gerrymandered this state to hell and back!" He was about to slam the receiver down when he heard a familiar voice.

"Asa?"

"Yes?"

"Hi, Asa, this is Charles . . . Charles Byrd."

He covered his face with his hand. "My apologies, Charles. I thought you were a telemarketer."

"Remind me never to try to sell you anything," Charles said, and in the long pause that followed Asa wondered why he was calling. Probably wanting to talk Asa into joining the reaccreditation committee.

"What's up, Charles?" Asa asked.

"With the weather, I wondered if we're still on."

"Still on?"

"For dinner tonight."

Then Asa remembered. They were supposed to have him over tonight. Charles's wife died three months ago, and the English department faculty had gotten together to take turns having him over to dinner. Tonight was Asa's turn.

"If tonight isn't good with the weather . . ." Charles said.

It wasn't good. Tonight might be the worst night of his life. Even so, the man's wife had just died. Plus, Melda Stern, the department chair, would ask Asa how it went.

"It's not supposed to get worse till later," Asa said. "And Betsy has a nice meal planned."

"Can I bring anything?" Charles asked.

"A bottle of wine?"

"I don't drink," he said.

"Maybe you should start."

Silence on the other end.

"You don't need to bring anything," Asa said, recovering himself.

"Seven o'clock still good?" Charles asked.

"If you could come later that would give us another half hour." He looked back toward the kitchen.

"You said the weather is supposed to get worse later," Charles said. "Maybe we should forget the whole thing."

Clearly Charles wanted to forget the whole thing, and Asa himself would have loved to forget the whole thing. But he didn't want to give Melda ammunition.

"Come at seven," Asa said. "Looking forward to it."

After he hung up, he looked out the window at the swaying trees. Melda Stern had had it in for Asa since he let slip that he no longer read his student evaluations. He stopped after years of working his butt off for his students, then being rewarded at the end of the semester by sitting down with student evaluations. While most were usually positive, occasionally one or two would be angry or even downright vicious. It was upsetting, even though he knew the vicious ones were usually from weak students resentful about low grades. Evaluations were anonymous, but he could usually tell who wrote the angry ones by how poorly they were written. Bad writers, he discovered, wrote badly in their own way. Nevertheless, he dreaded reading them at the end of every semester. The last straw was when an old friend who taught at a university in Tennessee and suffered from crippling depression shot himself one afternoon after reading his student evaluations.

Betsy came up beside him. "So I have a nice meal planned, do I?" She raised her eyebrows at him. "Tonight?"

"In half an hour." He braced himself for a well-deserved tongue-lashing, but by the way she chewed her lip he could see she was already figuring it out.

"I'll call him back and tell him tonight isn't good," he said.

She waved her hand dismissively. "The man just lost his wife."

Asa started to follow her back to the kitchen, but it thundered, and he detoured to the front window as lightning flickered. He heard Betsy in the kitchen, getting out pots and pans. They were going through with the dinner. Even with catastrophe loose in the house, they were going to go through with ordinary life and talk about ordinary things. That's what late middle age was. Right? Going through certain motions, regardless.

The hemlock swayed. He'd had Henry, their arborist, spray it, but it hadn't done much good. He told them it was time to take the tree down, but Betsy wanted to keep the tree as long as possible. It had overseen their children grow up, she said, and was part of the family. They chose their house in part because of the hemlock which, twenty-five years ago, was a lush, healthy tree shading the yard and the house. Lately, it looked to Asa that a good third of the tree might be dead. He'd called Henry to come out and take a look, but he never heard from him. He'd check in with him tomorrow.

In the kitchen Asa found Betsy looking through the refrigerator. "A baguette and plenty of romaine for salad. We'll be fine." She began chopping up carrots and mushrooms for the salad. "If you'll put the rice on."

He dug the rice out of the pantry, measured two cups of water into a little worn pot, set it on the stove, and waited for it to boil. There was no more talk about the other woman. The only sign of how deep this went was that Betsy hadn't gotten angry at him.

He picked up the old wine bottle on the counter.

"I was feeling nostalgic." She refilled the salt and pepper shakers, setting them on the table.

The rice boiled over on the stove, and as he turned down the flame and covered it, he realized this battered little pot was the sole survivor of a copperware set that had been a wedding present.

CHAPTER 2

Asa, Tuesday Evening

Charles Byrd was such a private person it was difficult to determine how well he was coping with his wife's death. Asa felt for him. Poor guy had probably been subjected to more socializing in the past couple of months than in the last thirty years.

"Some days are better than others," Charles said in reply to Betsy's question, then took another bite of salmon.

"I'm sure," Betsy said. She'd done most of the talking throughout dinner for which Asa was grateful. So when Asa passed Charles the salt and salt spilled all over the table, Asa wasn't irritated. It said something about his own distracted state that he'd broken the golden rule when it came to living with his wife: Never pick up any container by the top that Betsy might've come in contact with.

Betsy had been good friends with Charles's wife Isabelle—a lively, funny woman and a sanguine sociology professor. Charles and Isabelle were among the initial handful of Black faculty hired at Altamont College in the mid-eighties, several years before Asa was hired. Isabelle had clearly loved Charles, always hugging and kissing him, and Asa knew Charles, who would give in to smiles whenever she was around, had loved Isabelle in his own reserved way.

"Luna, stop pestering Charles," Asa said as the dog sniffed Charles's trousers. Luna liked guests, had greeted Charles when he first arrived, and followed him around ever since.

"She probably smells our cats," Charles said, petting Luna. "What a good dog."

"Except when it comes to chihuahuas and other little yappy dogs," Asa said.

"Oh?" Charles said.

"Luna is great with people," Betsy said, "especially children. She's very gentle and tolerant, but nervous little dogs . . ." She exchanged a look with Asa.

"She's sent two dogs to the vet," Asa said. "Setting us back thousands."

"Hard to believe," Charles said.

Asa told Charles they'd gotten Luna when the children were younger. They adopted her from a farmer, who had found her and a couple of other malnourished puppies wandering his field.

"After we adopted Luna," Betsy said, "as sweet as she was, she was very strong, too strong for the children, so either Asa or I would walk her."

"She was always pulling on the leash," Asa said. "Every time I walked her, I'd lose my temper."

"That's how Luna became my dog," Betsy said.

"Not that she hasn't sent you to the chiropractor half a dozen times," Asa couldn't help adding. He didn't say that he blamed his wife, at least in part, for Luna's attacks on those little dogs, because of her relaxed attitude about keeping Luna on the leash.

He noticed the dog still sniffing Charles's trousers. He opened the back door that led out to their fenced-in backyard, making sure the gate was closed. Luna paused on the doorstep, looking out at the windy night. "Go on," Asa said, shooing her out the door.

As soon as he sat back down, Asa knew putting the dog out had been a mistake. Luna had given them something to talk about. The silence they'd worked so hard to keep at bay settled over them. Asa had no choice.

"So, Charles," he said, "tell us about the book you're working on."

The way Charles straightened in his chair reminded Asa of that expression *Who put a nickel in you?* "I'm revisiting the work of Paul Dunbar and researching how his poetry shaped and continues to shape American poetry."

Simple enough, thought Asa, comprehensible and interesting. Asa had always included a poem or two by Dunbar in his survey of American lit, but he didn't know his work as well as he would have liked.

"I'm recontextualizing Dunbar's poetry, especially his dialectic poems, in terms of the metaphysical constructs and hierarchical oppositions of the nineteenth century."

Asa nodded, having only a vague idea of what Charles had said.

Then off Charles went, becoming far more animated, using the polysyllabic wordage Asa himself had used in his own scholarly papers and books over the years—the numbing language of tenure. He'd lost his tolerance for the big words and small-mindedness of his profession, but tonight he appreciated every solipsistic syllable. It kept Charles talking and gave Betsy time to make the decaf and serve the dessert, and time for Asa to polish off a third glass of wine.

The more he drank, the more difficult it was to keep Betsy's confession at a safe operating distance. How could he sit here and eat tiramisu when his world was imploding? Widower or no, Charles needed to go home so he and Betsy could get to the bottom of this. From the drowning look in Betsy's eyes, Asa knew she was thinking the same.

Charles seemed to have grown comfortable at their table, and the fact that both Asa and Betsy had stopped talking didn't seem to register with him. After all, here was a man who spent most waking hours ensconced in the stacks of university libraries.

Eons passed, and then as Charles contined to hold forth, the mouse shot from under the oven, across the kitchen floor, under Charles's chair, and veered into the living room. Betsy suppressed a smile. She'd seen the mouse too. Not long after the mouse's escape, Luna barked at the back door, and Asa got up to let her in. This loosened Charles from his mooring. He pushed back his empty plate and said, "I better go."

"At least the rain has stopped," said Asa, helping Charles with his coat.

Charles thanked them for the meal and petted Luna again. Then he flipped his collar up against the wind and turned to them. "I miss so many things, but you know what I miss most? Working the crossword with her over breakfast." Thanking them again, he walked down the drive, climbed into his little English Ford, and drove away.

• • •

"Thanks for pulling a meal together so last minute." Asa rinsed dishes and set them in the drain.

"It's really sad, isn't it?" Betsy put away the food.

He scrubbed burnt rice from the bottom of the little copper pot. "He's difficult to read."

"I don't think so," she said.

Outside the wind blew.

"I almost lost it when that mouse ran under his chair," she said.

"Apparently the mouse isn't a Dunbar fan. I'll dig the Havahart out of the basement."

When he put the garbage bag in the container by the side of the house, the trees swayed and fall leaves showered from the sugar maples. Had his earlier conversation with Betsy been a figment of his imagination? Some strange out of time dialogue he'd had with himself? All during Charles's visit, she'd appeared her same wifely self, laughing at a joke Asa made, reaching across the table and squeezing his hand. When they told Luna's story, they worked as a team, as they often did in social situations.

Perhaps all the talk about this other woman was a waking dream, a nightmare sent by his deeper self to remind him how much Betsy meant to him. He felt a little lighter when he went back inside and found her wiping the kitchen counter.

"We should get dressed up and go to that new tapas place downtown that everybody raves about," he said. "What's it called?"

She stopped and looked at him.

"That place below Malaprops," he said. "Zambras? I'll call them tomorrow and make a reservation."

She came over, gave him a long hug, then held him at arm's length. "We've kissed a few times."

He felt his stomach drop. "You said nothing happened."

"I meant we haven't slept together."

"Why now? After all these years?"

"I guess with the kids off at school and Mitchell better..." She looked up at him. "It's somehow freed up some part of myself I wasn't in touch with."

The wind moaned down the chimney, bringing with it the dry smell of soot.

"Is it Rosemary Brown?" He had been going through teachers in his head, teachers he could imagine his wife being attracted to. "Or Charlene Bolton? Is it Charlene?"

"I'm not the woman you married," she said.

He sat down in the kitchen chair, his mind having blanked on him.

"Neither are you the man I married," she said.

"What's that supposed to mean?"

"Asa, you've gotten cranky, depressive, and isolated," she said. "You never want to go anywhere or do anything. Even Charles is willing to risk going over to people's houses for dinner, and by himself, I might add." A dam had burst in his wife. "You, on the other hand, seem to care about little except whether we've gotten our flu shots or our mutual funds are adequately funded or if the paper carrier has thrown the paper into the abelias again." She shook her head in exasperation. "The older you've gotten, the more negative and judgmental you've become," she said. "You live a tight little life, Asa, and sometimes I find myself wondering, where did the man I married go? Where did my Walt Whitman go?!" She sounded at her wit's end.

Another moan down the chimney.

"Lately, I've felt like nothing more than a series of irritations to you," she said in a quieter voice. "It's like living with Silas Marner."

Of course, she chose the George Eliot novel. She assigned it every year to her tenth-grade honors students.

He plucked a little twig out of her hair and handed it to her.

"Did you even hear me?" she said, examining the twig, as if it were a clue.

"Is this about my writing?" He worried that even though she'd been so supportive of his writing, she might resent all the time it took away from being with the family.

"This is not about your writing." She looked him in the eye.

"Are you sure?" Several of his married writer friends talked about tension with their spouses who couldn't understand their partner's need to spend a portion of each day alone writing.

"I fell in love with your writing before I even knew the writer," she said. "I've always loved that you write because it makes you happy, and it's a big part of who you are."

"What is it then?"

"When I think about it, all those things I said about you have always been part of who you are. Maybe over the years you've gotten to be more like yourself. Maybe that's true for me too. All I know is that I have to find out about this."

"About you and her?"

A large thud shook the house and for a moment he thought a big limb had fallen.

"What on earth?" Betsy asked.

Asa went out the front door and found one of the heavy rocking chairs overturned by the wind.

Back inside, he put on his coat, picked up his satchel, and opened the back door.

"Where are you going?" she asked.

"I have to get these papers read."

"Don't go back out in this," she said. "Read them at the kitchen table."

"I need to get these papers back by tomorrow," he said as he headed to the back door. Luna followed him.

"Don't leave when I'm trying to talk to you." Betsy grabbed his arm, sounding angry and, at the same time, desperate.

"We've been talked to enough tonight, me and Silas," he said. He started to leave but then whirled around. "This is awful, Betsy. Really, really awful and makes me feel like a fool. And it's so fucking embarrassing!"

"I haven't told a soul."

"I'll be sleeping out there too."

"I'm the one causing all the trouble," she said. "Sleep in the bedroom, and I'll sleep on the couch."

"I'm surprised you would want to sleep in the same house as Silas Marner," he said.

"Don't be like this," she said.

"Once a misanthrope always a misanthrope."

"Asa, there's no place to sleep out there. The bed's not even made."

"Is the person in question a teacher?"

"Stop it," she snapped.

"She knows who I am, right?"

He stepped out into the yard. The wind had died some, but the air felt heavy, portentous. He opened the gate and started up the little lighted path beside the drive that led to the renovated garage apartment. Then he walked back to where Luna stood beside Betsy at the open gate.

"She's wondering where you're going," Betsy said.

"How could you?" Asa said.

"I hate how this has turned so melodramatic," Betsy said. "Please, come back. I don't want to leave it like this." Then she took his arm. "I will always love you, no matter what happens."

"What might happen?"

The trill of a screech owl carried across the backyard as Asa looked into the shadows of his wife's confused face.

"Are you going to have sex with her?" Asa asked.

When she didn't answer, he pulled away. As he walked out to the studio, he felt her watching him. He turned back around. "I was never anything like Walt Whitman."

"You were in your heart."

When he tried the studio door, it was locked. Then he remembered the key underneath an empty flowerpot. Unlocking the door, he walked in, turned on a light, shut the door, and listened to his pulse throb in his ears.

He had their garage converted to a studio office a couple of decades ago when they first moved in and he needed a place to work. Then this year, with them struggling to pay Mitchell's tuition, Betsy suggested they turn his office into an apartment. Even though they needed the money, Asa had been reluctant to give up his office. With Mitchell and his distracting energy out of the house, he didn't mind reading papers at their kitchen table, and Betsy often would join him, preparing her classes. After the kids had gone, he and Betsy enjoyed a new privacy that brought them closer together.

Or so he thought.

He looked around the studio. Bookcases crammed with books lined two walls. Two bookshelves were devoted to contemporary poetry, and more than half the books belonged to Betsy, who had the larger poetry collection when they met. Another couple of bookshelves of textbooks, anthologies, and books related to teaching. One bookshelf of his own poetry—small lit journals and magazines he'd published in over the years, as well as his books and chapbooks he published with one university press or another every few years as well as dozens of his notebooks. Most of his poems had been written in the studio.

His eye fell on *In Captivity*, his first collection, published back in grad school before he and Betsy met. He pulled a copy off the shelf and blew the dust off. He started to open it but decided against it.

Asa turned on the baseboard heat to take the chill off, then set his stack of papers on the little kitchen table. He put on the kettle and looked through the cabinets in search of a box of tea bags he kept out here. As he went over what had been revealed to him tonight, the anger and hurt reminded him of the unopened bottle of wine he kept in the back of the cabinet. But he already had a headache from the wine he'd had with dinner, and besides he'd promised his students their papers. He made himself a cup of tea.

He was sitting down to his papers when his phone rang. He saw it was Betsy. "I don't feel like talking about it anymore tonight."

"This isn't about that," she said. "Sarah called today with some news."

"I've had enough news for one day."

"This is good news."

"What?"

"She wants to be the one to tell you," she said.

"Okay." Why was she notifying him that their daughter was going to call him? It wasn't unusual for Sarah to call him. Now if it were Mitchell calling, that would have been unusual.

"When she does call," Betsy said, "please try to sound excited."

"What a strange thing to say."

"We need to be supportive."

"I'm supportive. Aren't I?"

"She's gotten a summer fellowship to the University of Copenhagen. The Niels Bohr Institute. It's a big deal."

"Oh wow," he said. "I have to say I'm not surprised. She's one smart cookie." Sarah had fallen in love with physics her sophomore year and never looked back.

"She thinks you'll say it's too far."

"Denmark is far."

"It's only for a couple of months. She doesn't think you'll be excited for her. We need to be excited for her."

"I understand," he said, "And it *is* a big deal."

"Another thing," Betsy said. "Josh is not being supportive and doesn't want her to go."

"What does she see in him?" he said.

If there was one thing he and Betsy agreed on, it was what a lame boyfriend Josh was. In fact, *lame* was too generous a word for the poor excuse of a boyfriend Josh was.

"He told her she had to choose between him and the fellowship," Betsy said.

"Did he?" He felt himself smile.

"He did indeed." He felt Betsy smile.

"In that case I'm over the moon about this fellowship," he said.

Betsy laughed. "I thought that might bring you around."

He laughed again, and then they were quiet. He knew she sensed it as well, the strangeness of carrying on a conversation and even laughing as their marriage might be ending.

After a moment he said, "I haven't made a dent in these papers."

"I don't like that you're sleeping over there." Her voice had gone softer.

"What are you saying?" He held the phone to his ear, listening to her breathe.

Finally he said, "We can talk in the morning."

"Okay." She sounded disappointed.

"Good night." He hung up.

For a moment, he sat trying to take in what had transpired in the last few hours. How strange, he thought, that their marriage might very well be ending, yet they could go in and out of the subject while at the same time seeing to things they'd always seen about.

As he plowed through the papers, occasionally he would get a faint whiff of something unpleasant. He traced the odor to a vase of chrysanthemums Betsy had set out on the kitchen counter to brighten the apartment, reminding him again that they had to rent out the studio.

Even though it had been a considerable strain on their finances, they sent Mitchell to Furman, a small Baptist school with a strong art department where he connected with the art professors and a handful of art students. Unlike in high school, he worked hard, thrived in the art department, and spent hours each day in the studio. He was a very different student than he had been. No longer was he depressed, at least not in the way he was in high school.

Spring semester, in her weekly Sunday night phone conversations with Mitchell, Betsy had gotten the distinct impression he was happy, and she suspected there was a girl behind it. Ordinarily a mother might simply ask her son if he had a girlfriend. Getting information out of Mitchell was a waiting game that required patience and restraint as well as a kind of feigned inverse attentiveness in which the information you sought was most likely to present itself when Mitchell didn't suspect you were seeking it. One day, Betsy was on the phone with him when out of the blue Mitchell mentioned someone named Wendy. Since then, he'd mentioned her only a handful of times, but Betsy sensed her presence.

After finishing grading a few of the papers, Asa made himself another cup of tea. Over the years he measured his paper grading, not in Eliot's coffee spoons, but in tea bags. He allowed himself a cup of tea after every three or four papers unless a paper was especially bad, which might require a couple of cups to work his way through. As a student, he remembered getting papers back from professors with nothing but a grade. His best teachers thoroughly marked up his papers and gave a lot of written feedback. Asa tried to do the same. What he really loved about teaching was being in the classroom with his students. Over the years, his teaching evolved to less lecture and more discussion. He talked less and listened more. He loved listening to his students arrive at new places in their thinking, surprising themselves with their own insights. Each class period became its own journey, one in which Asa never knew where they might end up.

Waiting for the kettle to boil, he looked out the window toward the house. Betsy had turned out the downstairs lights, leaving only their upstairs bedroom light on. He saw Luna's shadow in the bedroom window. When Asa looked over to the house later, the bedroom light was off too. He knew what Betsy meant about feeling freed up with Mitchell doing better. He felt freed up too. A weight that they both felt for the last few years had been, if not completely lifted, lightened. Asa wrote more poems, put more energy into his classes, and enjoyed being with his wife in a way he hadn't in years. It appeared they'd gone in different directions with their freedom.

The wind started up again, and thunder rumbled in the distance. Asa turned on WCQS, Asheville's public radio station that played jazz late at night. The announcer read the weather report in his mellow voice: "Looks like thunderstorms with occasional gusts will continue into the early hours. So batten down whatever hatches you may possess, then sit back and let me, your host, Jamal Williams, keep you company on *Round Midnight*, Asheville's only jazz programming." He played Lena Horne singing "Stormy Weather." Over the years, Asa had stayed up many a night reading or grading papers to Jamal Williams and his soothing music.

Asa didn't finish the papers until one in the morning. Like Betsy had said, the bed had no sheets. The little couch, a new love seat she bought to replace the pull-out sofa that dated back to their Atlanta days, was small and nearly impossible to sleep on. He curled up as best he could on the love seat, pulling a comforter over him. Lightning flickered and thunder rumbled. From where he lay, he could look up at their darkened bedroom. All these years of marriage and never had anything like this come between them.

He slept fitfully, waking to rattling shutters and the wind in the trees. He lay there going through all the possible teachers, and it occurred to him maybe it was Alice Stromquist after all. Even if she was matronly and loud, and he himself would have never been attracted to her, she was a thoughtful, kind, and genuinely good person. The idea of his wife being attracted to a woman made him feel less to blame. After all, he could be a lot of things, but he couldn't be a woman.

Unable to sleep, he rummaged through his satchel, found a bottle of sleeping pills, took a couple, then inserted earplugs he kept in a little side pocket. He had bought them at an American Lit conference in D.C. where he'd been kept up by a couple of rowdy Benjamin Franklin scholars in the next room.

He was climbing back into bed when his eye fell on the copy of *In Captivity* he had left out. If anything could put him to sleep this should. He flipped through the pages, pausing to read a line or two here and there. It wasn't his best work, but he felt fondly toward the book for bringing Betsy to him so many years ago.

He'd been thinking about Betsy's, *Where'd my Walt Whitman go?* She called him that in their early years out of affection and a gentle teasing, or so he'd always assumed, because his own reserved, reticent, and often downright taciturn nature was nothing like the Bard of Democracy's effusive, gregarious, sensual, boundless cosmic consciousness. Now he wondered if Betsy had been more sincere than he'd understood when she called him her Walt Whitman. Had it been without irony? How else to explain her words to him tonight: "You were in your heart." It surprised him and saddened him all at once. Surprised that she must've meant it all these years and saddened that she had used the past tense.

CHAPTER 3

• • •

Asa, Spring 1991

Asa had come down from Chapel Hill to the University of Charleston for a job interview, his first. His individual interviews with faculty and administrators went well, and he felt good about his demonstration class on Whitman's Lincoln elegy, "When Lilacs Last in the Dooryard Bloom'd." But that evening Asa sensed something amiss when two graduate students he recognized from his demonstration class had shown up at his motel instead of the faculty who were supposed to take him to dinner.

One was a loquacious heavyset man named Trip, a good ten years older than Asa and most interested in talking about Charleston cuisine, and the other was a quiet, distracted woman who never said her name. With her cheekbones and her electric blue eyes, she could've been Joni Mitchell's little sister. Asa guessed her to be a few years younger than him. She wore a skirt that showed off her legs and a blouse unbuttoned just enough that he felt his gaze being tugged all evening.

Adding to Asa's misgivings was the fact that in spite of Trip's monologue on Charleston's legendary restaurants, they ended up at a Chinese buffet called The Peekin' Duck, that had a neon sign out front of a Daffy-Duck-like-duck pressed against a wall peeking around a corner. Trip held forth through the meal, while the woman, who didn't say two words, occasionally tossed Asa a bored smile, obviously wishing she was anywhere else. The whole meal depressed the hell out of him, and on top of that, the place didn't serve alcohol.

They dropped him back off at the Harbor View Lodge, an old, slightly shabby but not unkempt motel that at one time must've offered a view of the harbor until it had been walled in by high-rise hotels and gleaming office buildings. On his way to his room, he passed two long-haired young men sitting in the bed of a pickup, drinking beer and discussing what Asa was pretty sure was Kierkegaard. They shared a bucket of Kentucky Fried Chicken, which would've been better than the tired chicken chow mein he'd pushed around on his plate tonight.

He laid his hand on the hood of his gleaming Corolla station wagon he'd parked in front of his room so he could keep an eye on it. He couldn't really afford a new car but had given it to himself to celebrate finishing his dissertation. Now, with this job possibility feeling less than a sure thing, he wondered if he'd jumped the gun.

When he walked into his room, he flipped the light switch, and the fluorescent lights clicked and flickered on, casting the room in cold light. The place faintly exuded stale curry. He couldn't get used to how unsettlingly big the room was, made more so by its scant furnishings pushed against the room's perimeters. A modest dresser occupied one wall, a lonely table with a single straight chair (the only chair in the room) stood against the opposite wall, and across from the bed, on the whole other side of the room, perched a small TV that would have required binoculars to watch from the bed.

He sat on his made bed and stared at the distant TV that he

didn't have the heart to turn on. He wondered what he had said or done wrong. Maybe he hadn't included enough discussion. Maybe he had overprepared and hadn't allowed enough time for questions. He had been counting on this job to get him out of Adjunctville. He checked his wallet to see if he had enough cash for a six pack. He had seen a 7-Eleven down the street. When he opened his door, the woman grad student stood there, Trip nowhere in sight.

A wolf whistle came from the direction of the philosophers in the truck.

She brushed past him into his room. "It's like some weird sixties time warp. I never knew this place was here."

"She speaks," he said.

"Oh, that." She rolled her eyes. "Trip has a way of sucking the air out of a room. I can hardly think when I'm around the man."

"Do you have a name?"

"Betsy. And what's up with this room?"

"It's not so bad," he said, not wanting word to get back to the department that he was in any way a complainer.

"Would you like to go for a drink?" she said.

"I was heading out in search of a six pack," he said.

"Oh, God! Don't drink alone, especially in here." She cast a disparaging eye around the room. "You might get lost." She turned to him. "Come out with me. Charleston is at its best at night."

He paused. "Is it appropriate?" he said.

"Appropriate?"

"A candidate going out with a student," he said. "A woman student at that."

She laughed. "I'm twenty-six." She put her hands on her hips, looking him up and down. "I think I can handle you. Besides, you've got nothing to worry about. They're not hiring you."

A dog began to howl in a room across the hall.

"They've already made up their minds?" he asked. "Was I that bad?"

"They were never going to hire you. This 'national search' thing?" she said, indicating air quotes. "A charade."

"I don't understand."

"The chair is having his way with the candidate they're hiring," she said.

"You're kidding?"

Asa fell back onto the bed, staring up at the popcorn ceiling. He needed this job.

She sat down beside him. She wore a dark, rich smelling musk.

"Don't look so glum," she said.

He sat up. "I have student loans and car payments.

"You'll get a job soon enough," she said.

"What makes you so sure?"

"I heard them talking," she said. "They wanted to hire you." She pressed her finger into his solar plexus. "They were impressed by you and were going on and on about your class. They haven't done that with anyone else."

"I suppose that's one consolation."

"And I'm another," she said brightly.

"I don't know," he said.

"You're in one of the most beautiful cities in the world," she said, standing, "and I refuse to let you squander it drinking Pabst in this Samuel Beckett set. Arise." She pulled him up off the bed with surprising strength. "Charleston awaits."

He gave in and went with her to a nice bar, one of the places Trip had talked about. They split a bottle of wine she insisted on paying for. He learned she was from Columbia, had gone to Emory undergrad, and was finishing her master's in English in Charleston. She wanted to teach high school English. She originally planned to get a PhD but her experience at the university turned her off the idea of teaching college.

"Academics are small-minded, big-ego-ed, backbiting, stoop-shouldered sons of bitches." She frowned into her glass.

"Don't hold anything back," he said.

"You're not any of those things." Her face softened. "You're different."

"How can you know that?" he asked.

"I just do." She looked him right in the eye.

He felt himself blush. He wasn't used to having the attention of women, especially striking women. Whenever he was around them, he seized up, his mind blanked. But the wine loosened him. He allowed himself to be more attracted to her as the night wore on, giving in to his eyes, which returned to her legs and her blouse, which generously came unbuttoned one more button.

They walked along the Battery as lightning flickered out in the harbor, followed by the distant rumble of thunder. Behind them stood the formidable grand homes of the Battery, their two- hundred-year-old facades spotlighted, like aged actors gazing out to sea.

"So they survived Hugo," Asa said, nodding at the immense homes. "Had you moved here yet when it hit?"

"I just moved here last year," she said. "The city was still reeling though. Lots of cleaning up, lots of construction, a whole lot of roofs being replaced."

When Asa came into town yesterday, he noticed a lot of construction that looked to him like repairing and rebuilding.

Asa had watched Hugo's grim progress up the coast on the news, along with the rest of the nation.

The wind picked up, whipping Betsy's hair across her face and pressing her clothes against her body. She looked in the direction of a low dark silhouette far out in the harbor. "Fort Sumter was a sitting duck. A seventeen-foot wall of water hit it and did a million dollars' worth of damage."

Asa told her his parents had taken him and his sister on a tour boat out to the fort when they were kids.

She guided him through the maze of close, dark downtown streets, the palmettos rattling in the stiff breeze and the thunder growing louder. They walked for some time, turning down more streets than Asa realized Charleston had, some so dark he would only catch the glimmer of Betsy's earrings during flickers of lightning.

"This isn't the way back to the motel, is it?" he finally asked.

"I want to show you something," she said.

After a couple more blocks, she stopped in front of an elaborate three-story house that he guessed was probably built in the early 1800s. At the rear of the house, they paused outside a wrought iron gate that looked into a brick-walled courtyard with a sprawling live oak at its center. The tree's heavy limbs, many of which grew along the ground, were strung with hundreds of tiny white lights suspended in the middle of the courtyard.

From beneath an old brick, she produced a single key and unlocked the gate, reminding him of Alice in Wonderland. The gate squeaked as she opened it.

"You live here?" he said incredulously, looking up at the big house.

"There." She pointed to a small two-story brick structure at the back of the courtyard. She said it was an old carriage house converted to a garage downstairs and an apartment upstairs. She held the gate open for him.

"I don't know if that would be a good idea," he said, standing at the gate. "Even if I'm not getting the job."

The buzz from the wine had worn off a little. Asa had it drilled into him that the teacher/student relationship should be above reproach. Teachers were in a position of power and should never abuse that power, and even though he knew he wasn't getting this job and even though he wasn't this woman's teacher or she his student, this whole thing made him uncomfortable.

"I'm not going to jump your bones, if that's what you're worried about," she said.

"I'm not sure I trust myself."

Every fiber of his being longed to go with her. A beautiful woman was asking him to come inside with her, and he was declining. Was this about following his conscience, or was it cowardice? "I better head back to the motel."

"Suit yourself," she said.

"Thank you for a great night," he said.

She nodded, not looking at him.

He smiled. "I'm glad I came to Charleston, even if I never was going to get the job."

She held out her hand in that awkward straight-armed way women shake hands when trying to keep as much distance between you and them as possible. "Good luck with the job search."

"Good luck with finishing up your thesis," he said. "You'll be a sensational teacher."

She clanged the gate shut, and as she started across the courtyard toward the apartment and away from him, he imagined the bard shaking his head at him in profound disappointment. Asa was left standing on the sidewalk, looking down the dimly lit street. Then he looked back in the other direction which was even darker.

"Betsy," he called.

"Yes?" She walked back to the gate.

"I don't know where I am," he said.

She put her finger to her lip. "Oh?"

"Can you give me directions?"

She rattled off street names, and when she was done, he was more confused than ever. Lightning flashed and a crack of thunder sounded on top of them. It began to drizzle.

"You sure you don't want to come in for a little while?" She glanced up at the sky, the heavy clouds reflecting downtown's lights. It thundered again, and then the heavens opened up.

"What about now?" she yelled over the din of the rain. She fumbled for the key, unlocked the gate again, and opened it. By this point it was raining so hard he could barely see. She took his hand and led him through the courtyard, past the live oak, and up a small flight of stairs. Although it had only been minutes, by the time she unlocked the door and they stepped inside, they were soaked.

She turned on a couple of lamps whose yellow light cast a warm intimate glow. It felt as if they had stepped into another world. The main room was paneled with warm knotty pine. The room included a kitchenette with a table by a window and a sitting area with a futon couch and a desk stacked with neat piles of index cards. Bookshelves lined one wall. Several large, thriving potted plants stood near the glass sliding doors that opened onto a small, covered balcony facing the live oak, making the apartment feel like it was up in the tree itself. And there was a sweet smell he couldn't quite identify.

"I feel like I've washed up in *Robinson Crusoe*," he said.

"I promise not to eat you." She stood beside him at the glass doors, the rain drumming on the roof.

Asa noticed his clothes dripping little puddles. "I'll ruin your floor."

"Don't worry about it," Betsy said. "I'm sopping too."

"Let's take these off," she said, "and I can throw your clothes in the dryer. I have something you can change into."

She came back with a large t-shirt and a pair of outsized sweatpants, which he changed into in the bathroom. When he came out, she was drying her hair with a towel, having changed, not into a robe, which would have suggested more possibilities, but into a blouse and jeans.

She filled a kettle with water and set it on the stove and lit a burner. "Isn't there a scene like this in *Jude the Obscure*?"

"It's been a while since I've read Hardy," he said, "but I can't picture Jude in sweats and a Clemson t-shirt." He tugged on his orange t-shirt, a grinning tiger strutting across it.

Carrying their wet clothes, she opened a door that led down a flight of stairs to the washer and dryer. While she was gone, he glanced at her bookshelves, noting how many contemporary poetry books she had, most by women. He was leafing through Rita Dove's *Thomas and Beulah*, a collection that had won the Pulitzer a few years ago, when a gust of wind drew his attention to the glass doors. Outside the great limbs swayed in the wind and, with them, the swarm of little lights. He felt gratitude to this woman for rescuing him from the Harbor View.

That's when he noticed a vase of purple flowers sitting on the kitchen table in a mason jar. He leaned over to smell them just as Betsy came back up from the basement.

"Lilacs," he said.

"I saw them at the market after your class today and thought it was a sign."

"They're beautiful," he said, wondering, *A sign for what?* Beside the vase he noticed a familiar book with a bookmark in it. It took him a minute to realize it was *In Captivity*, which had come out the year before last.

"I can't believe you unearthed a copy," he said, setting down *Thomas and Beulah* and picking up *In Captivity*.

"I read it when it first came out," she said. "When I learned that you were one of the candidates, I reread it. I liked your poems the first time I read them, and I liked them even more rereading them."

"Really?" He flipped to the back, seeing his picture on the jacket flap. He had tried his best to smile for the photographer.

"Are you working on anything now?"

"I slowed down on the poetry when I was writing my dissertation," he said, "but I hope to have a new collection ready to send out next year."

The kettle began to whistle. She turned it off and set out two mugs. "Would you like some tea?"

"Sure," he said, setting the book back down.

"I'm glad you're working on a new book," she said.

She nodded at *In Captivity*. "That's why I came back for you tonight. Don't get me wrong. You gave a good class. But I didn't come back for the teacher. I came back for the poet."

"I'm glad you came back," he said. As soon as he said it, he realized he sounded a little too . . . something. "Not that I expect to sleep here." In situations like these, he tended to dig himself deeper.

She poured hot water into the teacups.

"I'll go back to the motel as soon as the rain lets up," he said.

She took a bottle of whiskey out of a cabinet, sat back down, and without asking, poured several splashes into his tea and then into hers. "What if I don't tell you how to get back?"

Her bold look registered down into his thighs. "Then I guess it's out of my hands."

She looked away as if she had seen something wanting in him. "The futon folds out," she said, making it clear he wouldn't be sleeping with her. With this woman, he didn't know whether he was coming or going.

They sipped their tea, which warmed him and radiated through his limbs. "I saw you looking at *Thomas and Beulah*," she said.

"I've always wanted to read it. I saw she autographed it to you."

"She came here and gave a reading," she said. "An amazing book."

Then they were quiet. The rain drummed on the roof and the tree continued to sway in the breeze. A wave of depression settled on him. He hadn't gotten the job and had no idea when he might find one. Several fellow postdoc colleagues had been looking for jobs for years.

"Will you sign it?" She slid *In Captivity* toward him. "I have a pen around here somewhere." She started to look around her desk, moving piles of index cards. "My thesis in progress."

"On?" he asked.

"The working title is 'Emily Dickinson and the Underlying Eroticism of the Charged Imagination.'"

"Interesting," he said.

"Meaning it's anything but."

"I'm serious. I never really thought of Dickinson as erotic, especially compared to someone like Whitman."

"Don't get me wrong," she said. "I love Whitman. The man sings sex morning, noon, and night, and *Leaves of Grass* is 'The Star-Spangled Banner' of sex. But 'The Star-Spangled Banner' doesn't arouse me, at least not in the way Dickinson does. She never talks about sex yet somehow manages to infuse every word she writes with sensuality, as well as every word she doesn't write."

"You've lost me."

"With Dickinson, it's what she doesn't tell you, what she doesn't say, what she *withholds*." She paused. "Her poetry makes me horny."

In other circumstances Asa would have laughed, but Betsy's presence over the course of the evening worked on him in ways he couldn't explain.

She held a pen out to him, but when he reached for it, she didn't let go at first, then smiled a mischievous smile and let go.

Recovering himself, he signed the book. She turned off most of the lights and suggested they move to the futon couch. She poured more whiskey into their teacups. They sat next to each other on the futon, looking out at the lights, his senses on high alert as her bare arm pressed against his.

After a little while she said, "You're not how I expected you to be."

"What do you mean?"

"Your poetry is so sensual and sure of itself. And in your class today you were so animated and engaging and very much in charge." She sipped her tea.

"But?" he asked.

"Alone you're a lot quieter and reserved." She hesitated. "Maybe even tentative."

"I'm sorry," he said.

She laughed, then he laughed at himself.

"When I came for you tonight," she said, "I thought I was getting Whitman, but somehow I've wound up with Dickinson."

"Is that a bad thing?"

"Not at all." With that she leaned over and kissed him.

He started to kiss her back, but she put her finger on his lips.

"I'm not ready to have sex with you," she said.

"That wasn't even on my mind," he said, hearing how unconvincing he sounded.

"It was on mine," she said. "I would enjoy messing around, unless of course you'd rather not."

He leaned over and kissed her and then she kissed him back, and they embraced and kissed until their mouths were sore. Then she helped him pull out the futon, gave him some sheets and a pillow, then went to her room and went to bed. Unable to sleep, he stayed up a while listening to the rain and reading *Thomas and Beulah*.

The next morning, she made coffee and walked him back through the Charleston streets to his motel. The sky was clear and the air lighter and cooler. Asa felt a little hung over and assumed she did as well since she was quiet all the way back to the motel. Either that or she was recalibrating her attraction to him in the harsh light of day. He thought about asking for her phone number, but why would a woman like her want anything resembling a relationship with him? Poetry could only get you so far.

When they reached the motel, he walked around his car, finding not a scratch.

"Nice car," she said, touching the hood.

"A graduation present to myself," he said, aware that they were now standing on opposite sides of the car. "I hope I can still make the payments now."

"You'll find a job soon enough."

He walked around to her side. "Thanks for such a nice night, and thank you for rescuing me from the Harbor View. And if you're ever in Chapel Hill . . ."

"You can't just drive off into the sunrise."

"Pardon me?"

"I've never done one-night stands," she said. "And I'm not about to start."

"Last night wasn't really a one-night stand," he said.

"Well, if you're going to get technical about it."

"Are you saying you'd like to see me again?" It crossed his mind that she was mentally unbalanced.

"Are you still hung up on that whole teacher sleeping with student thing?" she said. "Technically you're not even a professor. You're just some guy with a PhD, like so many wanderers in the land of postdoc."

He felt his jaw tighten. "I need to get back," he said and was glad she didn't ask for what.

"I'm sorry," she said. "I was just kidding."

"I guess you hit a little too close to home."

"You'll get a job," she said. "I heard the faculty say they knew you'd be snapped up soon."

"Well, anyway, I have to get back," he said. "It was nice meeting you."

"It was nice to meet you," she said, sounding resigned.

After they said good-bye, he went into his motel room, packed up, and then put his suitcase into the trunk. He was backing out of the parking space when he was startled by someone rapping on his window. It was her. He rolled the window down.

"I want to loan you this," she said, pulling a book out of her purse and handing it to him. It was *Thomas and Beulah*.

"Oh, no," he said. "I shouldn't borrow this. It's autographed. What if something happens to it?" He tried to hand it back to her, but she folded her arms.

"I know you'll take good care of it," she said.

"How would I get it back to you?" Taking such a book would be a lot of responsibility, responsibility he did not want.

"Just bring it back, when you come to visit . . . Fort Sumter," she said, scratching her nose.

He smiled. He started to say something about not knowing when that would be.

"Or mail it back when you're done," she said, and without another word started walking away.

"I don't have your address," he called after her.

"Yes you do," she called over her shoulder, and then the next minute she disappeared around a corner.

Then he saw something sticking out of the book. He opened it, and there neatly printed on one of her index cards were these words he recognized from Dickinson's "Wild Nights–Wild Nights!":

Rowing in Eden -
Ah - the Sea!
Might I but moor - tonight -
In thee!

And beneath those lines were her name, her address, and her phone number.

* * *

On his way out of town, he decided to drive back down to the Battery where he sat on one of the benches, occupied mostly by young couples, many probably students from the university.

Next to him sat an elderly Black woman dressed in a hat and pearls as if she had been to church, an old sweet-faced Corgi lay at her feet. The sky was a solitary blue, and a breeze dotted the harbor with whitecaps. Fort Sumter occupied the same place on the horizon it had last night, but in daylight, he was struck by what a stark lonely place it must've been out there for those soldiers.

"What's your dog's name?" Asa asked the woman.

She turned to him, put her hand to her ear, and smiled in the way people do when they haven't heard what you said.

"Your dog," Asa said, raising his voice.

"Phineas," the woman said loudly, clearly hard of hearing.

"What a great name," Asa said.

"After *Finnegan's Wake*," the woman said. "Ever read it?"

"Let's put it this way," Asa said, "I tried."

"My husband named him." She paused. "He was a big reader, loved Joyce." This was tinged with melancholy.

Asa leaned down and petted the old corgi, who looked up at him with soulful eyes. "How old is Phineas?"

The woman put her hand to her ear.

"How old?" Asa pointed at the dog.

"Eleven," the woman said. "Seventy-seven in people years. That makes us the same age. He's been a good friend." Then they were both quiet, and after a little while she said, "We lost him in the storm. Like everybody else, we were evacuating, and he died of a heart attack."

It took Asa a moment to put together what she was telling him. "I'm sorry," Asa said.

"We had a good run," the woman said. "Nearly sixty years."

Asa could not fathom that kind of loss.

They were both quiet for a moment, and then she asked, "What brings you here?"

Asa looked at her. How could she tell he wasn't from here? "I came down from North Carolina to interview for a job." Then he added, "A job I didn't get."

"You already didn't get it?" she said, shaking her head.

"Must be some kind of record," Asa said.

"Why are you still here?"

Asa debated with himself whether to tell her. "I met someone yesterday."

"I see," she said. Phineas glanced up at the woman in a conspiratorial sort of way.

"It wasn't really like that," Asa said.

"It's hardly ever like that," she said. "At first anyway. It certainly wasn't with us." Her face looked as if she had gone off somewhere, but then she turned to Asa. "So where is she now?"

"Half an hour ago, I went to try to find her apartment but got turned around and wound up here." He sighed. "I'm thinking it's a sign I should give up."

"Do you want to see her again?"

With her watching him, he felt his heart race and a tingle ran across the top of his head. "Something tells me if I do see her again, I'll be in for heartbreak."

"So you do want to see her again," she said crossing her arms and turning back to look out at the harbor, as if he had made her point.

As Asa drove out of downtown, he felt depressed that he hadn't gotten the job and that for the foreseeable future he would be trapped in adjunct hell. Then he heard Betsy say, *You'll find a job soon enough*. He turned onto the exit ramp that lifted him quickly up onto the expressway, from where Asa looked out over a city of new roofs.

CHAPTER 4

• • •

Clare, Wednesday Morning

Clare turned down Montford Avenue, her favorite street in Asheville, with its renovated Victorian homes surrounded by manicured gardens and walking paths. The morning air was so clear that the storm's aftermath appeared in hyper focus. The streets were littered with leaves and branches. Yards were covered with large limbs, and she even passed a few toppled trees.

She thought of Henry at home, getting the girls' breakfast and making their lunches with his phone scrunched to his ear, talking with his customers, all wanting their arborist to come assess the damage. Normally, Clare would have been back at home by now. On most mornings she could deliver her route and be home in time to get the girls ready for Henry to drop off at school on his way to work.

She tossed a paper toward the Flowerses' house, but it landed beneath a bush. Being so late, she would have left it, but Dr. Flowers sometimes complained. Like his letters to the editor, he could be on the critical side. Henry, who did a lot of tree work for the Flowerses, said that Dr. Flowers wasn't a bad guy once you got to know him. Still, it didn't hurt that Mrs. Flowers sent Clare a card with a check for a hundred dollars each Christmas.

Clare had pulled over, picked up the paper, and moved it to the Flowerses' walk when she looked up at their house, a two-story arts and crafts home she'd always admired. What she saw took her breath away. A tree had snapped halfway down its trunk and crushed a corner of the second floor. How dark and eerily quiet the house seemed. She looked around. Had no one on the street noticed? The way the house was tucked back in the trees, she wouldn't have noticed either if she hadn't been standing in their front yard. She hurried up on the front porch and rang the doorbell, and when no one came, knocked, then knocked louder.

"Is anyone there?" The front door was locked, but she heard a dog inside, whining. That would be the sweet old chow Mrs. Flowers was often walking when Clare delivered the paper. Maybe the Flowerses were still asleep. But how could they be with that tree on their house? Clare went around to the back of the house, pausing at the gate with the worn sign that said, BEWARE OF DOG. She knew Luna was nothing to beware of. Besides, the dog was in the house, not the yard. She went through the gate, careful to pull it closed behind her. She knocked on the back door, calling out. She tried the door, and it wasn't locked. "Hello," she called as she stepped into the dark kitchen. There was no answer, but a black blur shot past her into the yard. Clare found Luna in the back, peeing. She waited till the dog was done and walked her into the house. As soon as they were inside, Luna started whining again.

"Hello?" Clare called. "Dr. Flowers? Mrs. Flowers?"

Clare found the light switch, and, to her surprise, the light came on. She looked around. Everything appeared to be in order, no sign of damage down here. She walked through the first floor, turning on lights and calling out. Maybe the Flowerses were on vacation and had left the dog for a neighbor to watch. But Mrs. Flowers always called to have their papers held whenever they went out of town.

As she moved through the house, Clare remembered an article she read a few months ago about a father who shot and killed his daughter, mistaking her for an intruder. The girl had come home from college a week early, wanting to surprise her parents, and had been tiptoeing through the dark house in the early morning hours.

Standing at the bottom of the stairs, Clare felt a breeze come from up above. She heard a voice upstairs. What if someone was in the shower and found her walking around in their house?

"Hello?" she called up the stairs. She paused on the landing, looking up. From where she stood, she saw twigs and branches scattered in the hallway. Slowly, she walked up the stairs, but Luna remained at the bottom. When Clare reached the top, there was no sign of damage in the hallway, but when she looked into the first bedroom, she saw nothing but tree and blue sky.

The tree had fallen halfway into the room, bringing with it limbs and the trunk itself, which ran across the length of the bedroom. It smelled of evergreen. *Hemlock*, she said to herself, fingering a branch of needles with cottony wide patches underneath. The woolly adelgid. This tiny aphid from Asia that had been decimating the hemlock population throughout Southern Appalachia. How out of place the great trunk looked. She patted it as if it were a whale that had somehow beached itself on the second floor of the Flowerses' house. She pulled away a few limbs, ducked under the trunk, and went deeper into the bedroom. Much of the room was intact, down to framed pictures of children that sat on the dresser. The voice was coming from the radio on the dresser, an announcer reading the news. She cleared away another limb and when she did, she gasped.

In her nightgown, Mrs. Flowers stared up at her with lifeless eyes, her body pinned to her bed by a branch that had run her through where her heart might be. In the empty space beside Mrs. Flowers, the bed was skewered with several more limbs.

"Oh Lord, Lord, Lord." Trembling, Clare dug her phone out of her jeans pocket, and after a few failed attempts managed to call 911 and ask for an ambulance. After she hung up, she tried looking around the rest of the upstairs for Dr. Flowers, but as far as she could tell, he wasn't there. He could be pinned somewhere under the great tree, but her instincts told her he wasn't.

She sat back down on the bed, next to Mrs. Flowers. Someone should be with her till the EMTs arrived. She took Mrs. Flowers's cold hand and held it. Amazingly, Clare saw no blood anywhere, and the longer she looked at Mrs. Flowers, the more it seemed as if the branch was a physical extension of the woman, as if the tree had somehow grown out of her chest. That was when the tree branches that had run through the empty side of the bed fully registered with Clare. Wherever Dr. Flowers was, it was a very good thing he hadn't been sleeping beside his wife last night.

Somewhere a phone began to ring. She spotted it through the limbs on the night table on the far side of the bed. She scrambled over several limbs and picked up the receiver.

"I was inquiring about the apartment listed in the paper," said a woman. "Is that still available?"

"This isn't my house," Clare said, her voice shaky. "I deliver their paper."

"Could I speak with the owner then?"

"She can't come to the phone," Clare said.

Sirens wailed down the street, coming closer.

"Could you take my number and have her call me back?"

"I have to go," Clare said as tires screeched to a stop outside. She hung up, picked her way over the limbs, and hurried down the stairs.

CHAPTER 5

Asa, Wednesday Morning

Groggy from the pills, it took all his willpower to unfold himself from the love seat, massaging the crick in his neck. He heard the buzz of a mosquito in his ear. He removed the earplugs, and the buzzing turned into a maniacal roar. He looked at his watch. Nearly 8:30.

His mind shifted to all that had happened last night. It wasn't a good sign that Betsy hadn't come over to the apartment this morning. She didn't like to leave things stewing. She insisted they talk things through whether Asa wanted to or not. He looked at his watch again. She would have left for school forty-five minutes ago. He checked his cell. No calls or texts.

The roar started again. Jack Hodges, looking for an excuse to break out his chainsaw, was no doubt cutting last night's windfall. What was it about middle-aged men and chainsaws? What did it say about Asa that he never had any desire to touch one?

Asa splashed water on his face in the kitchen sink and began to think more rationally about last night. Yes, Betsy had said she wanted to explore her relationship with this person. She also had wanted to keep talking, and he had been the one who cut it off. Also, she never said she wanted a divorce. She had even gotten upset when he brought it up. As usual, she was right. He was a Four, overly dramatic, making her confession into something insurmountable. Plenty of couples survived dalliances. Betsy was also right about who he had become—cranky, depressive, and isolated. All things he could work on. Heck, even Silas Marner came around in the end.

He gathered up the papers he had finished grading last night. At least he had only one class today, American Lit, which didn't meet till 2:00 p.m. That gave him plenty of time to go back to the house, shave, shower, down a pot of coffee, and prepare for class. Tonight, he would apologize to Betsy and see where to go from there.

As he started back to the house, he noted how cool the morning was, the front having passed through, transforming the sky to a deep forgiving blue. Asa felt an unexpected surge of hope. They would get through this.

Halfway up the walk, he saw a small crowd with their backs to him, watching an ambulance pull out of their drive. Flashing lights but no siren. Asa came up behind the group of neighbors, a few police and firemen. Police cars and two ladder trucks were parked in front of his house.

"What's happened?" Asa said.

Everyone turned around and looked at him as if they had seen a ghost.

"Thank goodness," said their neighbor Norma Hodges. "We've been looking all over for you. Where have you been, Asa?" Her tone went from one of relief to something guarded.

"What's going on?" He walked around to the front of the house. An immense ragged section of the hemlock lay sprawled across the crushed front of the house. As he stared up at the tree, he saw the great black rotted sections of the tree's interior where it had split. Rotted to the core. How much of this would insurance cover? Had he updated their policy?

"They've taken her to Mission," said a lanky short-haired woman in jeans who he recognized as the paper carrier.

"Why have they taken my wife to the hospital?" Asa asked.

Two firemen stepped out the back door, one carrying a chainsaw, their faces grim. A third fireman came up to Asa. "Dr. Flowers, we've cut off the electricity to your house till Duke Power can check out the situation. Would you like an EMT to look you over?"

"An EMT?" Asa said.

"I'm very sorry for your loss," the fireman said, looking into Asa's eyes, then walked over to a policeman standing on the curb.

Loss? Was the damage worse than it looked.

"Where's Luna?"

"She's okay," Norma said. "She's fine. We've got her at our house. Just thought it best."

"What's happened?"

Norma looked away and Jack stepped up. "Betsy's been taken to the hospital, buddy."

Maybe the sleeping pills hadn't worn off. Whatever the reason, Asa felt strangely calm. Oddly detached from the whole scene. Like one of the dead in *Our Town* watching the living act out their lives below. He was only vaguely aware that his legs had slowly given way and that he had knelt down hard on the drive.

A big hand reached down and pulled Asa to his feet. Jack Hodges was a monolith of a man who had once been a semipro linebacker.

"Asa," he said in his tender gravelly voice, "let me drive you to the hospital."

As Jack led Asa next door to his pickup, Asa became aware that the papers he had graded last night had slipped out of his hands when he fell. He started to collect them, but a breeze scattered them along the walk.

"Let 'em go, buddy," Jack said, leading Asa over to his truck.

"I have to get those back to my students," he said.

"Y'all go on to the hospital," Norma said, "I'll get them and put them in the house."

And with that, Jack opened the passenger door of his truck and helped Asa in.

CHAPTER 6

Sarah, Wednesday Afternoon

Sarah nearly floated down the steps of Phillips Hall, her lab presentation having gone much better than she had expected. Professor Zimmerman, an intimidating, no-nonsense German, who had the reputation as the department hard-ass, had said to Sarah in front of the entire lab that her investigation into the manipulation of electron spin was "very intriguing." Parsimonious with her praise, Professor Zimmerman never talked like that.

As Sarah started across the quad, she glanced at her phone, which she had silenced for the lab, and saw that she had gotten a couple of calls from her dad. Probably calling about the fellowship, either to congratulate her or tell her she couldn't go. Who was she kidding? Her mother would have already drilled into her dad that the fellowship was an honor, that Sarah should definitely go to Denmark, and that he needed to be encouraging. In such situations her dad didn't stand a chance. In fact, Sarah was willing to bet her mom had instigated her dad calling to congratulate her.

She dialed his number, and as soon as he answered, she said, "I know Denmark is far, Dad, but it's only for a couple of months."

Her father was quiet.

"Dad?"

"Something's happened," he said.

"Dad? Are you okay?"

"Darling," he began. She couldn't remember the last time he had called her *Darling*. "Late last night a big section of the hemlock fell on the house."

"Oh no," she said. "Did it do much damage?"

"It fell into our bedroom," her father said.

She gasped. "Are you okay? Is everybody okay?"

"Your mom." His voice shook.

"Mom was hurt? How bad? How bad was she hurt, Dad?"

Silence.

"Is she in the hospital? Don't tell me she's in the hospital." She pictured her mother in a hospital bed all bandaged up. "Did she break anything?"

Her father's silence began to terrify her.

"Dad, exactly how is she? Is she in the hospital?"

"Oh, Sweetie," he said.

"What?" Sarah sank down on a low wall that curved up to the entrance of a humanities building.

"The doctor said she didn't suffer. She said it would've been instantaneous, that she wouldn't have felt a thing."

"She's dead?" In her shock, Sarah became aware of a barefoot student slacklining on a low strap tied between two maples. Like a tightrope walker, except only two feet off the ground.

"Jack Hodges took me to the hospital to be with her," her father said. "But that was afterwards."

"So you saw her."

"I did, but she wasn't alive anymore."

"How did she look?" She needed to picture her mom.

"Like herself," he said. "No blood to speak of. A tree branch, a small one, pierced her heart. She looked asleep. She looked peaceful, Sarah."

"Oh god," she said. She pictured her mother lying with the branch through her heart. "How is Mitchell?"

"He doesn't know."

"You haven't called him?" she said.

"I left a message but didn't say what happened, of course," he said. "He hasn't called back, and knowing him, he might not call me back. It might be better if you call him, if you don't mind."

"I'll call him." She and Mitchell had been close since they were little. Back then she was the only one who could understand what her brother was saying. He would mumble something, and their parents would turn to Sarah, who would translate.

"I'll be home as soon as I can," Sarah said.

"Come in the morning," he said. "You shouldn't make that drive tonight."

Her dad was a worrier, their mother not nearly as much. Sarah wished he wouldn't worry so much. She found it tiring, but she also knew that worrying was the way their father expressed his love.

"I won't be able to sleep," she said. "I might as well come on."

"Drive safely then," he said. "If you become the least bit distracted or sleepy, pull over and get some coffee, or better yet call me and I'll come get you, wherever you are."

After she hung up, she became aware of her heart pounding. She felt dizzy and everything looked too bright, like the time when she was a little girl and fell from her bike and had a concussion. She had managed to walk her bike the few blocks home but cried the whole way, not because anything hurt but because nothing looked like itself. Scared to death, she dropped her bike on their front walk and ran into her mother's arms, sobbing, "I don't know what's happening, Mom. I can't think. I just can't think!"

Her heart slowed as she watched the student on the slackline climb on again, holding his arms out, keeping his balance longer than Sarah thought possible.

She walked across the quad, wiping her eyes and thinking how much she had to do now. Having to call Mitchell. She knew her dad really should do it, but she also agreed with her dad that Mitchell would probably rather it come from her. It was a terrible feeling, what she had to do. With her finger poised over Mitchell's number, she understood that for as long as she didn't call Mitchell, their mother would still be alive to him. Wanting to allow her brother just a little more time with their mother, she slid her phone back into her jeans pocket. An hour later, after she'd contacted her professors, told her roommates, packed her suitcase, and loaded up her car, she called Mitchell and sat in the dimming light of the dorm parking lot telling him, in the gentlest way she knew how, that the world they knew had unraveled.

CHAPTER 7

Asa, Wednesday Evening

Asa sat across from his old friend Ben Berkowitz at the candlelit kitchen table, listening out for his daughter's car. It was nearly nine o'clock, and the only sounds were the tick of the woodstove and the flap of the tarp upstairs. Henry's men had already gotten the hemlock off the house and hauled most of it away, leaving a good fifteen feet of trunk standing. Henry said they would remove the rest when his crew, swamped with work, had more time. Henry's crew stretched a giant blue tarp over the exposed section to protect the upstairs from the elements. Ben met Asa at the house after Jack had brought him back from the hospital and then stayed with him.

Luna had sat down beside Asa's chair as soon as he got back home and had shadowed him ever since. Usually, Asa would have been the last person she would've followed. In the dog's younger, wilder years, Asa lost his temper whenever she'd jump the fence and roam the neighborhood, refusing to come when he called and getting into trouble. Even though Luna had mellowed considerably, as had Asa, and even though Asa and Luna had come to a more amiable place in their relationship, she still maintained a certain wariness around him.

Asa checked his watch.

"She'll be here soon." Ben sipped bourbon from a jelly glass while Asa nursed a cup of hot tea. Ben had brought the Jack Daniel's, and as much as Asa appreciated the gesture, he didn't want to be buzzed when Sarah arrived.

The phone rang in the hall, and Ben answered it. He had been screening calls, letting family and close friends talk to Asa and telling the rest that they would be in touch regarding the memorial service. Asa had called Betsy's mother. When she had cried out, it felt like he had stabbed her. Then he called his sister and his father. His family loved Betsy. His mother, who had died six years ago, had been very close to her.

After Ben hung up, he sat back down, his face full of flickering shadows from the candles they had set around the kitchen. The power wouldn't be back on till tomorrow at the earliest. Ben poured himself more whiskey and held the bottle out to Asa, but Asa shook his head.

"An affair," Asa said. "I can't believe it."

"From what you told me it sounds like nothing happened," Ben said.

"Something was about to happen."

"Thinking about having an affair isn't the same as having an affair, unless you're Jimmy Carter," Ben said. "Stop worrying about who it is and distracting yourself from the fact that you've lost your wife and your children have lost their mother."

The candle on the table hissed and a river of wax spilled down its sides.

"Who do you think it was?" Ben asked.

"You just said . . ."

"It must've been another teacher," Ben said.

"It might've been her best friend," Asa said, "a woman named Alice Stromquist. They've been close friends forever."

Ben got a funny look on his face. "It's not Alice Stromquist."

"How do you know?"

"I'm not at liberty to say," Ben said.

"Don't tell me you're having an affair with her."

"God no. My cheating days are over."

"Then how do you know it's not Alice?"

Ben balled a piece of the candle wax in his fingers.

"You're her therapist?"

Ben looked up at him.

"So what?" Asa said. "You don't know everything about your clients."

"Cross Alice Stromquist off your list," Ben said.

Asa had started getting used to the idea that it was Alice. She was a nice person and had a good sense of humor. Plus, if Betsy had been attracted to Alice, it couldn't have been for sex. Could it?

Another car went by out front.

"Betsy said she saw no reason to tell the children about the affair," Asa said.

Sirens started up in the distance and neighborhood dogs howled. Luna pricked up her ears and then lifted her head.

"Why don't I feel anything?" Asa said.

"You're in shock."

"You think so?" Asa found himself staring at his own hands, surprised how veined and wrinkled and frail they appeared. The hands of an old man.

"A tree falls on your house and kills the love of your life?" Ben said. "Of course, you're in shock."

Asa looked around the room, the candlelight giving the

house the feel of an earlier era—a good century ago, when the house was first built.

"Sarah should've reached Mitchell by now." Asa glanced at his watch. "I hope he's okay."

"Is he still on meds?"

"He was till he started dating this Wendy."

"Ah, sex," Ben said, "Nature's antidepressant."

"I hope this doesn't derail the progress he's made." Asa felt a familiar knot in his stomach that came up whenever he worried about his son.

"Sometimes we underestimate what our kids can handle," Ben said. "Mitchell has a lot going for him. He's smart, talented, and a genuinely good boy. As hard as it is, he'll deal." Then he added. "And you'll help him."

The phone rang and, sure it was Sarah, Asa jumped up to answer it.

"Hi Asa, this is Amanda from Videolife." Amanda was the owner of the last DVD store in Asheville, only a few blocks away. He and Betsy had rented movies there for years. "Could you let Betsy know she has a movie overdue?"

He said he would let her know, hung up, and went to the kitchen to get down another glass but while in there noticed Luna hadn't eaten. Asa knelt down beside her. "Not hungry, girl?" He petted her and could feel her trembling, which she'd been doing since the accident.

With Luna following, he rejoined Ben at the table and held out the glass.

Ben poured him a finger of Jack Daniel's.

"Just the one." Asa sipped the bourbon slowly, as it warmed the back of his throat.

They sat for a while and listened out for cars.

"Betsy said coming home to me was like coming home to Silas Marner."

They sat sipping the Jack Daniel's. Upstairs the tarp fluttered.

Asa caught his hand moving to his chest as if feeling for a sympathetic wound. Betsy's injury, which he had insisted on seeing when they showed him her body at the hospital, wasn't as formidable as he'd thought a mortal wound should be. On first sight it looked to him like a small, ragged rose blooming in the center of her chest.

"How am I to live in this town while somewhere is the person she was ready to leave me for?"

"She didn't say she was leaving you," Ben said.

"She sort of did."

They heard a car come up the street, but then it passed by the house.

"Concentrate your energies elsewhere, as in being a good father."

"I'm a good father."

Ben gave him a skeptical look. "Good fathers don't ask their daughters to call their sons about their mother's death."

"He'd rather hear it from Sarah."

"You can't count on Sarah to take over where Betsy left off," Ben said. "It's not fair to Sarah, and it's certainly not fair to Mitchell."

"Right now, I'm the last person he needs."

Ben leaned across the table, looking his friend in the eye. "The mother's gone, the father steps up."

Outside a car passed and Asa hurried to the window, but the car continued up the street. He thought about calling Sarah to see where she was but didn't want her taking her eyes off the road. He caught his friend stifling a yawn.

"Go home," Asa said. "Linda will wonder where you are."

Linda was Ben's current wife. A sweet-natured woman with a generous figure and a nature to match, the very antithesis of Ben's two previous high-strung wives.

Ben said he would be happy to stay, but Asa insisted he go home. He knew his friend had a full day tomorrow at work.

"If you need anything, anything at all, call me," Ben said. He stopped on the kitchen doorstep. "And will you allow your old friend one more bit of advice?"

"No," Asa said.

Ben gave him a tight hug and walked down the drive.

With the aid of a flashlight, Asa found clean sheets in the hall closet and headed over to the studio with Luna behind him. Outside the air felt colder and lighter. Autumn was coming on, full bore. Ben had meant well, but Sarah would be better talking with Mitchell. Sometimes being a good father meant being less of one. Inside the studio he turned on the lights. The power company hadn't cut off the power to the studio since it hadn't been damaged. He turned on the baseboard heat and had finished changing the sheets when he glanced through the window back at the house, saw flickering light, and remembered the candles. As he hurried back through the garden and into the house to blow out the candles, the phone rang. He picked up the receiver. "Sarah?"

"Dad." By the catch in Mitchell's voice, Asa knew Sarah had reached him.

"She died in her sleep, Honey," Asa said.

Asa heard a woman's voice in the background.

"I can't believe it," Mitchell said.

A long silence, and he thought he heard his son cry a little.

"I called her the day before yesterday," Mitchell said. "About Thanksgiving plans. She asked if I wanted her to make the green salad, you know with the walnuts and cream cheese and pineapple." Another silence.

"When can you come?" Asa asked.

"Tonight," Mitchell said. "You'd need to come get me."

Asa hadn't given any thought to the fact that Mitchell didn't have a car.

"I could do that," Asa said, but as soon as he said it he realized he was in no shape to drive down to Greenville tonight.

"When's the service?" Mitchell asked.

"I imagine Sunday afternoon," Asa said. Mark Ward, their minister, had come by, given Asa his number to call if he needed anything, and said he would help plan the memorial service. Betsy was a Unitarian, and Unitarians didn't have funerals per se—no fancy caskets, no viewing of the body, no over-the-top flower arrangements.

"Sarah and I could come down in the morning and pick you up," Asa said.

Asa heard the woman's voice in the background.

"Wendy'll bring me up. She'd like to meet you and attend the service."

Asa felt a little ripple of impatience. "Where would she stay? Upstairs is unusable, and the power's out. I'm not sure it's such a good idea."

"I want her to come," Mitchell's tone hardened.

Asa heard Wendy talk in a gentle tone in the background.

"She wants to be there," Mitchell said softer, but still with an edge, "and I want her there."

Although this was no time to meet the girlfriend, neither was it time to have a blowup with his son. "We can find a place for her."

"Dad?" Mitchell asked. "How are you doing?"

The question almost undid him. It wasn't one he would have expected from his son.

"Numb," Asa said.

"Me too," Mitchell said.

After they hung up, Asa felt aggravated that this girl was coming at such a private family time. Still, Mitchell had sounded reasonable, even thoughtful.

Asa heard a car pull in the driveway. He recognized the rattle of Sarah's old Volvo. Luna barked a high excited bark and ran out the door. Outside, Asa found Sarah crouched down hugging the dog.

Sarah stood and pointed a flashlight up where the tree had fallen and where the tarp now lay. "Oh God," she whispered, looking up at the house. "I don't understand. How can this have happened, Daddy?"

She hadn't called him Daddy since middle school. As he hugged her, the emotional scaffolding that had sprung up to keep devastation at bay came crashing down.

CHAPTER 8

Sarah, Wednesday Evening

The leaf-strewn, tree-ravaged bed floated in the beam of Sarah's flashlight. The city hadn't given the okay that the upstairs was structurally sound, but Sarah had gone upstairs anyway. Her dad, being her dad, had come with her.

No blood, just like he said.

Her father reverently placed his palm on the mattress. "It's more upsetting to see the bed than it was seeing her in the morgue." His voice was quiet and sad. "Her wound didn't look that bad. The doctor said that sometimes there's very little blood with impalements. A word I'll never forget."

Sarah had already looked it up. "The limb must've lodged in her heart in such a way that it blocked the bleeding."

"That's what the doctor said," her father said. "Exactly what she said."

"How long were you with Mom in the morgue?" Sarah asked, already thinking she wanted to see her too.

"Not long," he said. "I sat with her a little while and held her hand and even caught myself squeezing it, as if she might squeeze back."

Sarah turned her flashlight on the blue tarp flapping above their heads, the upstairs chilly with the breeze slipping in. She aimed her flashlight back on the bed, training it on what would have been her dad's side where three branches remained stuck in the mattress as if it were a giant pincushion.

"Where were you?" she asked.

"Out in the studio grading papers," he said.

"Why were you out there?" Sarah had been under the impression that her parents had gotten into the routine of grading papers together at the kitchen table.

"I had a lot of papers to grade," he said, "and I didn't want to keep your mom up, so I decided to go out there instead."

They walked out to Sarah's car, Luna keeping close. Despite Sarah's warning that it was heavy, her father insisted on carrying her suitcase. He groaned as he heaved the suitcase through the studio door.

"Textbooks," she said. She knew she'd need to stay a while to help her dad. He would need it, especially with the funeral arrangements. Her mother had been the arranger, the planner, the organizer. Her father didn't have an organizing bone in his body.

"Are we sleeping here tonight?" She looked around the studio, which she always thought of fondly. When she and Mitchell were in elementary school, they would come to the studio every afternoon after school and have tea and cookies with their dad, do their homework, and then go out and play with their friends and roam the neighborhood, their dad always being a base if something should come up.

"I'll sleep in the house," he said.

"You'll freeze!"

"I've got the woodstove," her father said. "I need to keep an eye on things over there."

"Dad, it's not your fault."

"I should've been there," he said.

"I'm glad you weren't." She turned to the oven. "What's that wonderful smell?"

"I'm toasting some bread."

With her dad making tea, she went to the little bedroom and unpacked.

If anyone was to blame for her mother's death, she was. Her parents had been arguing about the hemlock for as long as she could remember. Henry, who regularly sprayed the tree for adelgids, had for a while warned the tree was sick. Her dad wanted it down, but her mom thought of the tree as a member of the family and kept delaying. Sarah could see for herself that the tree wasn't well. The cottony white growths on the limbs were thicker, while many of the limbs themselves had become spindly and others, some fairly large, had fallen off altogether. Even so, her dad had become so opinionated that almost without thinking Sarah sided with their mother on most issues, including the fate of the tree. She remembered chiming in more than once, "What could it hurt to leave it up one more year?"

When she came back to the kitchen, her dad slid a pan of toasted golden squares out of the oven and set them on a plate beside the teapot with three bags of tea steeping. Sarah and her dad sat at the little kitchen table, and Luna lay on the floor beside them.

"She's trembling." Sarah sat down on the floor and took Luna's head into her lap.

"She hasn't eaten," he said.

Sarah hugged Luna and kissed her head and saw her father watching.

"Remember that time when you were little," he said, "and you took her for a walk, and she pulled you off your feet?"

She pulled her jeans leg up, showing him the shiny crescent on her knee.

"That's when we stopped letting you walk her," he said. "She was too much dog for a little girl."

"Say 'I didn't mean to hurt Sarah,'" she said petting Luna. "'I was chasing a squirrel, and Sarah just happened to be attached.'" Sarah buried her nose in Luna's fur which smelled dusty and sweet.

"How'd Mitchell sound?" She sat back up and came to the table.

"Better than I would have expected." Her dad poured tea into her cup. "The girlfriend is driving him up. She wants to come to the service."

She heard exasperation in his tone.

"That's a good thing," Sarah said. Mitchell had predicted that their father would be resistant to the idea of Wendy coming. During crises, their dad couldn't countenance anything more than the crisis itself. To their father Wendy would feel like one more thing to deal with.

As they drank their tea, her dad slid a folder over to her marked *Betsy's Last Wishes*. "I haven't had time to read them," he said.

Sarah took out the few pages of notes and instructions. Her mother had chosen poems she wanted read and music she wanted performed at the memorial. As Sarah read, she took a bite of bread.

She opened an envelope marked *Obituary*, dated *Christmas 2015*. "I'll read this over," she said, "and update it and then type it up."

"Go to bed," her dad said. "This can wait till the morning."

"I'm not sleepy," she said. "Besides it'd be good to get this to the paper tomorrow. I'll call Mark first thing and set up a meeting."

"Okay," he said, kissing her cheek. "Don't stay up too late." As he started to leave, Sarah noticed that Luna had watched him with a look of confusion.

He came back and petted Luna. "You stay here and be with Sarah, Girl," he said. "I'll see you in the morning." He closed the door after him.

Luna lay back down on the floor at Sarah's feet. Sarah poured herself another cup of tea, ate a second piece of toast, and opened the envelope, which turned out to be two spare typewritten paragraphs of facts her mother had put together about her life. It felt overly modest to Sarah. Using her mother's paragraphs as an outline, she got to work. She wrote, drank tea, wrote, ate toast, and otherwise lost herself in a fuller distillation of their mother's life.

As she wrote in the quiet of the studio, she became aware of a throbbing in her ears, a sound she had been hearing off and on since her father had called to tell her about their mother. It wasn't an earache, just a pulsing that at first she thought came and went but then realized was constant, but she could only hear it when she listened for it. How bizarre to be writing her mother's obituary. More than once, she started to call her and double-check a few details.

CHAPTER 9

• • •

Asa, Late Wednesday Evening

When he got back to the house, Asa dug a sleeping bag out of the closet and rolled it onto the floor beside the couch. He lit a candle on the coffee table beside him and lay there, his hands behind his head, watching shadows play on the ceiling. Outside, the quince scraped against the kitchen window and the candle beside him fluttered.

Watching Sarah read through Betsy's last wishes, she reminded him so much of her mother. His daughter had inherited her mother's planning gene. For Betsy planning was her way of being in the world. She especially enjoyed planning family trips—studying maps, sending off for materials, reading travel books, finding places to stay, places to hike, places to explore. She would research the history of whatever place they happened to be traveling to. When they arrived, she would find the visitor center or the historical museum and read everything, absorbing all the exhibits. Betsy spent her life orienting herself and everyone around her. She was the family compass, and now, without her, they were lost.

Asa wasn't sure how long he had been asleep when he heard the front door open and in walked Sarah, Luna behind her. Sarah carried a blanket and pillow.

"What time is it?" Asa glanced at his watch. "You've been writing all this time?"

"We want to sleep over here with you."

He helped her get settled on the couch.

"I can't take this in," she said.

He hugged her, and Luna nosed her way between them.

"I think she might have PTSD." Sarah leaned her head against Luna's.

Asa pulled the blanket over his daughter, and as the dog settled between the couch and his sleeping bag, Asa blew out the candle.

He was glad Sarah was home. Even as a little girl she had been good company, running errands with him or helping him in the yard or going with him to the office. She'd been a talented conversationalist who filled his natural reticence with the generosity of her words. Being with Sarah then had been like being in the presence of thought itself. Like opening up his daughter's brain and looking down upon a constellation of firing synapses as she said one thing, then another until, after half an hour or so, she arrived at a new place. What had impressed Asa about Sarah when she was little was how she would ask him how his day had been. Asa himself had been such a reserved child. He had never dreamed of asking his parents about their day. It had never occurred to him adults had days of their own to ask about.

Only when Mitchell came along did Asa recognize his child self. As a baby, Mitchell had watched tree leaves flutter in the breeze, seeming to send him into an almost ecstatic contemplative state. His eyes would shift to the leaves and his face empty out, and he would remain still for several minutes, staring. He had been an inscrutable boy, telling them next to nothing. Asa and Betsy became highly attuned to their son's tone of voice, his expression, the way he entered the room, the way he sat at the dinner table, the way he participated in a conversation or, more often, did not. They became domestic detectives piecing together their son's interior life.

Asa thought of the time he had picked up Mitchell from elementary school, and as he walked him back to the car, he noticed he was unusually quiet. Asa worried something had happened. He strapped Mitchell into his booster seat, and as they drove home, he could see Mitchell in the rearview mirror brooding about whatever it was. Asa knew something awful had happened and was on the verge of asking him about it when Mitchell met his gaze in the rearview mirror and said, "Which way do tornadoes turn?"

As Asa lay in the dark, he heard Sarah's breathing and knew she was asleep. He had moved to the edge of sleep himself when the breeze outside picked up. He heard Betsy say, *I don't want to leave it like this.* The tarp upstairs began to flap, a great bird trapped in the house.

Asa woke in the middle of the night, trying to remember a name, a teacher Betsy worked with on the yearbook staff. Asa had never met her, but evenings when Betsy came home late from school, it was always because of working with students and this other teacher on the yearbook. Betsy had been on a few hikes with her and some other teachers.

Not wanting to wake Sarah, he slipped outside, went over to the studio, sat down at the little kitchen table, and opened his laptop. He scrolled down the Asheville High School faculty directory until he saw the name Heather Greene. That was it. Heather Greene was a firm-jawed, athletic-looking woman identified as an eleventh-grade English teacher and coadvisor for the Asheville High Annual. Asa looked at her picture then got the wine bottle from the cabinet and poured himself a jelly glass full. He sat back down and studied Heather Greene's picture some more.

CHAPTER 10

Asa, Fall 1991

Asa had spent what spare time he had over the past week getting ready for Betsy's visit—dusting, mopping, scrubbing, and putting out enough roach motels to accommodate a convention. He had moved to Atlanta in August where he had gotten a two-year gig teaching comp to wall-to-wall freshmen. He liked freshmen. He liked their energy and their openness, even if their writing left something to be desired. With benefits and an actual salary, the job was a step up from Adjunctville. But since his move to Atlanta, he had discouraged Betsy from visiting. He drove to Charleston once a month. If she came to Atlanta, she would take one look at his apartment, hightail it back to Charleston, and never be heard from again. But this time she had insisted on coming to Atlanta.

To make things worse, two nights ago an old girlfriend had called out of the blue, said she was in town, and wondered if he would like to meet. She had snagged a job at a liberal arts college in north Georgia.

Elly was a pale, thin waif with curly hair and big glasses, overly serious but sweet and kind. A girlfriend he liked more in retrospect. At Manuel's Bar in North Highlands, their conversation centered on the trials of teaching. As the pitcher of beer between them drained, she asked more personal questions, including was he seeing anybody.

"A woman from Charleston," he had said.

"Good for you," she said.

"How about you?" he asked.

"Not at the moment. With teaching five classes, heading up the curriculum committee, and advising the school newspaper I don't have time for much else." Her eyes lingered on him. "I miss us though."

Me too, he almost said, but he didn't because he didn't miss them. They talked a little longer, and he walked her out to her car. The buzz from the beer had him feeling nostalgic. He opened her car door for her, and she turned back to him, and he was reminded why he had been attracted to her. In the right light, from the right angle she reminded him of Diane Keaton. He leaned in to hug her, but they veered into a kiss. It wasn't a long kiss, but it wasn't a peck on the cheek either. She smiled and said, "Take care of yourself, Asa."

"You too, Elly." They hugged, he closed her door, and she drove away.

• • •

Since Betsy wasn't getting in till nine, he told her he would have dinner ready. After a phone consultation with his mother, he decided on something simple—baked chicken with rice and green beans. For hors d'oeuvres he bought port wine cheese and a box of ak-mak crackers. He splurged on a couple of eight-dollar bottles of wine that the clerk had said were even better than Mateus.

At 8:30, he set out the folding chairs and covered the card table with a tablecloth. He dug out candles and set the table.

Then he checked on the chicken. It was the first time he had used the oven other than to heat his apartment. With the oven light burned out, he had to use a flashlight to inspect the browning chicken pieces.

With everything under control, he opened one of the wines and poured himself a jelly glass full. He couldn't have told the difference between a merlot and a cabernet if his palate depended on it, but Betsy liked wine, especially with meals, and as he took another sip, he swished it around in his mouth.

He went back out to the main room, turned off most of the lights, and lit the candles. He carefully slid a record out of its jacket, making sure not to get fingerprints on the tracks. He gently set the record on his turntable. He had come across the Wendy Waldman album at Wax 'N' Facts, the used record store a couple of blocks up from his apartment. Waldman's voice was a scratchy, urgent growl. He and Betsy had first heard her on the University of Charleston's station the night they had met.

He cast a glance around the apartment and had to admit he had done a good job. He didn't need to tell Betsy about the kiss since it had meant nothing. Telling Betsy would be overindulging his overactive conscience, which his $25-an-hour intern doctoral student therapist at Georgia State pointed out was Asa's way of distracting himself from what mattered.

There was a knock, and he threw open the door. There she was, standing in the hallway's blinking fluorescent light. In faded jeans and a blue denim jacket she looked even more like Joni Mitchell. Her little suitcase could've just as easily been a guitar.

"I told you not to go to any trouble," Betsy said when she saw the candlelit table. He could tell she was touched. "Something smells really good. You actually cooked?"

"I said I would have dinner ready," he said taking her suitcase.

"I thought you meant takeout. Aren't you full of surprises."

"I bet you're hungry," he said. "Ready to eat?"

"I'd like to see the rest of your apartment first."

"Oh, the *rest*," he said. "I hope you have some time."

He showed her into his bedroom, setting her suitcase on his double bed, which took up most of the room. On his desk sat his used IBM Selectric. This tank of a typewriter weighed forty pounds and would've survived a nuclear blast. It had seen him through six years of grad school, its motor's industrious little rumble keeping his spirits up during the rise and fall of a handful of predominantly scholarly, bespeckled girlfriends—not to mention two years of dissertation composition.

He showed her his bathroom. "I call it Phone Booth with Shower." Then he directed her into a kitchen so small he had to stand in the bedroom doorway while she checked it out.

"Cozy," Betsy said.

He had her take the opened wine bottle into the living room. He served their plates and carried them into the main room, where he found her standing by the stereo, looking at the album cover.

"Wendy doesn't look like what I expected," she said as he came over and stood behind her, looking over her shoulder at the album cover. Betsy's hair smelled of Herbal Essences. A smell he couldn't get enough of.

They sat down, and as she put her napkin in her lap she said, "Your apartment has a lot of character."

A siren wailed in the distance then grew louder. From where they sat, they couldn't see the police car, but the blue lights flashed off the apartment building across the street, and they could almost feel the displacement of air as the car whizzed past.

She held up her jelly glass. "To life in Atlanta."

Whose life? His or theirs? He held out his glass and they clinked.

She took a sip. "I like this wine," she said, turning the bottle so that she could read the label. "Thank you for making such a nice meal."

He smiled. "Pretty basic," he said.

She buttered her rice, then cut a piece of the chicken, pausing to look at it in the flickering candlelight. "Chicken amandine," she said. "You're quite the chef."

Amandine? He leaned over his plate to take a closer look in the dim light and saw little brown ovals glistening in the candlelight. He grabbed her arm that held the fork on its way to her mouth.

She examined the bite of the chicken on the end of her fork, then set it down slowly. She leaned over her plate. "I can even see their little antennae." She said it like an observation, as if taking a scientific interest. "They must've crawled onto the chicken in the oven while it was cooking."

Asa was mortified.

"What an awful way to go," she said.

"I don't think it would've killed us," he said.

"I meant for them," she said, nodding at the toasted roaches.

He carried the plates back to the kitchen. Whatever had given him the idea he could pull off a nice meal, especially in this dump? When he returned with a plate of cheese and crackers, she stood at the window, looking down on Euclid Avenue and drinking her wine. They sat on the plaid couch, an old sleeper sofa. Asa held out the plate with the cheese and crackers to Betsy.

"I'll stick with the wine," she said.

"Why don't we go out?" He started to get up, but she pulled him back down.

"First," she said, "let's sit here and finish our wine." She took his hand, and they sat in the candlelight, listening to the music. How lucky he was to be with this woman who, upon being served chicken garnished with roach, had not made a scene. After a little while, the wine began to relax him. He leaned over to kiss her, but she laughed.

"I keep seeing the expression on your face," she said.

"Not every guy serves up chicken a la cockroach to his girlfriend."

"You called me your girlfriend."

"I heard that," he said.

They had been sleeping together for months, talked on the phone at least once a week, and yet this felt somehow presumptuous. He had blundered across some tacitly agreed upon line. "It was the wine talking," he said.

"You didn't mean it?" she asked.

He looked at her. "Do you want me to mean it?"

"Do you want me to want you to mean it?"

He paused counting the *wants* on his fingers. "Do you want me to want you to want me to mean it?"

"The question is," she said, "Do you want me to want you to want me to want you to mean it?" The smile on her face was the same as when she had just laid down a seven-letter word in Scrabble.

"I give up."

"Oh, don't give up." She stood. "Let's go get something to eat."

As he picked up the cheese plate to carry it back to the kitchen, a roach that had stowed away under a few crackers hurled itself off the plate and skittered under the couch.

Outside, the night was chilly, and leaves scuttled across Euclid Avenue as they walked up the sidewalk toward Little Five Points. Asa felt himself calm in the evening air. Betsy shivered and pulled herself against him.

"It's a full moon," he said, nodding at the fat, bright moon rising over the trees.

"Not quite," she said.

"Looks full to me," he said.

"It'll be full in the next couple of days," she said.

It being a Friday night many apartment doors were open, and people sat out on porches, talking and drinking and laughing, stereos blasting from open windows.

"I wanted to make you a nice dinner," he said.

"You did," she said. "The roaches just beat us to it."

They ended up at the Rainbow, an all-night diner catty-corner from The Pub. The Rainbow was cheap and good. Asa was a regular. He liked correcting papers at the diner, surrounded by people he didn't know.

They both ordered the vegetable plate. When she chewed, her jaw did this little popping sound that he found endearing. They were finishing up the last of their buttered corn muffins when the middle-aged waitress came over and topped off their coffees.

"Glad to see he brought something in beside his papers tonight," she said to Betsy, peeling off their check and putting it on the table. "I hope we see more of you."

They sat and sipped coffee and talked about what they might do tomorrow. Asa had always wanted to see the High Museum. There was a new Chagall exhibit, and a friend of Betsy's in Charleston had told her about the DeKalb Farmer's Market where they sold food from all over the world. She wondered if he would like to climb Stone Mountain, something she'd always wanted to do.

"I kissed a woman two nights ago," he said.

"Oh?" she said her face hardening.

He told her about meeting up with Elly and what he had come to think of as the grazing incident. "It didn't mean anything."

"Is that why you haven't wanted me to come?" she snapped. "Because you have something going on here?"

"This woman called me out of the blue. I hadn't seen her in years."

"Don't worry about it." She shoved her empty plate back. The look on her face went from angry to something else.

"I shouldn't have let that happen," he said, "but I didn't want to keep it from you. My therapist says I tend to let my overactive conscience distract me from what matters."

"You see a therapist?"

"Do you think that's weird?"

"If you ask me, more men should see therapists."

"He says I spend so much time feeling guilty about every little thing that I let the big things, in this case you, pass me by. I don't want that."

She smiled at him but then looked away. "Don't give the grazing incident another thought. If it makes you feel any better, I'm married."

He laughed, but she didn't even smile.

As they looked at each other, it seemed the conversation level in the restaurant rose several decibels. A guy bussed a table behind them, the dishes clattering so loudly it sounded as if everything was breaking. They started walking back to the apartment in silence. It had gotten colder.

"We're separated," she said after several blocks. "We haven't lived together for over two years, and for a lot of that time he's lived with another woman. In South Carolina you have to wait a year before filing for divorce." She stopped walking. "It'll be final next month."

"Why didn't you say anything?"

"I didn't tell you when we first met because I didn't want to scare you off. As time passed, I didn't tell you because I thought you'd be angry that I hadn't told you."

They walked along a little bit farther and he stopped again. "Married."

"We've covered that," she said.

He was quiet, not knowing how he felt. It had all been too good to be true.

"Just for three more weeks," she said.

"All this time you've been married. I don't mean to be weird but . . ." He looked at her. "It changes everything. Doesn't it?"

"I haven't lived with him for two years." She sounded frustrated. "I'd written off men altogether till you showed up with your poetry and your fucking endearing ways." She blinked back tears. "Want me to get a room somewhere tonight?"

"Of course not."

They walked a little farther.

"I should've told you sooner," she said.

"How long were you married?" he asked.

"Not even a year."

He nodded.

"If it helps any, he was a Buddhist."

"All this time I've thought of you one way," he said, "and now I need to think of you another way."

"That's called being in a relationship."

Asa insisted she sleep in his bed while he slept on the pullout sofa. He lay awake staring up at the streetlight outside his window. Married. Why had it bothered him so much? She hadn't lived with the guy for a long time. Why did it matter? Had he studied so many Victorian novels he had internalized their strictures? Was he going to forfeit this spirited, beautiful woman to a fusty set of mothball mores? Was he at heart a self-righteous judgmental prick right out of a Thomas Hardy novel?

The next morning, he woke to the sound of a door closing. It took him a minute to gather his wits, remembering all that happened last night and how ridiculous he had been. He went into his bedroom to apologize, but the bed was made and there was no sign of her anywhere.

He pulled on his clothes and ran outside, but Betsy's car was gone. Waylon, a friendly young guy who worked as a realtor downtown and lived in the apartment next to Asa's, was carrying a garbage bag out to the curb.

"You didn't see a woman leave a few minutes ago, did you?"

"She asked where a good breakfast place was, and I told her The Flying Biscuit."

Asa started jogging in that direction, but Waylon grabbed

his bike off the porch and told him to take it, said it would be a lot quicker.

"She your girlfriend?"

"I hope so," Asa said and pedaled down Euclid Avenue for all he was worth.

CHAPTER 11

• • •

Asa, Thursday Morning

The headline read, *Beloved Teacher Killed in Storm.* The paper ran a photo of the hemlock on their house. The cutline read: *The sole fatality attributed to the storm was that of longtime Asheville High School teacher Betsy Flowers, killed when a tree fell onto the family home. Her husband, Asa Flowers, escaped injury.*

That last line had felt like an accusation. The photographer hadn't bothered to warn them the photo was coming out. Exactly *when* had it been taken? While Asa was still asleep in the studio and Betsy pinned by the tree? The photo had already prompted phone calls, and a couple of flower bouquets along with notes addressed to *Mrs. Flowers* had appeared at the foot of what remained of the hemlock.

On their way back from meeting with their minister they stopped by Riverside. Like a park with headstones, Riverside Cemetery, in the heart of the Montford neighborhood, stretched across nearly ninety acres of rolling hills and thick-trunked oaks and tulip poplars. People came to walk or jog or eat their lunches on one of the wrought iron benches. This morning city crews cleared the storm's aftermath—several immense fallen trees, a slew of limbs, many more branches, and a carpet of brilliant red and yellow leaves.

A cold breeze made his daughter shudder, even though she

had put on her mother's workout hoodie. Asa had on his UNC fleece that Sarah had gotten him last Christmas.

"I think Mom will be pleased with the service," Sarah said.

The three of them had sat in Mark Ward's office going over Betsy's instructions, but Asa had found his mind wandering. He sensed the strange, disorienting calm that had been visiting and revisiting him these past days. What a contrast to how intensely he had felt and how angrily he had reacted all those years ago when Betsy had told him that she was married.

"Dad, are you paying attention?"

Asa had looked up to see his daughter and Mark looking at him.

• • •

"It's a lovely spot," Sarah said when they came over a hill and arrived at a little grassy area, and Asa agreed. He and Betsy bought the plot the same day they had closed on the house. They used to walk over on early summer evenings and stroll through the cemetery, making a point to go by and check on their "property." With Asa being older than Betsy and coming from a long line of early deaths, he had always assumed he would go first.

Sarah's phone rang, and she answered it. It was Mitchell, she said. They were forty minutes away and wondering if they should meet at the house for lunch or go out somewhere or was Asa up to going out in public?

"Go out," Asa said to Sarah, thinking that right about now the house would be crawling with insurance adjustors, city inspectors, friends, and neighbors.

She spoke into the cell. "Let's meet somewhere." She paused, and Asa could hear his son's voice. Sarah turned to Asa. "Freda's?"

Asa nodded. He hadn't been to Freda's in a little while, but he'd always liked it. And even if it was vegetarian, it wasn't militantly so.

"See you at Freda's," Sarah said into the phone.

The wind blew and pine needles showered down around them. Asa plucked a pine needle out of his daughter's hair. The two of them faced the grave.

"Do you know the odds of being killed by a tree?" she said. "One in twenty million. You're twice as likely to be struck by lightning. And six hundred times more likely to be killed in a car accident."

He handed her his handkerchief. She dabbed her eyes and blew her nose, but seeing his daughter had nowhere to put it, held out his hand to take back the handkerchief.

"It's all snotty now," she said.

"I've been holding your snotty Kleenex since you were knee high to a katydid." As Asa and Sarah left the cemetery, Sarah said she was worried about Luna and wanted to take her to their vet, Regina Hill. Sarah, like Betsy, was an animal person. She had always connected with Regina, often taking Luna to her appointments. Although Regina was a little eccentric, Asa felt fondly toward her. She had saved their family from giving up Luna in the dog's younger, more aggressive days when she had viciously attacked a couple of small dogs. Asa was grateful for Regina's intervention since, at the time, he had been the one lobbying to give up Luna, which would have been a terrible mistake. Regina had saved his children and his wife from heartbreak and kept his family from resenting him.

Sarah's phone rang again, and when she pulled it out of the hoodie, a folded piece of paper fluttered to the ground. As Sarah answered her phone, Asa picked up the paper and unfolded it. He read the couple of lines neatly printed on notepaper:

Good luck tonight! I can't get my head around that you're actually doing this!! I know it won't be easy! Call me after you've told him!!

Asa recognized it as one of the scores of notes Betsy was always intercepting in class. She said teenage girls were living exclamation points. As Asa stuck the note in his jacket, he overheard a little of Sarah's phone conversation. She was talking to Josh.

"He called to see how I'm doing," Sarah said when she got off the phone.

Then he remembered the last conversation he had with his wife.

"Your fellowship!" Asa said. "Mom told me about it. Congratulations." He hugged her. "I should've said something sooner. With everything that's happened it slipped my mind."

"It slipped mine too." She bit her lip and shook her head, and he put his arm around her shoulder as they walked out of the cemetery gates.

CHAPTER 12

Wendy, Late Thursday Morning

As Wendy drove along the edge of Jones Gap, thinking about the notices from the accounting office piling up in her email, she told herself that now wasn't the time to worry about that.

A gust of wind nudged the car closer to the edge, and she gripped the steering wheel tighter. Having grown up in the piedmont, she loved the mountains for their dramatic terrain, no matter the weather or time of year. The storm had cleared the sky, leaving it intensely blue with low puffy clouds whirling along the tops of the bent bare gnarled trees, reminding her of the Japanese landscape paintings they had studied in her Asian art history class, the very class where she and Mitchell had met.

"Wendy?" Mitchell was looking at her.

"Hm?" She turned her gaze back to the road.

"What are you thinking?"

"I hope your dad likes me," she said. She glanced over at him. "Maybe it isn't the best time for me to visit. Maybe I should drop you off and go back to Furman this afternoon."

"We've been through this," he said. "I want you to meet my family."

Mitchell's eyes flickered as it registered that the family he referred to was missing a key member. Ever since he had gotten the news Wendy saw the shock revisit his face, the realization of his mother's death coming in waves. He was in that shut down mode that came over him when he was sad or depressed. Wendy reached across the seat for his hand, but he stared out the window.

When Sarah had called with the news yesterday, Wendy and Mitchell had been eating with the rest of the cafeteria workers before their supper shift. She followed him outside where they sat on one of the picnic tables and watched the sun set as a pair of swans glided across the lake. She tried her best to comfort him. Talk didn't do much for Mitchell. Later that evening, they snuck across campus into the faculty lounge, which, early in the semester, they discovered was mysteriously left unlocked at night and always empty. On the couch where their professors drank coffee and complained about students during the day, she gave Mitchell what she had been giving him most of the semester.

Premarital sex was a sin, but she had talked it over with the Lord and concluded it was a greater sin to deny Mitchell what he needed. She didn't confide to the Lord how good the giving felt. When Mitchell made love to her, he inhabited every inch of her body. It was like being filled with the Holy Spirit on a subatomic level.

Wendy knew she played a role in Mitchell's improvement. She also knew pride goeth before a fall. That wasn't exactly what it said in the Bible. In the Bible it said, "Pride goeth before destruction, and an haughty spirit before a fall."

"So you'll stay for the funeral?" Mitchell said.

"If that's what you want."

His eyes darkened. "I want them to get to know the woman I intend to spend the rest of my life with."

"Probably not a great idea to bring that up right now," she said.

They had discussed getting married the summer after Mitchell graduated. While that was a while off, it made her rest easier about the whole business. Premarital sex didn't feel as sinful knowing it would eventually lead to marital sex.

"It's so bizarre. A tree." He looked at her. "And that it missed Dad."

Mitchell was really saying that if either of his parents had to go, he wished it would have been his father. Of course, Mitchell had no idea this was what he was saying. Still, it was plain as the loss on his face. He had lost the wrong parent. Wendy had gathered Mitchell's father wasn't a bad man, just moody, remote, and quick to anger. Not unlike someone else she knew.

"You know about this kind of thing." Mitchell kept his eyes on the mountains.

"Little kids are resilient," she said. "They accept things." Her father had been a drug rep and was away a lot, but when her mother died, he quit that job and started his church and stayed home.

"In the end," she said, "I lost a mother but gained a father."

Mitchell went back to looking out the window.

When she and Mitchell first got together, she was often hurt by his lack of attention. Then he began sending sketches of her through the campus mail. Those drawings revealed an almost unnerving attention, as if he could see through to her soul.

Ever since Mitchell had gotten the news, Wendy had been remembering her last visit to her mother's hospital room. How it had taken every fiber of her four-year-old self to lean over and endure the sour breath and kiss the papery cheek, how it took every ounce of courage to stay in that stultifying room and look into the remnants of her mother's face, her eyes blazing. Her father prayed at the bedside in his strong calm voice about how he looked forward to the day when they would be together again. Even later, when he became a minister, her father would talk about the afterlife in the same way, not like some gaudy dream with harp-strumming angels hovering over streets of gold, but like a real place, a quiet little town just off the map, where families, when they had become separated, knew to meet up.

CHAPTER 13

Asa, Noon Thursday

Freda's Diner sat on Montford Avenue, across from Lola's Salon, Almost Downtown Books, and Hip Replacements, where manikins modeled vintage clothes, their pelvises thrust forward. As Asa and Sarah started into the diner, Asa noticed the newspaper rack. There it was again, the damn photo of the tree on their house. It made him feel conspicuous. Sarah and he scooted into one of the booths in the back that felt a little more private.

"Mom said you were only one of a handful of students in the country who received the fellowship. I'm really proud of you."

"Thanks, Dad."

"I want you to go," he said.

She looked up at him. "Mom got to you." She smiled a sad smile.

"I genuinely want you to go."

His daughter had started out as a chem major but in the middle of sophomore year had shifted to physics and never looked back. She said physics engaged her creativity in a way that chemistry didn't. She was obsessed in the best of ways, always scribbling equations in the margins of everything.

"But now it all seems beside the point." Tears shone in his daughter's eyes.

"Tell me about Wendy," Asa said, trying another tack.

Sarah said Wendy was an art history major and her father was a minister of a little church in Traveler's Rest, South Carolina. Her mother had died when Wendy was little, and she and her father were close.

A waitress Asa guessed to be in her late twenties who looked vaguely familiar handed them plastic-coated menus, then came back to the table with a coffeepot, turned their cups over, and filled them.

"Didn't I teach you?" Asa asked her.

She smiled.

"Erica, right? From Baton Rouge!"

"Very impressive." She seemed pleased.

"You were in my poetry class and wrote good poems. I remember one about a copperhead."

"Wow," she said. "I can't believe you remembered that." She took their orders and headed back to the kitchen.

Sarah sipped her coffee, and they sat there a little while not speaking. His daughter had that look he recognized when she was hesitant to tell him something.

"What?" he asked.

"There's something else you might want to know about Mitchell's girlfriend."

"Yes?"

"She's one of *them*."

Asa looked at his daughter, going through all the possibilities and alighting on the one that rose to the level of car wreck. "Very funny." But his daughter wasn't smiling.

"Like a Susan Collins?" he said.

She shook her head.

"A Murkowski?"

She looked at him.

"A McCain? A Romney?"

"She is a pro-life, pro-NRA, card-carrying member of That Party Which Must Not Be Named, and one of her favorite pastimes is deer hunting with her father, an evangelical preacher."

Asa sat there, trying to absorb this news. "Republicans don't major in art."

"This one does."

"And Mitchell likes her?"

"*Likes* is a feeble word for how your son feels about her."

"How can this be?"

"She's warm, she's pretty, and she's smart."

He stared down at his coffee. "Never did I imagine one of our children would date one of them."

"You sent him to a Baptist college and surrounded him with smart, sweet, sexy conservative girls. What did you expect?"

"Your mother and I wanted him to be happy," he said.

"You got your wish," she said.

A vein throbbed in his neck. "My own flesh and blood."

"Stop being such a Four." Sarah had taken the same Enneagram workshop her mother had. "Mitchell's the happiest I've seen him. You need to be nice to her." She looked away. "Even if she did vote for . . ."

Asa put his head in his hands, stared down at the table, and groaned. "Shoot me now."

"We'll have to wait till Wendy gets here."

Sarah's phone vibrated on the table. "Speaking of which," she said, texting something back. "They're almost here."

"I'm glad your mother didn't know about Wendy's party affiliation."

"She knew."

"She never mentioned anything to me about it," Asa said.

"I wonder why?" she said.

"She was afraid I'd overreact?" he asked.

She scratched her nose. "Let's put it this way. Your son came by his emotional intensity honestly."

He raised his hands as if surrendering. "So where will everybody sleep tonight?"

"The three of us can camp out in the living room, but Wendy should stay in the studio to give her some privacy."

Sarah's gaze shifted to someone behind him. "There you are." She jumped out of her seat before Asa had time to recognize the dark-eyed boy she hugged was his own.

CHAPTER 14

Asa, Spring 1992

Soaked and miserable, Asa and Betsy sat inside the tent, staring out at the drenched world. They had hiked an hour and a half in the rain to reach the campsite, put up the tent as best they could, and now sat looking out.

The rain was hypnotic, and after a few minutes, Betsy shrugged off her poncho, slipped off her damp shorts, rolled out her sleeping bag, crawled inside, and fell asleep, snoring with a bad cold. Making sure she was asleep, Asa opened his pack and checked on the wine he smuggled along and the filet mignon wrapped in an ice pack.

He took off his poncho, leaned back on his elbows watching Betsy, then looked out at the rain and the rushing little creek beyond. Betsy had moved in with Asa after his first year at Georgia State, and it had been nearly a year now. She had found a job teaching English at an inner-city school only a mile from their apartment.

They got past the weirdness about her husband, officially her ex now that the paperwork had finally come through. Betsy fell in love with the Buddhist in college, but not long after they married, she realized it was Buddhism she fell in love with, not the Buddhist. Eventually she asked the Buddhist for a divorce, and the Buddhist, being a Buddhist, was not resentful or angry or petty. They had divorced amicably, although the divorce papers didn't come through until two weeks ago. This was the initial reason Asa planned to bring along the wine and the steak.

Asa sat over Betsy, watching her breathe with her mouth open. Why hadn't he told her as soon as he got the call? She knew he'd been applying for tenure track jobs in the Atlanta area and a few other places in the Southeast. She went with him on some of those trips, including the one to North Carolina, where they had him up for an interview at a little college in the mountains. He wasn't surprised when he received a short but thoughtful letter from the department chair saying he hadn't gotten the job. But day before yesterday, the same department chair called and said the first candidate had taken a job elsewhere and asked if Asa might still be interested. Asa's heart leapt with the news, and although he wanted to tell her yes, he asked if he might have the weekend to decide.

Betsy liked her job, and they never really discussed what they would do if he got a job somewhere besides Atlanta. Yet Asa didn't see how he could turn down this offer. They might have to go back to a long-distance relationship. He had enjoyed living with her these past ten months. He looked forward to the end of the day, when he could go home to their apartment, discuss their day, and then go out for a beer at the Little Five Points pub. He was more than fond of their life together, and the idea of interrupting it depressed him. Another idea occurred to him, but he didn't know how Betsy, who had just extracted herself from one marriage, would receive it.

He fell asleep and woke a half hour later to find Betsy on her knees looking out the tent flap at the rain, which had slackened some. He came up beside her, hugging her, and she leaned back into his arms.

"I slept two hours," she said.

"You've been sick."

"I do feel better," she said. "In fact, I'm a little hungry." She reached for his backpack. "Did you bring those ak-mak crackers?" She started opening his pack.

"Hey, don't go in there." But he was too late.

She pulled out the bottle. "Wine! And some very nice wine at that," she said, looking at the label. "I know that wine. The Buddhist used to buy it."

"Hold on there," he said, seeing her reach into the pack again.

She pulled out the filet and gave him a mystified look. Then she pulled out two potatoes wrapped in aluminum foil. "What's going on? Is this about the divorce papers?"

"Sort of." That had been the initial reason for buying all this, until the phone call. Since then, he had greater ambitions for the expensive wine.

"That's sweet of you to haul all this for five miles, so we could have a nice meal in the woods."

"If we get to cook it," he said, looking out at the rain.

"It's letting up." She looked out at the lightening sky. She pulled on her boots. "I gotta pee." Looking hopelessly cute in her t-shirt, bare legs, and hiking boots, she disappeared behind the tent.

By the time Betsy came back, the sun had slid out from behind a bank of early evening clouds, turning the dripping trees a shimmering green and brightening the campsite. A good omen?

"Let me get this fire going," he said. "You sit back and relax."

"I'm not an invalid."

They gathered up dry sticks and twigs they snapped off the underside of bushes. Betsy built a little teepee in the middle of the fire circle previous campers had made of flat river rock.

The damp limbs hissed and smoked but eventually dried and caught fire, and in a bit, they had a steady blaze going. Good timing since night had come on quickly, and it had gotten even chillier. Asa buried the cooked potatoes in the hot coals. Half an hour later, he had enough coals to lay his campfire grill across the rocks and then set the steak on it.

Betsy sat beside him on the log and held her hands out toward the fire. The collective thrum of the crickets and katydids echoed around them in a thunderous pulse.

"Want me to open the wine?" she asked.

"Sure." He turned the hissing steak over with a fork.

She came back with the wine bottle. "Did you bring a corkscrew?"

"Oh, shit."

"I take that as a no," she said.

"I went to all that trouble and didn't even bring anything to open it with."

"Pocketknife." She held her hand out like a surgeon waiting for a scalpel.

He dug his pocketknife out of his pocket and handed it to her. She slipped the knife blade into the cork, twisted it, and popped out the cork intact.

"Where'd you learn to do that? Let me guess. The Buddhist."

"What can I say? The man knew his way around a bottle of wine."

Asa knew it was silly. She had divorced him and talked at

length about how frustrating it was to live with a guy who refused to enter into an argument of any sort and would instead go off to his study and meditate. Even so, this talk about the Buddhist had made him uncomfortable, especially when it turned out he bought the wine the Buddhist used to buy. And now they owed the Buddhist for saving this meal. Next thing he knew the Buddhist would step out of the woods and join them for supper.

Of course this wasn't really about the Buddhist, this was about losing his nerve yet again. If he didn't ask her now, he might never.

Betsy brought two metal camping mugs from the tent, set them on the ground, and filled them with wine. They each lifted a mug. Before he could get the words out, she clinked her mug against his and said, "To freedom."

"To freedom," he said.

She took a sip and added, "From the shackles of matrimony."

To this he said nothing. His heart sank, but recovering himself, he dredged up a smile and took a sip of wine which, after all the expense and labor involved, tasted a little bitter. They sat on the log, eating steak and potatoes and watching sparks from the fire drift up into the starry night.

"There's nothing like food cooked on a campfire," she said, "especially if it happens to be filet mignon." She gave him a greasy kiss on his cheek.

Asa got up to put more limbs on the fire. It had gotten colder, so he built up the fire to throw more heat. "How are you feeling?" He sat back down beside her.

"Much better," she said. "This is such a nice meal. Thanks so much for going to all this trouble."

"Sure," he said, looking at the fire.

"Are you okay? Did I say something that weirded you out? Did I steal your thunder with my toast? You brought the wine. It was yours to toast with. Or maybe it was wine for its own sake. Nontoasting wine."

He looked up at her. "There's something I need to tell you."

"That doesn't sound good." She set her plate down. "You don't have cancer or something do you?"

"I've been offered that job."

"What job?"

"At Altamont College."

"But they turned you down."

"The first candidate ended up taking another job, so they asked me."

"That's fantastic, Asa!" She kissed him.

"I couldn't believe it when they called."

"When did they call?"

"Yesterday," he said.

"You've been sitting on this news since yesterday?"

"I didn't know how to tell you," he said.

"What's that supposed to mean? You have great news. You tell me."

"I didn't know what you'd think."

"I think it's awesome. Why would I think anything else? It's something you've wanted a long time. A tenure track job at a good college. Great school, great town. Are you kidding me? So why didn't you tell me?"

He poked at the fire sending sparks drifting up into the night sky and noticed the moon. "So is that a full moon?" he asked. "Looks like a full moon to me."

"Don't change the subject," she said.

"I'll have to move there," he said. "If I take it."

"Of course you'll take it. This means the world to you."

He looked back at the fire.

"Oh." Her face fell. "You don't want me to go with you. Are you breaking up with me?"

"I know how much you love your job."

"I've known all along that you might get a job away from Atlanta, and that if you were offered a good job elsewhere, you'd have to take it. You've been working toward this for years. It's how we met."

"You think I should take it?"

"You and I both know offers like this—a great school, hip little town, in the mountains even—don't come along every day."

"You're saying I should take it."

"I'm saying *we* should take it," she said.

"And you'd be okay with leaving Atlanta?"

"It wouldn't be easy giving up the couch-size vermin, the muggers, the traffic, the smog, the heat, and the urban sprawl for a cool town in the mountains of North Carolina, but I'm willing to make that sacrifice."

"Why didn't you tell me this before?" he asked.

"I didn't want you to feel bad if you didn't get the job. And I guess I didn't want to get my hopes up."

"So you'll go?"

She picked up her mug and he picked up his. "To Asheville." They clinked and drank.

"So all this, the nice wine, the nice meal, was about your new job?" she said.

He got up, put another log on the fire and stood on the other side, looking at her over the flames. A burning log popped, scattering sparks. The firelight made her face glow. *Beautiful* was too static a word to describe her. Her beauty was more of a verb, something that had acted on him over the time they were together.

Asking her might foul the whole thing. In fact, you might lose her if you ask her. Or what if she says no but will still go with you. Won't it feel weird to live together after that? She said she'd go with you—don't ask for more. Don't be greedy. What can it hurt to wait a little bit and see how it goes in Asheville? Give it six months.

"Would you be at all interested in marrying me?" he asked her.

"Oh, that." She looked off in the direction of the creek, now roaring with rainwater. "That's what the wine and all this was really about?"

"Not at first," he said.

She looked at him on the other side of the fire. "Asa?"

"Yes?"

"Why are you way over there?"

He shrugged. "It's easier to ask you from over here."

She glanced at the moon. "It is definitely a full moon," she said.

"Don't change the subject," he said.

After a little bit she began to nod slowly. Then she looked up at him. "I might be interested in marrying you."

"But?"

"You'll have to come over here and ask me."

CHAPTER 15

Asa, Noon Thursday

Seeing the lost look on his son's face, Asa hugged Mitchell tight, smelling that same dusty boy smell his son always had. He became aware of a woman behind them.

"We're so glad you could come," Sarah said.

Then Mitchell said, "Dad, this is Wendy."

"My prayers have been with you and your family." The woman took his hand. She looked him in the eye and gave his hand a firm grip.

"Thank you for delivering our son to us," he said.

Correction. No more our. *No more* us.

With Mitchell's eyes on him, Asa knew he should say something more. "We've heard a lot about you."

No more We've. *Loss it seemed was in the pronouns.*

Sarah moved over to Asa's side so Mitchell could sit with Wendy. The moment Asa set eyes on Wendy, he saw why his son fell for this girl who could've stepped right out of a book of Irish folktales. A willowy girl with long red hair, a wide freckled face, sunburned cheeks, and intelligent blue eyes.

Still, her presence miffed him. Wasn't it presumptuous that she, a relative stranger, had waded into this? He would have talked it over with Betsy if he could have. He had always talked things over with Betsy—the children, work, anything that mattered. In fact, the one person Asa kept thinking he should talk with about Betsy's death was Betsy.

"I hope you don't mind that I came, Dr. Flowers," Wendy said.

"Of course not," Asa said. "And please call me Asa. But I'm afraid we're a bit cramped with the upstairs bedrooms unsafe to sleep in."

"I understand," Wendy said.

"It might be better if you visited another time."

"Dad!" Mitchell said.

"I'll head back this afternoon," Wendy said, not batting an eye.

"You're not going anywhere." Mitchell put his arm around her shoulder.

"This is a family time," Wendy said. "I said that to you, Mitchell."

"It's important you be here," Mitchell said. "That they get to know you."

"Dad?" Sarah leaned over to Asa, "We agreed she'd sleep out in the studio."

Asa took a breath and tried to calm himself. He thought of what Betsy would say. She wouldn't say anything. She would glare at him. She would be furious.

"That's right," Asa said. "I forgot that's what we decided. I know it's important to Mitchell that you stay."

Sarah took Wendy's hand. "It's important to all of us."

"I should go back." Wendy looked at Asa in a calm direct way that unnerved him.

"I'm sorry if I was rude," Asa said.

"*If*?" Mitchell said.

"Listen, I don't want to get in y'all's hair," Wendy said.

How long had it been since Asa'd heard anyone use that expression? In that one sentence Wendy's accent had unfurled, sounding richer and thicker, a soft upstate South Carolina lilt that reminded him of his own mother's.

"You'll stay?" Mitchell said.

Wendy looked at Asa. "As long as you'll let me know if I get underfoot."

Then Wendy rested her hand on Mitchell's arm. Asa thought it was a comfortable gesture with a whiff of possessiveness about it.

After lunch Sarah had to go by the newspaper a few blocks away to drop off Betsy's obituary she'd written up. Mitchell was going to show Wendy around Montford.

Wendy turned to Asa. "Would you like to come, Asa?"

One glance at his son's face told Asa this was the last thing Mitchell wanted. Besides he didn't trust himself right now and wanted to avoid making another misstep.

"I need to get back."

Everyone agreed to meet back at the house. Asa went up to the register to pay the check. As the waitress rang it up, she said, "Your son looks so much like the jacket photo of you on your first book. What was it? *In Captivity*."

Asa looked up, surprised. "You've read my book?"

"I have most of your books, Professor. All but a couple I haven't been able to find."

"Really?" Asa was always surprised when anyone was interested in his poetry, especially interested enough to read them. But obscurity had never really bothered him. Poets knew what they'd signed up for. Unlike novelists with their outsized egos, their brag fests over agents, editors, fat advances, and three-book-deals, poets talked about the work. That's all they had to talk about.

"Tell me which books you don't have, and I'll bring them to you."

"Of course I'll pay you for them."

He shook his head. "I have too many copies of my books as it is," he said. "I don't know who I'm saving them for. It's a common affliction—writers hoarding copies of their books. In the basement, in the attic, under their beds. Posterity is a voracious reader."

He'd started walking home when he ran into Judith Gant, a short, sturdy woman and the principal at Asheville High. She gripped his arm. "Asa, oh my God. Everybody's so upset at school." An emotional woman and a beloved principal, Judith was a mother figure and a real leader to students and faculty. "How are you?"

"I don't know," he said.

"Of course, you don't." She hugged him. "We've called in counselors for students and staff. In fact, as I was leaving school Heather Greene came into my office. You know Heather. She works with Betsy on the yearbook. They're two peas in a pod. She's beside herself. Betsy's close to a lot of people. She makes herself available to whoever needs her. That's what made Betsy Betsy. And there's a whole lot of hurt going on at school over the loss of your sweet wife." She hugged him again. "You and Mitchell and Sarah are in my prayers."

Two peas in a pod. Two smart, beautiful women. Asa watched fiery yellow and red leaves drift down from a nearby maple, transforming the damp sidewalk into an immense Rorschach inkblot, and at its center, a skewered heart.

CHAPTER 16

Mitchell, After Lunch Thursday

They were barely out of Freda's when Mitchell, who had done his best to contain himself, said, "I can't believe you asked him to come with us!"

Wendy looked taken aback.

Mitchell berated himself for jumping on her. How was she to know that the whole reason he wanted a walk was to get away from his father? "Sorry," he said, putting his arm around her. "I know you were being thoughtful."

She pulled away. "He is your father after all."

"I didn't like him being rude to you," he said.

"He wasn't."

"All that about not having room for you? Sarah'd worked it out ahead of time that you'd stay out in the studio." He snatched a branch dangling from a rhododendron and snapped it in two. "Didn't you see the deer in the headlights look when you asked if he wanted to come with us?"

"To your dad," she said, "I'm an unknown quantity arrived in your family's midst at the worst possible time. So no, he didn't make me feel bad. What does make me feel bad is how shattered he looks. My father had the same look."

They walked along in silence, passing a sad, old, desolate-looking boarding house with NO TRESPASSING signs posted on the porch. Mitchell felt his anger at his father recede and the knot in his chest loosen.

"I know, you're right," Mitchell finally said. "He's got to be devastated. They've been married longer than I've been alive." His parents quarreled like all married couples, but mostly they seemed to enjoy each other. They got together with friends, had date night most Saturday nights, going out for dinner or to a movie. And they shared a certain way of looking at the world.

Mitchell slipped his arm around Wendy's waist, and she kissed his cheek. He liked the way they didn't stay mad at each other.

They passed a few blocks of large, ornate old homes, several turned into B&Bs. Others were law offices, doctors' offices, or spas of one kind or another. Occasionally an opensided tour bus would pause in front of one of the houses and the driver would narrate its history over the bus intercom, a history Mitchell could practically recite in his sleep.

Wendy stopped in front of an old white clapboard building that had been a church but was now a restaurant. "This looks like my dad's church," she said.

As they walked on, Mitchell said, "What worries me is that Mom was our buffer. Without her as go-between, I don't know how my dad and I will get along."

"He's probably worried about the same thing," she said.

He and his dad hadn't always fought. They had been close when he was a kid. His father was the one who realized how much he loved art and would bring art books and artist biographies home from the university library. His father enrolled him in art classes and started taking him to museums and galleries. Whenever their family had gone on trips, they'd always visit a museum. His mom and Sarah would get tired after a little while and go do something else while his dad stayed as long as Mitchell wanted.

"I loved those museum years," Mitchell said.

"Why'd they stop?" she asked.

"When I became a teenager, I was depressed. I didn't know I was depressed. I just knew I felt bad. And I was getting into fights with my folks, especially Dad."

"How did he react?"

"I think he was as surprised as I was," Mitchell said. "We'd have some terrible shouting matches, and it was sad because we'd been close. Then came the time when everything changed. After that, Dad basically stopped talking to me. I think he and Mom decided it'd be best if she did most of the communicating. So my dad and I stopped fighting, but we also stopped talking. At least when you're fighting, you're talking, even if it's loud."

"He's afraid, Mitchell."

He frowned. "Afraid?"

"That he might cause you to try to hurt yourself again."

"But that was a long time ago. I hardly think about it anymore." He shrugged.

She gave him a skeptical look.

"So maybe I think about it now and then."

"Have you talked to him about it?"

He paused. "Like I said, we don't really talk anymore."

"That's going to have to change."

Mitchell couldn't begin to see how that was going to happen. "The good thing is that he and Sarah are close."

"He needs you too."

Mitchell squinted his eyes at her. "Back there at Freda's when you invited him to go on this walk with us, you knew good and well I didn't want him to come."

She watched a group of tourists being led down the street by an overly enthusiastic tour guide.

"You invited Dad anyway," Mitchell said. "You invited him because you thought it was the right thing to do, even though you knew it would make me anxious."

She levelled her gaze at him. "Get used to it."

Staring at her a moment, he wasn't sure what he felt. Then he looked around and realized where they were. "I want to show you something."

He led her down a little alley obscured from the street. They came to a fenced-in area with an open gate. A sign said, *WELCOME TO MONTFORD COMMUNITY PEACE GARDEN*. They entered the garden, a place that had always felt like a refuge and a little bit of a second home to him.

In his school days, he spent countless hours among its tangle of paths woven around and between little sheds and outbuildings, adorned with a good twenty large paintings of famous Black historical figures like Nelson Mandela, Martin Luther King, and Malcolm X, who held a rifle and peeked around a corner. Among the buildings were flower beds and various plantings. At the center of the garden was a little library with doors made from a huge Texaco gas station sign cut in half and hung so that the two pieces slid open and shut like doors. Inside was a long table with chairs and shelves of books—picture books, children's books, and books for adults about African Americans. In the back was a row of small painted portraits of four girls.

"The 16th Street Baptist Church Birmingham bombing," Wendy said, looking at them. "Those poor girls."

"Sons of bitches from the KKK," Mitchell said. "Wasn't till decades later two of the bastards were finally prosecuted."

Wendy looked at Mitchell, as if caught off guard by the intensity of his anger.

He showed her around the rest of the garden, taking her down paths bordered by found-object sculptures made of street signs, traffic signs, and even realtor signs, as well as old children's toys, dolls, play kitchens, building blocks, toy mowers, little play cars and bikes, trikes, and wagons. Hundreds of objects, arranged, grouped, stacked, and interwoven.

"This is the peace garden?" she asked.

"And the Reverend Barton's backyard," Mitchell said.

"That would be me," said a large man wearing a suit and clerical collar. He walked down from a house toward the back of the property. "I thought I heard your voice." Reverend Barton hugged Mitchell, then as he did, he got a sober look on his face. "Your mama, Lord." And for a moment no one said anything. A wind chime hanging from an MLK Boulevard street sign rang in the breeze.

"You going to introduce me to your girlfriend?" The Reverend looked over his glasses at Wendy. "I notice you don't deny you are his girlfriend, but neither do you own up to it."

Wendy smiled.

"Reverend, this is Wendy, and Wendy, this is Reverend B-Love Barton, pastor of Stephen Grover AME Church."

"I love your garden," she said. "And your artwork."

"It's the neighborhood's garden," the Reverend said, "and the neighborhood's art, including some of this fellow's right here." He nodded at Mitchell. Then he glanced at his watch. "I better hustle. I'm attending a protest at the abortion clinic. They're shutting it down. The last one in this part of the state. Want to come along? We could use a couple more protestors."

"Sure," Mitchell said but then noticed Wendy looked uncomfortable. "On second thought we need to get back to the house," he said apologetically.

The Reverend smiled at Wendy. "A lot of folks in my congregation don't believe in abortion, but a lot of them have them anyway. Black women are four times more likely to seek abortions than white women." Then he shook his head. "Sorry. Didn't mean to start preaching at y'all. An occupational hazard."

He took Wendy's hand. "Very nice to meet you." The Reverend started out of the garden but stopped and turned around. "As far as this fellow goes, you could do worse."

They started down the sidewalk when Wendy said, "I like him."

"I'm glad you were able to meet him," he said. The Reverend had played a key role in helping Mitchell survive his hard high school years as a male figure he'd actually been able to talk to.

As they walked along, Mitchell noticed Wendy had gotten quiet.

"What?" he asked.

"Do my beliefs embarrass you? The way you were back there, saying we had to get back instead of telling him the truth."

"You don't embarrass me. I didn't see any reason to get into your views on abortion. Besides, he knows what you think. The expression on your face spoke volumes."

She pulled away. "I embarrass you," she said.

"Sometimes I just don't want to get into it, especially with my friends."

"*Because* I embarrass you."

He stopped on the sidewalk and unable to hold back said,

"How can you not see how important it is for women, especially women in poverty, to have access to abortion?"

"It's a life," she said. "Mitchell, we've talked about this. For me, abortion is wrong and always will be. It's murder, and I'm not going to change what I believe to suit you or any of your friends or your family. It's part of who I am. And if you're embarrassed, that's your problem. You understand that, right?"

"I'm not going to change what I believe either."

"Did you ever stop to think that your beliefs might embarrass me?" she said.

They looked at each other, and Mitchell felt uncomfortable things going on. He didn't like it when they fought.

"How are we ever going to do this?" he asked.

"I don't know," she said.

Mitchell didn't know either. They walked along without speaking. At times like these Mitchell didn't see how they could stay together, but he didn't see how they could be apart either.

CHAPTER 17

• • •

Asa, Fall 2014

That afternoon, Asa had gotten a call, one of several they had received over the past two years, from Mitchell's high school counselors about their son's plummeting grades. "He's in danger of failing several subjects, Asa," Xanthene Norris, the junior class counselor said. "I meant to talk to Betsy at school about it but remembered she's at a conference." Xanthene also said Mitchell had been skipping class. She said they should set up a meeting. "He's such a bright boy," she said. Asa thanked her for calling and then, furious and embarrassed, drove straight home and waited for Mitchell.

Betsy had been at a day-long conference for high school English teachers. Otherwise, she would have handled it. They had agreed ever since Mitchell's second year in high school when their son's grades had first begun to drop that she would handle problems that came up at school, especially since Betsy taught there.

Betsy was convinced Mitchell was depressed and should see a therapist. Asa thought it was laziness. Asa did his best to keep his comments to himself. Mitchell refused to see a therapist but agreed to see their family doctor who diagnosed Mitchell with mild depression and prescribed a low-dose antidepressant which, Asa had to agree, seemed to help.

This time, though, Asa could tell by the seriousness of the counselor's voice there was a chance their son could actually fail the grade—something he couldn't imagine any child of his would ever do. The longer Asa waited for Mitchell to arrive home, the angrier he became. He worried that Mitchell's grades would be so poor he wouldn't get into college. Asa was about to head back to work when Mitchell walked in the door.

"Everything all right?" Mitchell asked, clearly surprised to see his father home so early.

"Mrs. Norris called again," Asa said. "She said you're about to fail."

"She exaggerates," Mitchell said. "Don't worry about me, Dad."

"I'm not worried about you as much as I'm worried about me having to worry about you," Asa said.

"I'll get my grades up," Mitchell said. "I always do." He poured himself a glass of milk and without another word headed upstairs to his room.

Asa stood dumfounded. *Get out of the house, go back to work, let Betsy deal with it when she gets home. Get out of the house, get out of the house, get out of the house before you say or do something you'll regret.*

He was leaving, headed out the front door when he heard loud music blasting from Mitchell's room. He reminded himself that Betsy should deal with this, but she wasn't here. Next thing he knew he was banging on Mitchell's door and, not waiting for a response, walked in. Mitchell was sitting up on his bed, listening to music from his laptop and reading one of those eight-hundred-page sci-fi juggernauts.

Mitchell turned the music down. "What's up, Dad?"

"You're grounded." Asa tried to control his voice.

Mitchell gave an incredulous laugh. "I'm not in fifth grade."

"I wouldn't care if you were a PhD postdoc. You're grounded. For the next two months, you're not going anywhere but school, Mister."

"Two months!"

"Home and school," Asa said. "That's it. You're going nowhere with friends or anyone else. No football games, no movies, no cruising around town."

He snatched Mitchell's car keys off his dresser. "We'll be driving you to and from school."

"We'll see what Mom has to say about this." Mitchell went back to reading.

Asa grabbed the laptop off his bed and snapped it shut.

"Hey!" Mitchell said.

"You'll get it back when your grades improve." He tucked it under his arm.

"Don't take my laptop, Dad, please!"

The panic in his son's voice told Asa he had hit a nerve. "Maybe in a couple of weeks if your grades improve."

"A couple of weeks?" Mitchell said, his face reddening. "I'll kill myself."

"Stop being melodramatic."

Asa was reminded of when Mitchell was a little boy and he would throw a tantrum in the grocery store aisle or restaurant, hurling himself to the floor and wailing like he was in real pain.

"Dad, don't take my laptop," he said, pleading now. "Please, please don't take my laptop. It's my only oxygen in this suffocating house."

"I'm about to be late for class." Asa started out of the room with the laptop.

"Dad, please," Mitchell said, "I'm not kidding. I'll kill myself!"

"Be sure to get your grades up first," Asa said. He shut Mitchell's door and walked down the stairs, his son screaming from his room. Asa was heading out the front door when Mitchell ran downstairs saying, "Please!" Shaking, Asa got in his car, set the laptop beside him, and had pulled out of the drive when Mitchell ran up to the car, slapping Asa's driver-side window. "Please, Dad! I'm begging you!" Asa was startled to see tears in his son's eyes. Even so, he pressed on the gas and drove away, seeing Mitchell in his rearview mirror, standing in the middle of the street, his hands on top of his head.

About an hour after Asa returned to school, he got a call from Sarah, who he thought was in Chapel Hill. She was in the ER at Mission Hospital. Mitchell had taken an entire bottle of Tylenol. If Sarah hadn't happened to come home from Chapel Hill that afternoon, he might have died.

Asa was so shaken he distanced himself even more from Mitchell and let him do whatever he wanted. The irony was that Mitchell didn't want to do that much. He seemed different too. Mitchell became, if not exactly mellow, less angry. He became more responsible, which saved his grades, and that, along with his remarkable art, got him into Furman. Asa gladly left all significant discussions with Mitchell for Betsy to handle. For much of Mitchell's senior year Asa and Mitchell treated each other like polite strangers.

CHAPTER 18

• • •

Asa, Thursday Afternoon

When Asa pulled up to his house, a handful of cars and trucks were parked out front, some from the fire department, a couple from the city, and a few others. The guy from State Farm was walking around the house, taking pictures of the damage.

A couple of neighbors walked past, neighbors he only vaguely knew looked toward the house then looked at him as if they weren't sure what to say. In no mood to accommodate their sympathy, Asa crossed the yard and was about to go inside when he noticed more flowers around the base of the hemlock, a lot more. And there were notes and poems too, all dedicated to "Mrs. Flowers." A revered teacher, Betsy taught a popular creative writing class and was advisor to the school lit magazine, which held a poetry contest every year that Asa judged. Some of Betsy's students went on to Altamont College, and some of those wound up in Asa's classes. He could nearly always tell when someone had had Betsy—by their knowledge of poetry, by the depth and insight they brought to their papers, and by the awareness of form and craft reflected in their poems. In many of her students, she instilled a love of poetry that would last them a lifetime.

Asa went inside, shut the door behind him, leaned back against it, and closed his eyes. He felt a nudge at his leg. Luna stood beside him. "How did you get in, Girl?" He had left her in the fenced-in yard when he left earlier.

"I let her in, Dr. Flowers. Hope that was okay." A young man walked in from the kitchen—the city engineer, short and stocky with a neatly trimmed beard. Asa had met him yesterday when he had come to begin assessing the damage. "I thought she'd rather be inside," he said, "with all the activity out there."

"She and I would both rather be in here," Asa said.

The inspector told Asa the house was structurally safe to occupy but that the power company wouldn't have the electricity back on until sometime tomorrow.

"So it's safe to sleep here tonight?" Asa asked.

"You won't have power, and it's supposed to get cold tonight. But I see you've got a woodstove and a good pile of wood," he said.

After the inspector left, Asa went upstairs. Luna remained at the foot of the stairs watching him. He stood before the closed bedroom door. How odd. Betsy could've easily been in there taking a nap. He put his hand on the doorknob but hesitated. He heard a rasping sound from within like someone struggling to breathe and pictured his wife pinned to the bed, the red bloom in the middle of her chest.

He opened the door. The sound turned out to be the tarp being rattled by the wind.

The room had been straightened a bit. His wife's nightstand had been righted and the books she had been reading neatly stacked. Underneath a Louise Penny novel, Pema Chodron's latest book on meditation, and a Rick Steves travel book on

Iceland was a guide to the Enneagram, a book his wife read periodically as if it were the Bible.

Someone had removed the branches from the mattress and taken off the bedclothes, leaving the bare, forlorn mattress. It was an old mattress. He and Betsy had talked about getting a new one but hadn't gotten around to it. It had a number of stains, most old and faded, including a few bigger stains from tea spilled over the years while reading in bed. A few others, including a collection of small but more pronounced stains near the head of the bed from several nights of his bleeding after the deviated septum surgery he had two years ago. Both their children had been conceived on this bed. Looking down on the whole thing, it was a canvas of their marriage.

Asa was surprised to hear Luna come up the stairs. She came into the bedroom, for what Asa was sure was the first time since the tree fell. She went all around the room, smelling and sniffing, even in the closet. Then she went to the mattress and smelled all around it. Then she sat down beside Asa and let out a long sigh.

CHAPTER 19

Asa, Late Afternoon/Early Evening Thursday

Asa had timed his arrival so everyone would be gone for the day, but when he walked down the English department hall and turned the corner, Jillian Johnston, the department's longtime assistant, was at her desk, typing away. "Let me finish this sentence," she said without looking up.

Jillian was a tall angular woman who usually wore jeans, a blue work shirt, and lace-up hiking boots and often came into the office smelling of woodsmoke. She and her husband lived on a fifty-acre wedge of land they bought thirty years ago for a song, way up a mountain cove off the Blue Ridge Parkway.

"Asa!" She came from behind her desk and hugged him. "What are you doing here?"

He put his finger to his lips and nodded in the direction of the faculty offices.

"I think everybody's all gone home," she said.

He dug the papers out of his satchel and set them on her desk. "I'll email the class they can pick them up in your office."

"I can't believe you came in to return some papers with all you've got going on."

"I thought I'd hide out in my office," he said. "What are you doing here so late?"

"Getting caught up on everyone's accreditation notes," she said. "Melda wants them ASAP."

Asa knew Melda had used the *ASAP* too. *ASAP* was a bullying word, a word that made Asa want to slap whoever said it. Jillian worked harder and longer hours than most of the faculty and, yet, as department assistant, made half what the lowest paid faculty made.

"You've gotten a lot of mail," she said.

Asa glanced at the faculty mail cubby and saw that instead of the usual textbook catalogs or an examination copy, his box was full of actual mail. They appeared to be cards and notes. He opened one—a sympathy card from a professor across campus, a woman in the anthropology department he knew only in passing.

"That's not all." She pulled another box from under her desk. All these would be from people at the university. Campus mail didn't have to be stamped or mailed in the conventional sense. Many faculty kept a supply of cards for various occasions in their desks, so all they had to do was pull out a card for the appropriate event, scribble a note, and pop it into campus mail on their way to class. Asa had given up sending cards after he had accidentally sent a Congratulations card to the chancellor when her cat died.

Asa walked into his office, set down the box of letters, turned his desk lamp on low, and closed his door. He sat down and looked out his window. He'd inherited this office from Lamar Mustian, a spooky old Southern lit scholar Asa thought of as an aged misfit who, after visiting murder and mayhem upon the south Georgia countryside, had gone on to get his PhD.

Not only had Asa inherited Lamar's office but he'd inherited the view along with it. Since he'd last looked out his window, which felt like years ago, the lines of brilliant orange and red sugar maples bordering the quad had been ravaged by the storm. One tree had been snapped in two, many had lost limbs, and all had been stripped of their bright leaves. It broke his heart a little. Beyond the grassy quad was the deepening silhouette of the Blue Ridge mountains, presided over by Mount Pisgah, a mountain their family used to hike. Next to the window was a watercolor Mitchell had painted in middle school of the Mount Pisgah trail winding up a mist-shrouded, steep-stepped incline through thick rhododendron.

Asa sat at his desk, watching the clouds slip across the early evening sky, throwing shadows across the quad like traveling ponds. He was relieved to be alone.

He'd always needed time to himself. Ever since he was a kid. But it hadn't been till high school, as a shy boy who couldn't screw up his courage to actually talk to girls, that he wrote them poems instead. His high school poems never helped in the romance department. They tended to be an amalgamation of Kahlil Gibran, e. e. cummings, and Jonathan Livingston Seagull. Even so, his failed efforts eventually led him to discover a passion of a different sort.

He'd worked on poems in the middle of class, pretending to take notes. He scribbled poems on his napkin at lunch in the cafeteria while all around him kids picked at their food and chattered away. He even wrote poems at night after he'd finished his homework and the rest of his family was asleep. He'd pull out his poetry notebook that was nearly full and write till he couldn't keep his eyes open. Poetry became a structured way to be alone with his thoughts and, at the same time, a very real if vicarious way of being in the world.

In college, he continued to write poetry and became editor of the literary magazine. In grad school, he shifted to literary scholarship but continued to write and publish poems. When it came time for him to apply for teaching jobs, he was cautioned to leave his poetry publications off his resume. Many English departments, he was warned, weren't interested in faculty devoting their energies to anything other than teaching and scholarship. After he was hired at Altamont, he kept his poetry writing under the radar. The prevailing department sentiment, at least among many of the old guard, was that the only good poet was a dead poet, preferably a century or two. Still, he would wake up at five every morning and go out to the studio to write. As long as he could get in an hour or two, whatever else the day brought, he could handle. In fact, and he wasn't quite sure how, but he sensed that the act of writing made him a better person—a better husband, a better father, a better friend, and even a better colleague. Whenever his schoolwork became too much and he didn't have a chance to write, he felt out of sorts. Some nights at dinner Betsy would tilt her head, squint at him across the table, and ask, "You haven't had a chance to write, have you?" and he knew he was being cranky.

The longer he was in the department, the harder it was to hide the fact that he wrote poetry. He couldn't very well hide that he published regularly in journals and magazines, once even in *The Atlantic*, or that he published a book every three or four years. All pretense went out the window when he won an NEA grant, the only winner in the state that year.

News of his grant seemed to have emboldened other faculty to own up to their own creative writing. A Chaucer expert let it be known that she was the author of a popular cozy mystery series she'd been publishing under a pseudonym for years. And then a medieval literature scholar received a six-figure advance for his memoir about growing up gay as a Mormon in the South Carolina Lowcountry. And there were others. With creative writers coming out of their scholarly closets, Asa no longer felt so conspicuous. Creative writing courses and even creative writing majors had begun to catch on across the country. With several of the school's senior faculty retiring, the department decided to offer a handful of creative writing courses and, much to Asa's surprise, they asked him to teach a regular poetry writing course.

But even after all this, when Asa put in for a sabbatical, the chair of the sabbatical committee, a crusty old Coleridge scholar, tried to deny him, saying, "He's only going to write poetry with it!" If several faculty friends hadn't spoken up for him, Asa was sure he wouldn't have gotten his sabbatical.

The academic world's resistance aside, even after years of writing and publishing poetry, Asa had his own inner resistance. He could never get used to admitting to people he was a poet. It almost always insured a surprised "Oh" then an awkward moment of silence followed by the inevitable question, "What kind of poetry do you write?" Asa could never think of what to say and would come up with something innocuous like, "I write about family, nature, life, stuff like that." When asked what he did, Asa usually said he taught English, which wasn't much better since the response was often "I better watch out how I talk around you" or "I hated English" or sometimes "Can you even get a job with an English major?"

* * *

Asa wasn't sure how much time had passed when there was a knock on his door. It was Jillian in her long sweater coat, her pocketbook slung over her shoulder.

"Hope I didn't disturb you." She glanced around at his low-lit office. "I'm going home, and now you really do have the joint to yourself." Her eye caught the cards stacked on his desk. "Why are you sorting the sympathy cards, Asa? Tell me you're not grading them."

He raked the notes back into the box. "Do you want to sit down?"

"Only a minute," she said. "Sam will be waiting dinner on me."

"I'm afraid I'm all out of Glenlivet," he said. Sometimes, at the end of the week, he and Jillian sat in his office and drank a glass of whisky before going home.

"I find all this exhausting," he said. "The public part of it. Whose business is it anyway?"

They looked out at the mountains.

"I keep thinking of things I need to ask her," he said, "like what's our Wi-Fi password, or how often does she water the jade plant in the kitchen window, or on what setting should I wash my shirts?"

"On delicate," she said.

"I want to ask her how she thinks the kids are handling it," he said.

They heard footsteps down the hall. Asa felt as if they had gotten caught at something. "Melda?" he whispered to her. Melda was the last person he wanted to talk to. She would have faculty lined up to have him over to dinner before you could say William Wordsworth.

Jillian listened to the footsteps. "Charles coming back from the library."

"Sarah seems to be coping," he said, "although sometimes it's difficult to know whether she's just approximating coping. Mitchell seems to be better than I would've expected. Still, one never can be sure."

"Boys," she said. "We never know what our Eric is thinking."

"Mitchell brought his girlfriend home," he said, "Even though I've been less than welcoming, she seems unfazed. Sarah thinks she's at least part of the reason Mitchell is taking this better than he might've." He shook his head. "Still . . ."

"Still what? What's the problem? She sounds great."

"It's no time for the girlfriend, and she's a die hard Republican."

"Asa Flowers." She leaned close to him, her voice going steely. "Do not, I mean do not risk alienating Mitchell over his girlfriend's party affiliation."

"I almost blew it with her today," he said, "and Mitchell looked like he was a breath away from strangling me."

"Get your act together and be nice to this girl who sounds exactly like who Mitchell needs—who you all need!"

He couldn't remember Jillian raising her voice to him before. "You don't want to lose Mitchell too."

The sun slipped behind the horizon. Dark blues, reds, and purples radiated across the mountains, bruising the sky. Betsy was always dropping everything to run outside and watch the sunset. Didn't matter if she was cooking or on the phone. She'd stop whatever she was doing and often drag him along, and he was usually glad he'd come.

Jillian took his hand. A tremor travelled up his back, followed by a wave of sadness. A long moment passed in which he nearly told her Betsy had been seeing someone. But it seemed unfair to talk about it. Unfair to Jillian. Unfair to Betsy. Unfair to the kids and to himself for that matter.

A lone female student crossed the quad with her head down, cradling books in her arms, the last light catching in her hair.

Jillian stood and, digging her keys out of her purse, said, "We'll be there on Sunday."

"Sunday?"

"The service," she said.

He shook his head at himself. "I'm so out of it. All I can manage is to put one foot in front of the other."

"That's all you need to do," she said. "That and help those sweet kids of yours do the same."

"I can't help thinking the wrong one of us died," he said.

"Asa, honey," she said, "while that might be an interesting mind game, it doesn't have a damn thing to do with the price of eggs. You're the one still here."

Asa sat in his office, watching the walkway lights flicker on across the campus. His eye went to a black-and-white photo in an old drugstore frame that sat on his desk. It was of a sunburned Betsy some twenty-five years ago. In her bathing suit, she'd draped herself across his car's hood, one hand on her hip, her cheeks sucked in like a model fawning for the camera.

It was from his second visit to Charleston. They had talked on the phone a few times since their first meeting when he'd gone down to interview. Their phone conversations had been filled with long, painful silences. He wasn't sure why, but talking on the phone felt different than when they'd been together in person.

One day he'd gotten off the phone with her after one such halting conversation thinking this wasn't going to work. He sat down to write her a letter saying that very thing. But before he knew what he'd done, he'd written her a long letter about nothing more than his uneventful day teaching hungover freshmen, including one student who had lifted her essay on Huck Finn pretty much whole cloth from CliffsNotes and signed it as her own.

A few days after Asa mailed it, a letter from Betsy showed up in his mailbox, in which she talked about her Eudora Welty landlady who smoked and cursed and told bawdy stories. They wrote each other once or twice a week after that. He looked forward to the mail in a way he hadn't since he was a boy away at camp. He would write Betsy back the very night he received one of her letters. He began including a poem or two he had been working on. And that's how they got to know each other, through their letters. It's also how their phone conversations loosened up and why a couple of months after that first night in her apartment, she invited him back down and he was eager to go.

On that second visit to Charleston, Betsy took Asa to the beach, and after a long swim, they spread their towels between the dunes for privacy. They'd lain in the sun for a while when he looked over and saw Betsy peeling off her bathing suit. The next thing he knew she was on top of him. When they finished, they rolled back on their towels, listening to the cry of gulls overhead and the rattle of the sea oats in the breeze. And the sky was so deep he felt in danger of falling in. It was then that a black lab came racing up out of nowhere, squatted beside them, laid a big turd in the sand, and ran off.

"Foreshadowing," she said as they pulled their bathing suits back on.

"For what?" he asked.

"Our relationship," she said.

"We're in a relationship now?" he asked.

"The dog seems to think so."

CHAPTER 20

Wendy, Thursday Night

Wendy put on a long-sleeved Furman t-shirt and flannel pajama bottoms but, not yet ready for bed, went into the kitchen. She was relieved to get away from the family, especially Mitchell's father who half-heartedly tried to apologize. Ever since she and Mitchell had arrived, she'd felt in the way. Their family was in the throes of the worst kind of loss, and she was an interloper traipsing through an emotional minefield.

She rummaged in the cupboard, found a box of Raisin Bran, filled her bowl, and walked around the studio eating cereal, looking at Mitchell's paintings. They had spiritual depth. Almost everything she had seen of his did. She had given up trying to convince him of this. It only irritated him whenever she brought it up. Still, she hadn't an iota of doubt that Mitchell's talent was a divine gift and that everything he painted, in one way or another, was an evocation of the Holy Spirit. Unlike the nineteenth-century landscape painters she studied in art history, painters like Cole, Church, and Bierstadt of the Hudson River School, Mitchell never intentionally sought to instill the divine in the natural world he portrayed; the divine was just there, a natural occurrence in the natural world, a natural occurrence in Mitchell.

She switched on the radio on the kitchen counter and tuned it to a country station down the mountain in Greenville. Her roommate, a music major, preferred the classical station. So tonight, as Faith Hill and Tim McGraw finished up "The Rest of Our Life," Wendy cranked up the volume, happy to have a place to herself.

Earlier, when Doctor Flowers had gone over to the university, Mitchell, Sarah, and Wendy had sat at the table together in the main room of the house, working a jigsaw puzzle of Paul Klee's *Fish Magic* by candlelight.

"It's getting chilly," Sarah said, turning a puzzle piece to fit.

Mitchell peered into the woodstove.

Sarah watched her brother leave and after he shut the door turned to Wendy.

"He hasn't talked a whole lot about it," Wendy said. "But he wouldn't."

"No," said Sarah.

"I can't always read him," Wendy said.

"I'm his sister, and I have no idea what he's thinking half the time."

"It's not hard to read your father though," Wendy said.

"Dad knows you've been good for Mitchell, and while he might have a funny way of showing it, he's grateful."

"Mitchell's been good for me too. Did he tell you about my ankle?" Wendy told her that she and Mitchell had only been dating a couple of weeks and hardly knew each other when she broke her ankle in a club soccer match and was on crutches for nearly two months. "Most boys would've been out of there in a skinny minute, but Mitchell looked after me the whole time."

"Really?" Sarah said, sitting back in her chair. "Our Mitchell?"

"He helped me to class, carried my books, carried my tray in the cafeteria, helped me dress, even helped me in the bathroom. He washed my clothes and folded them, neatly mind you. I've never been so taken care of."

"He never said anything about that." Sarah looked out the window where they saw Mitchell gathering wood.

"I would've had to go home if it hadn't been for him helping me." Then she added, "That is, when I let him, which isn't always easy for me. I'm used to doing things for myself."

Sarah nodded, but Wendy could tell her mind was elsewhere.

"Will you promise me one thing?" Sarah asked. "Could you let me know if anything about my brother's behavior starts to worry you. He has a history of depression."

"He told me." Not that Wendy needed to be told.

"Did he tell you about the time in high school?" Sarah asked.

Wendy nodded.

"The Mitchell back then is different from the Mitchell today. Still, if you wouldn't mind keeping an eye on him. I hope I'm not going to run you off with more responsibility than a girlfriend should be saddled with," Sarah said.

"I'm into your brother for the long haul." What Wendy didn't say and would probably never admit to anyone, not her father, certainly not Mitchell, and not even herself on some level, was that part of her attraction to Mitchell was like that of a painter to a blank canvas or a sculptor to an uncut stone. She loved Mitchell, loved him with all her heart, and that love bent toward the hope—even the need—over time, years if it took it, and without spooking him, to save his beautiful soul.

Mitchell walked in, laid an armful of split wood on the floor, then, smiling up at Wendy, began to load the stove.

* * *

Wendy was rinsing out her bowl when she heard a knock. She turned the radio down and cut on the porch light. Mitchell stood hugging himself against the cold. She unlocked the door and let him in.

"Couldn't sleep," Mitchell said. "Looks like you couldn't either."

"I was eating some cereal," she said.

"And rocking out to Taylor Swift."

"Kacey Musgraves," she said.

"I wanted to apologize about my dad."

"He's trying," Wendy said.

"I think he actually is, and that's what's so pathetic."

"Don't talk that way about your father."

The hardness in his face gave way to sadness. "So you won't leave or anything?"

"No." She squeezed his hand.

"Besides, you'll soon be part of the family," Mitchell said.

"Don't bring that up with him now. It'll make everything harder."

"I want him to know," he said. "I want everybody to know." He gave her a deep kiss.

She pulled away. "I don't think that's a good idea."

"Dad doesn't care." He kissed her again, sliding his hands down her t-shirt. Mitchell was a good kisser. She could feel his charge all the way down to her toes. She wanted to lead him back into the little bedroom but instead took his hands and kissed them and then turned him around by the shoulders and guided him toward the door.

"Please," he said. "It's all so sad."

"Do you want to pray about it?"

"If we pray about it, can I stay?"

"Go back to your family. They need you." She tried to shut the door, but he held it open.

"Is something up with you?" Mitchell asked.

"Just because I don't want to sleep with you?"

"You're not telling me something. Does it have to do with school?"

She cocked her head at him. "Just some financial aid form I forgot to submit. I'll figure it out."

"I'm not sure what it says about us that you won't talk to me about things you're dealing with," he said.

"I'm tired and need to go to bed." She closed the door and watched him walk toward the house, stopping to look up at the moon. He disappeared into shadow while on the radio Kacey sang, "If you want to find the honey / You can't be scared of the bees."

Later, when Wendy was climbing into bed, she texted him. "I love you and God does too."

He texted back, "Leave Him out of it."

She woke in the middle of the night, unable to sleep. She opened her laptop and scrolled through the school bills. For some reason, her scholarship money had been reduced, and she was supposed to pay several thousand dollars to make up for it. Being a straight-A student, she always paid her way with scholarships and assistantships. She was proud of never having taken a dime from her dad, who didn't make much as a minister.

A feeling of helplessness overcame her. She had a little less than a thousand dollars in her savings account. That wouldn't even touch these bills. What could she do? She'd have to quit college and get a job. Her father would be upset.

Then she paused, took a breath, and reminded herself she had always been able to figure things out before, and she would this time too. She wasn't alone with this. She was never alone.

CHAPTER 21

Mitchell, Friday Morning

The next morning Mitchell was woken by a text from Wendy: *Go for a run?*

He sat up in bed and texted back. *No thanks. Didn't sleep so great.*

I'll come over when I get back.

Okay.

He climbed out of bed, his room chilly. He pulled on a sweater and went downstairs, where the woodstove ticked with heat. Mitchell found his sister in the kitchen putting Luna's harness on her.

"How is she doing?" Mitchell yawned.

"She's not herself," said Sarah. "I'm glad we're taking her to see Regina this afternoon."

He knelt down and petted her. "You not feeling well, Girl?" He kissed her head. Then he poured himself a cup of coffee, sat at the table, and yawned again.

"I didn't sleep well." She clicked on the harness. "When I first came down this morning, I expected to find Mom already back from her morning walk."

"And I wondered why the radio wasn't on," he said. Their mother was a huge NPR fan and always had the radio on as everyone was grabbing breakfast and getting ready for work and school in the mornings. NPR was part of the soundtrack of their childhood.

"Want to walk with us?" Sarah asked. "We're just going around the block."

He grabbed his coffee and followed Sarah and Luna out the door.

Mitchell was struck by what an uncannily beautiful day it was. Crazy blue sky and a chilly breeze. They paused and took in the emptiness where the hemlock had stood all their lives.

"Strange," Mitchell said.

"Very," Sarah said.

As they started down the sidewalk, they saw Wendy disappearing down the road.

"She's fast," said Sarah.

"So fast."

Wendy could outrun him, and he had always thought of himself as fast.

"I'm glad you brought her."

"Clearly not everybody feels that way." He glanced back at the house.

"She's good to have around, and it's obvious she makes you feel better. I think she's a mellowing influence on all of us."

"I'm glad you like her," he said. It had always been important that his sister like whoever he dated, and that was especially true of Wendy, considering their plans.

On their walk they passed an arborist's truck as helmeted men wielding chainsaws cleared limbs and other storm debris. When they passed by the Hodgeses' house, Norma had just dropped an armload of sticks at the curb.

When she saw them, she came over and hugged them both. "I'm so sorry."

Mitchell thought how Norma and Jack had been such fixtures in their lives from the time he and Sarah were little. They felt more like an aunt and uncle than neighbors.

"It was kind of Jack to go with Dad to the hospital to be with Mom," Sarah said.

"How awful that your father had to find out that way," Norma said.

Sarah and Mitchell looked at each other.

"What do you mean?" Sarah asked.

"That he woke up to an ambulance in the drive and a yard full of people," Norma said, "then watched the ambulance pull away with Betsy."

"Dad was the one who found Mom," Sarah said.

"Clare found her," Norma said.

"The woman who delivers our paper?" Sarah asked.

Mitchell looked at his sister, whose curiosity had been roused. Not always a good thing.

"She saw the tree on the house when she was delivering papers, went inside, and found your mom," Norma said. She paused, her eyes reddening, as if she could see the whole thing. "Clare called the EMTs. Most of us were still asleep." Norma scratched Luna's head. "When I finally did go over, I found Luna in the yard and brought her over to our house. But she'd wanted to stay with your mother."

Norma glanced at her watch. "I'm late for my quilting group."

"Thank you again for all you and Jack have done," Sarah said.

As Norma headed inside, Mitchell started up the drive, but

noticed Sarah still stood there. She was thinking something, and he was pretty sure he knew what.

"Why didn't Dad tell us he wasn't the one to find her?" Sarah asked.

This would bother his sister, a stickler for details. It would nag at her that their father hadn't made clear to them who found their mother.

"Dad never claimed he found her," Mitchell said.

"Still," she said, as they started up the drive, "he had to know that's what we would've assumed."

"Maybe he didn't think to tell us. Or maybe he's like me and would rather not talk about it."

"Are you serious?" she said. "Of course, he's like you. More to the point, you're like him. Either way, it's odd he didn't tell us."

"What are you going to do?" he asked, following her back to the house.

"Ask him."

"Sarah," he said, lowering his voice as they walked inside, "leave the man alone.

His wife just died."

They found their dad in the kitchen, loading the dishwasher.

"How was your walk?" he asked.

"We just went around the block," Mitchell said, feeling a little sorry for their dad, who didn't suspect Sarah was about to give him the third degree.

"How's Luna this morning?" their dad asked.

"Not herself," Sarah said. "I'm glad we're taking her to the vet." Sarah paused then said, "So Dad?"

He closed the dishwasher and turned around. Mitchel noticed deep circles under his eyes, how much older he looked.

"We ran into Norma," Sarah said. "She told us Clare was the one who found Mom."

Their father crossed his arms. "That's right," he said.

"I guess we thought you found her."

Mitchell didn't like being included in Sarah's *we*. He wanted no part in interrogating their father.

"It sounded like you actually slept out there in the studio that night," Sarah said.

A chainsaw started up somewhere in the neighborhood.

"There were a lot of papers to grade, and I didn't want to bother your mom."

"We have a big house," she said.

"Meaning?" His voice took on an edge.

Mitchell couldn't stand his sister's cross-examination of their father.

"I find it difficult to believe that you went out there to keep from bothering Mom," Sarah said. "She'd be sleeping upstairs, and you'd be grading downstairs."

"Leave him alone," Mitchell said under his breath.

Their father dropped his head then looked up. "We had a fight."

"About?"

"Let's not do this, Sarah," their father said. "It's not the time or place." The way he said it didn't sound angry to Mitchell, just very tired.

Sarah looked at their father for a minute, and Mitchell was sure she was about to ask him again what the fight was about. When it came to getting at the truth, his sister was like a dog worrying a bone.

Their dad started upstairs, and Sarah watched him. "Dad?"

"Yeah?" He stopped, clearly braced for more interrogation.

"Will you come with me to take Luna to the vet this afternoon?" she asked.

He looked at her a minute. "Sure," he said, then went on upstairs, his footsteps heavy as he crossed the floor above them.

CHAPTER 22

Asa, Friday Afternoon

The waiting room at MoonVet was crowded with dogs on one side and cats on the other. The dogs wagged their tails nervously or lay on the floor, casting a doleful eye up at their owner. On the other side, cats crouched deep in their carriers, mewling eerily.

An assistant who Asa vaguely remembered called for Luna. He was a tall olive-skinned man with a goatee and an earring. He wore scrubs with smiling frogs and grinning turtles.

"Sarah," he said.

"Hi, Deno," she said.

He bent down and petted Luna, then started to lead them to the examining room. Sarah looked back at Asa who'd remained seated and waved for him to come too.

"You should hear what she has to say," Sarah said, "since you'll be the one taking care of Luna."

With everything going on, this hadn't crossed his mind. It had never been his job. Sure, he fed her, and if Betsy was away, he looked after her and took her for walks, but mostly Betsy cared for her.

In the examining room, Deno squatted down and petted Luna again. "Not feeling well, Girl? We'll get Dr. Hill to examine you." He looked up at them. "We're all so sad for your family."

So were a lot of people, judging by the students and former students, not just Betsy's but Asa's as well, who had been coming by the house, setting more flowers, posters, and candles around the foot of the hemlock. This afternoon as Asa and Sarah had left for the vet's office, a group of Altamont students were in the yard, tacking up notes and poems around the tree trunk. When Asa asked them about it, Yvonne, a student from Asa's poetry class last year, said they were members of the school literary club and that the president of the club had the idea to send out an email to students, saying anyone who wanted to write something about Mrs. Flowers could leave it in a box in the English department office.

"Who's the president of the school literary club?" Asa asked.

Yvonne looked in the direction of a student with his back to them, handing sheets of poems and notes out to students to tack onto the tree. Asa walked over to him and put his hand on his shoulder. The student turned around.

"Dr. Flowers. We're all so sorry about Betsy."

"Quentin? You're the president of the literary club?" Asa asked, astonished.

"We wanted to do something for Betsy."

Asa was flabbergasted. Betsy had always said he was a terrible student, an awful writer, and a bully in class discussions who browbeat classmates into piling on in excoriating whatever great writer they happened to be studying at the time. He had tried to do this in Asa's class as well, but with debriefing from his wife, Asa was able to short-circuit at least some of Quentin's classroom antics. The boy was a piece of work, and Asa couldn't fathom why he would ever do anything to honor Betsy. And why the hell was he referring to his wife by her first name as if she were a friend?

Once Asa recovered himself, he thanked Quentin and the other students who by now had papered the entire trunk with poems. When Asa got back into the car with Sarah and Luna, he didn't pull out of the drive at first but watched the students work their way around the tree with Quentin directing them.

"How is Quentin president of the literary club?" he said to himself. "Probably bribed a bunch of English majors." He shook his head. "What's the world coming to?"

"That's Quentin?" Sarah said. "The Quentin?"

"The one and only," Asa said.

"He looks innocent enough," she said.

"That's his superpower."

Asa started to back out of the drive, but there was a knock on his car window. It was Quentin.

Asa rolled down his window.

"Dr. Flowers, I wonder if we could set up a time to discuss the C you gave me on my Whitman paper. I made a real effort with that paper. I think it deserves better."

"Do you?" It took every last ounce of Asa's restraint not to tell the boy to go fuck himself.

Apparently, Quentin had read Asa's expression. "I can see now isn't the best time to discuss this. I'll reach out to you in a few days when things have settled, and we can set up a time to meet."

"You do that, Quentin," Asa said between clenched teeth.

"You just do that." He continued to stare at the boy, who seemed to grow uncomfortable.

"Okay," Quentin said, nervously patting Asa's car door. "Glad we could have this little talk, and I look forward to our discussion. You have a good day, Dr. Flowers." He paused. "Not that it can be that good with your wife's demise and everything."

Asa rolled up his window before Quentin could say anything else and backed out of the drive.

"Oh my God!" Sarah said, laughing into her hands. "Your wife's demise? What a weird dude."

Asa hit the heel of his hand on the steering wheel.

"What?" she asked.

"He organized this memorial for your mom to butter me up," he said. "He wants a better grade. All this because he wants a better grade."

"He can't be that low."

Asa raised his eyebrows at her. "First lesson in Quentin. Quentin never ever does anything not for Quentin. Plus, he's a grade grubber. A terrible student and a grade grubber. The worst combination."

She smiled to herself.

"What?"

"Back there you sounded just like Jack Nicholson. 'You do that, Quentin. You just do that.'" His daughter imitated Asa perfectly, so perfectly he realized she had probably been imitating him behind his back for years.

• • •

Regina hurried into the examining room in her white coat that showed off her dark complexion and jet-black hair. Sometimes

Regina's eccentricities distracted Asa from seeing what a striking woman she was.

"Dad should hear what you have to say," Sarah said, "since he'll be the one taking care of Luna now."

Regina gave him what felt like an appraising glance.

"She's not eating," Sarah said. "We're convinced she was sleeping with Mom when the tree fell. I think she might have PTSD."

"That's very possible," Regina said. "Asa, can you lift her onto the examining table?" But Sarah was already doing it. Sarah stroked Luna's head as Regina pulled her stethoscope out of her lab coat pocket and listened to Luna's heart and lungs. She opened the dog's mouth and checked her tongue and her teeth. She ran her hands gently over her back and ribs and legs. And, finally, she took Luna's temperature in her rear which Luna clearly didn't like.

Regina asked Sarah to set Luna on the floor. She knelt down beside her and began swinging a crystal. Asa had seen Regina use the crystal with Luna a few times before, yet could one ever be fully prepared for such a spectacle? He had to admit that as soon as she had started with the crystal, Luna sat up with raised ears, alert.

"She's letting me know that she's wondering where Betsy is," Regina said, "and if she's coming back." She looked at Sarah. "And I'm letting her know that she died and isn't coming back." Regina wiped a tear from her eye. "She seems to be feeling bad because she believes it was her job to keep Betsy safe."

Sarah stroked Luna's head. "There's nothing you could've done, Sweet Girl."

Regina continued to swing the pendulum. "She seems to be wondering what will happen to her now that Betsy's gone."

"You'll stay here like you always have," said Sarah. "You'll be with Dad."

Asa came over and gave Luna a hug.

Regina swung the pendulum a bit more. "I'm asking her if there's anything else she wants to know."

Asa worked hard not to roll his eyes.

After a moment, Regina let out a big sigh. "She's sending me an image of Betsy and you together, Asa, and I'm letting her know again that Betsy is gone." Regina continued to swing the crystal and, as she did, appeared frustrated.

"I'm not sure she understands," Regina said. "She's showing me the image of you and Betsy again." Regina stood up abruptly and said, "Okay, that's enough."

"What was she trying to say?" asked Asa.

"I don't know, Asa!" snapped Regina. Then in a more measured, businesslike tone she said, "I'm going to prescribe St. John's Wort for her anxiety and depression."

"Is that real medicine?" Asa asked.

Regina gave Asa another one of her glances.

"I think my dad's right," Sarah said. "Could you prescribe a more conventional antidepressant?"

A surprised look crossed Regina's face.

"I'm very worried about her," Sarah said.

Regina's expression softened. "I'll prescribe a course of Prozac, and we'll see how she does."

Asa had noticed that the longer Sarah had been a physics major the more assertive she had gotten about science.

"Prozac is one thing we can do," Regina said, "and Asa, I know you're not a dog person, but you'll need to take Luna on walks, give her treats, sit with her in the evenings, and give her plenty of love and affection. Do you think you're up to it?"

She sounded dubious. Why did she think he wasn't a dog person? Because he didn't bring Luna to the appointments? Had Luna said something in their crystal session? *Rein it in, Asa, you're losing your grip.* The woman wasn't Doctor Dolittle.

"Dad," Sarah said, "if it would help, I can take Luna back to Chapel Hill with me."

"That might be a good idea," Asa said.

"I could keep an eye on her," she said, "at least for a while."

It would be good for his daughter and good for Luna too, he thought. And one less thing for him to worry about.

"That's what should happen," Regina said.

"Why do I feel like an incompetent pet owner or worse?" Asa said.

"There is nothing worse," Regina said. "Some people, through no fault of their own, aren't animal people. If Betsy were here, she would want Luna to go with Sarah."

Asa felt his face flush. It was one thing for Regina to speak for the animals but another to speak for his wife.

"Here's the Prozac prescription." Regina scribbled something on a prescription pad and handed it to him. "I can't get my head around it."

As he slipped the prescription into his jacket pocket, he found a crumpled note, the one that had fallen out of Sarah's pocket in the cemetery. He opened it: *Good luck tonight!! I can't get my head around that you're actually doing this!! Call me after you've told him.*

Asa felt the earth shift under his feet. He read the note a second time. This was no note written by one of Betsy's students. This was a note to Betsy, and not from a student. Then he looked at the prescription and compared the handwriting.

He looked up at Regina. "It's you," he said.

"Pardon me?" Regina said but then saw the note in his hand.

"It's you," he said again.

"Asa," Regina said under her breath, cutting her eyes toward Sarah.

"What?" Sarah asked. "Is there something you're not telling me? Are we going to lose Luna too?"

A hair-raising howl came from the hallway, followed by shouts and someone crying. There was a quick knock, and Deno poked his head in, his scrubs covered in blood. "Dr. Hill," he said, "We need you."

"Coming," she said. She gave Sarah a hug. "Luna's going to be fine." She looked at Asa, but another howl went up and she was gone.

• • •

Asa threaded through afternoon downtown traffic, in the direction of the drugstore, his mind going a mile a minute. It wasn't Heather Greene or Alice Stromquist. It wasn't a teacher at all.

"Did you say something?" he asked.

"It's sad they had to put that dog down." Sarah reached back and petted Luna who lay in the back seat panting.

"He was in bad shape," he said.

"I could never do her job." She looked out the window.

Her job. *Her.* Right under their nose? This intense, New Age veterinarian who Asa had never felt particularly comfortable around and now understood why. But even now, he felt indebted to her for saving him from making a terrible mistake nearly fifteen years ago, and it would have truly been a terrible mistake to get rid of Luna.

"You do know they're serious," Sarah said, watching him.

"Who?" Had his daughter figured it out too?

"Wendy and Mitchell," she said. "I don't think you understand how important she is to Mitchell. They're serious."

"How serious can undergraduates be?" he said.

"I won't dignify that with an answer," she said.

"No son of mine is marrying a fundamentalist nut, even if she is pretty."

"Can you even hear yourself?"

"I'm being honest," he said.

"Honestly pigheaded. First, she's not a nut. She's a level-headed intelligent girl. Second, she's not a fundamentalist, she's evangelical, there's a difference. And last, you're being incredibly sexist. And if Mom were here, she'd say you're catastrophizing."

"Good thing she's not here then."

The look his daughter gave him was of complete and utter horror, and it skewered his very soul.

"I didn't mean it like that."

Sarah's face had gone stony. "What was all that about back at Regina's office? Between you and her. Something happened. Something upset you."

There it was, his daughter getting to the bottom of things.

"Regina gets under my skin sometimes," he said, looking away.

"It felt like more than that." Sarah reached back and petted Luna again. "You were angry."

They rode along in silence.

"Was it because she said you weren't a dog person or that

she thought Luna should go with me? Or both? Regina can be pushy."

"It's true that Luna would be happier with you in Chapel Hill," he said.

"This is where Luna grew up," Sarah said, "where she's lived her whole life."

"Sarah," he said, "I don't want to care for Luna. Maybe she's right. Maybe I'm not a dog person."

Sarah looked at him. "So if it wasn't about either of those things, what was it back there between you and Regina that you're not telling me?"

He pulled into the drugstore parking lot, and Sarah started to go in and get Luna's prescription, but Asa grabbed his daughter's hand.

"What I said about your mom. You know that's not what I meant."

She pulled away and without another word hurried inside the drugstore. Luna began to whine, looking toward the store where Sarah had disappeared.

"She'll be back, Girl," he said, petting her. "She'll be back in a minute."

CHAPTER 23

Asa, Summer 2009

"We can't keep her anymore," Betsy said to the veterinarian, a Dr. Hill, who specialized in animal communication and was in the middle of the living room, petting Luna. Betsy had heard about her through a friend.

"No matter what we try she either jumps the fence or gets away somehow," Betsy said. "Yesterday she attacked the neighbor's dog."

Asa fought the impulse to say, *You left the gate open, what do you expect?* "It's not the first time she's attacked a dog," he said. "She's become a neighborhood menace."

Dr. Hill looked at him as if she had heard something in his tone.

"She's attacked a couple of small dogs," Betsy said, "but this was the worst." Betsy had been working in the yard, left the gate open, and Luna escaped, then came upon a neighbor's shih tzu loose in his backyard. The vet's bill: $2,000.

Asa stood watching his children: Sarah, who was twelve then, and Mitchell, who was eleven. Sarah wiped her eyes, and Mitchell's jaw was working. It was their mother's last-ditch effort to keep Luna, who they had had for seven years. With this being Luna's most expensive attack yet, Asa had convinced himself they had to get rid of her.

Dr. Hill had pulled out a crystal on a string, waved it in front of Luna, and whispered to her. Mitchell shook his head and left to go visit a friend up the street. Sarah, too upset to keep watching, went upstairs to her room. Disgusted by the whole production, Asa went out to cut the hedges. How could Betsy have paid this woman, this charlatan, $200 to make a house call? As he worked to rein in an overgrown abelia, his anger receded, and a deeper sadness slipped in. What Betsy hadn't told Regina was that they had gotten Luna in response to Sarah, who had been only five at the time, and had had pretty extensive surgery to remove a premelanoma on her thigh. It hadn't upset Betsy nearly as much as it had upset Asa. Betsy had an evenness when it came to the children. She seldom let herself be overwhelmed by worry, which made her a good mother, always present and able to cope. It also helped Asa to see how she carried on despite whatever came up, because when it came to the children, he had no such evenness.

So when their five-year-old daughter found a black mole on her thigh one day in the bathtub and it turned out to be a premelanoma, he was terrified. She had wanted a dog for some time. After the surgery, everything had taken on a new urgency. A week after the surgery Asa drove Sarah to the Humane Shelter and they picked out a cute year-old puppy and brought her home.

After Regina's visit, Betsy told them at dinner that Luna had told Regina she was very surprised they were thinking of getting rid of her. She told her she loved living with their family and wanted to stay. She told her that she had mistaken those small dogs for rabbits and that she hadn't known she shouldn't chase them and that she didn't mean to hurt them.

It was clear Betsy had taken the animal communicator's conversation with Luna dead seriously. It was also clear that the children hadn't believed a word of it but, seeing a ray of hope for Luna, resisted uttering a single cynical word. Asa could feel the mood at the table lighten, and as both Sarah and Mitchell volunteered to walk Luna more to keep her from jumping and Betsy talked about a kind of cattle wire Dr. Hill told her about that they could string along the top of the fence to keep Luna from jumping.

Even so, Asa couldn't get past the $2,000 they had to pay their neighbor for the vet's bill. But the evening after Regina had come to the house, the doorbell rang and there stood Muriel Ruber, the owner of the shih tzu.

"I've been thinking, Asa. Luna's always been such a sweet dog. I've decided she thought my dog was a rabbit or some other critter." She held out a piece of paper, a check he realized—for a thousand dollars. Half the vet bill.

"You don't have to do that, Muriel," he said, trying to hand it back.

"I want to," she said. "I'm partly to blame. I shouldn't have left him loose in the backyard."

So they kept Luna, and over time Asa became grateful to Regina. He couldn't believe he had ever considered getting rid of the dog. Not after those early days of bringing Luna home after his little girl's surgery. Not after the big furry puppy tore through the house wreaking havoc—snatching food off the kitchen counter, destroying everything in her wake, pooping and peeing everywhere. Not after she infuriated Asa so often and in so many ways that once in the middle of the night when she had woken Asa for the hundredth time, he picked her up and hurled her out into the pitch-black yard. Not after Luna had bounded into their household like the life force she was, returning them to themselves again and again.

CHAPTER 24

Wendy, Late Afternoon Friday

Wendy swept the sawdust out of the drive and neatened the flowers and candles around the memorial while Mitchell picked up branches and raked the front yard. With Sarah and Dr. Flowers at the vet's, they had the house to themselves. It was good to be outside, doing something physical, especially in this mountain weather. She had inherited her love for the mountains from her mother. Wendy would have been only three, but she had dim memories of her father driving her and her mother, already sick, up windy, shady mountain back roads, taking them along creeks, past little waterfalls, stopping at overlooks that opened onto waves of receding mountains. They rode with the windows down, breathing in the cool air that seemed lighter and richer than the air back home. Even as a little girl Wendy had preferred shade to sun, cool to heat, forests to fields, probably why, in spite of the emails from the accounting office piling up, her mood had improved as she and Mitchell had driven out of the school gates and headed up the highway to Asheville.

Watching Mitchell rake, she could see how deep inside himself he had gone. Wendy loved Mitchell with all her heart, but it troubled her that she often couldn't track him when he disappeared into himself. This bothered her so much she had called her father early this morning when she knew he would be up studying his devotional. He was a good person to talk things over with. And as a pastor, he dealt with a lot of death. This morning he told her that it was his job to comfort his parishioners, but he couldn't do that if he was constantly being overwhelmed by their loss.

"If a doctor felt he had to get sick every time he saw a sick patient," he said, "he'd be a mess and a lousy doctor. Like doctors, pastors need a little distance to be able to do their job. And it's the same with helping our loved ones. Somebody has to stand outside the suffering to help the other through it."

"So I don't have to feel bad because he feels bad," Wendy asked.

"All you can do is be present for him."

She thanked him and was about to hang up when her dad said, "How's school?"

It caught her off guard, and she nearly told him about the bills.

"Fine," she said. "School's fine."

* * *

Watching Mitchell stuff a big plastic bag full of leaves, Wendy came over and hugged him. He stood there, holding the rake like she had pinned him. After a few moments she felt his body relax, and he dropped the rake.

"Want to go back to my place?" She glanced toward the studio.

"How come you never told me about the bills?" he asked.

"What bills?" She let go of him.

"Your bills from school."

"How do you know about those?" she said. "Have you been snooping around on my laptop?" She'd had a creepy boyfriend in high school who'd done that kind of thing.

"About a week ago, when we were in the library, you left your laptop open to an email from the accounting office."

"You shouldn't have read it," she said. "It's not your business." She hugged herself.

"Are you kidding me?" he said. "We're planning to spend the rest of our lives together, and you don't tell me about something as big as this?"

"I'm figuring it out myself."

"How?" He picked up the rake. "It looks like you owe the school a lot of money."

She took a deep breath and watched an empty tour bus go down the street. She turned back to him. "I can take a couple of semesters off, go back home, get a job, and save up some money." It made her feel sick to hear herself say that. She had worked so hard to get where she was.

"Doesn't sound like much of a plan," he said. "Have you talked to your dad?"

"All it'd do is make him feel bad that he couldn't help. Ministers don't make squat, especially ministers of little churches like my dad's."

"What about taking out a student loan?"

"My dad hates loans and has always preached that I should never take out a loan. My grandfather took out so many loans when my dad was little that he finally sent his family into bankruptcy."

"Talk to him. He'd want to know what's going on. Parents want to be helpful."

"You're an expert on parents now?" She scoffed.

He looked hurt.

"I'm used to figuring things out on my own," she said. "But I'm beginning to think I can't figure this out alone." She sighed. "Maybe I need to pray harder."

"You don't have to figure it out by yourself," he said. "Your problem is my problem. We're in this together. If we're going to last, you need to trust me," he said. "You don't need to pray harder. You need to talk to your dad."

• • •

Dr. Flowers pulled into the driveway with Sarah and Luna, Luna's head out the window, her tongue lolling out of her mouth. Mitchell opened the car door, and Luna hopped down.

"Well?" Mitchell asked, petting Luna.

Sarah came from around the other side. "She thinks Luna has PTSD and prescribed an antidepressant. But she thinks she'll be okay."

"That's a blessing," Wendy said, but as soon as she spoke, Dr. Flowers shot her a look and without a word headed toward the house.

"What's with him?" Mitchell asked.

Wendy wondered if she had said something to upset Dr. Flowers.

"He's been like that ever since we left the vet," Sarah said. "Regina said something that upset him."

"If I'm making things harder here . . ." Wendy began.

Sarah put her arm around Wendy. "Stay."

Wendy felt a nudge at her hip and saw Luna beside her, wagging her tail.

"Luna wants you to stay," Mitchell said.

Dr. Flowers came back out of the house and passed by without a word.

"Dad?" Sarah said.

He climbed into the car and started to back out, but Sarah tapped his window.

"Where are you going?" she asked.

He paused for a moment as if he had to think. "To meet Ben for a beer."

"We need to go over the plans for the memorial service," she said.

"I'll be back in a little while." He backed out of the drive and was gone.

"Ben?" Wendy asked.

Luna plopped down at their feet.

"Our dad's best friend," Sarah said.

"About his only friend," Mitchell said.

"That's not true."

"I can count his friends on one hand," Mitchell said.

"A lot of dads are like that." Wendy wished Mitchell wouldn't be so hard on his father.

"Being a minister, your dad must have a lot of friends," Mitchell said.

"He knows a lot of people, but parishioners aren't friends. They're work, sometimes a lot of work. At the end of the day when he goes home," Wendy said, "my dad fixes himself dinner, goes for a walk, then sits in the den and reads, or watches a little Netflix. He prefers his own company when he can get it. And your dad sounds kind of like my dad except instead of parishioners your dad deals with students all day."

After Wendy's mother died, she became closer to her father. She wondered if the same might end up being true for Mitchell and his father. She had never liked the phrase *The Lord works in mysterious ways*. It sounded bumper-stickery. Also it wasn't in the Bible like everybody thought. It was from a hymn by William Cowper, a poet from the 1700s who wrote hymns, and the line actually went *God moves in a mysterious way, His wonders to perform.* But her favorite line from that hymn was *God is His own interpreter*. What was interesting about the hymn was that it was written between suicide attempts. Cowper, having struggled with depression all his life, spent time in an asylum and tried to kill himself many times. These words weren't written blithely to reflect some Hallmark card sentiment. They were the words of a desperate man who never knew from day to day how long he could bring himself to live.

A gust of wind picked up the pile of sawdust Wendy had swept up, and enveloped them in its cloud, getting sawdust in their eyes, their noses, their hair, and coating Luna's fur.

CHAPTER 25

Asa, Early Evening Friday

The Turnpike Tavern, a long, close, pine-paneled room, was only blocks from their house. After work he and Betsy would often walk over and meet up with friends. Asa pulled into the crowded parking lot. Being a Friday evening, the place was packed. He threaded his way to the bar. The big TV, mounted in an upper corner ever since 9/11, showed a baseball game.

"What'll it be, Asa?" Roger, the bartender, was an affable, sturdily built older man, maybe a few years older than Asa, and a dead ringer for Holling Vincoeur, the bartender from *Northern Exposure*, a show Betsy and Asa had both loved.

"The Green Man," Asa said, glancing at the chalkboard where his go-to stout was listed among other local IPAs.

Roger filled the glass to brimming, then wiped the sides down. He looked up at Asa, his eyes sad, "My condolences." He handed Asa the beer, but as Asa reached for his wallet, Roger gave him a pained look as if he was insulted that Asa was trying to pay for it.

Asa found Ben at their usual table tucked far enough back in the bar that they could hear each other talk. Ben was eyeing the Coke on the table in front of him.

"On call?" Asa asked.

"Afraid so."

Asa had always been impressed by how disciplined his friend was whenever he was on call.

"Do you mind?" Asa picked up his beer.

"Not at all."

Asa took a sip, which tasted unusually good, and then took a bigger swig.

"So what's up?" Ben asked. "You sounded upset on the phone."

"In case you hadn't heard, my wife died," Asa said.

"It didn't sound like this was about that."

"It's about Regina," he said quietly.

"Who?" Ben cupped his hand to his ear.

"Regina Hill," Asa said louder, looking around to see if anyone heard, ridiculous given the general din of the place.

"The veterinarian?"

"She's the woman Betsy was seeing." Asa told Ben the story about taking Luna to the vet and what had happened this afternoon, and how he'd made the connection.

"Sarah still doesn't know?" Ben asked.

"If not, she's closing in."

"What does all this really change?" Ben took another sip of Coke, then pushed the glass away.

"Betrayal now has a face," Asa said.

"That sounds pretty dramatic."

"I've started having thoughts," Asa said.

"Thoughts?"

Asa leaned in. "Murderous."

"You want to murder the vet?"

"Of course not," he said, "but I would like to do something to her."

"You mean hurt her? Physically?"

"Not *physically*," he said. "What kind of person do you think I am?"

"Asa, jealousy makes people do crazy things. I have filing cabinets full of such things."

"Mental anguish was more what I had in mind," Asa said.

"If she loved Betsy at all," Ben said, "it's safe to say she's in considerable anguish."

Asa glanced in the direction of the baseball game and then looked back at his friend. "I'm thinking about telling the kids."

"You decided not to."

"It's not fair," Asa said. "They think of Betsy as some motherly saint and me as some acerbic crank."

"Then they think right," Ben said.

"If they only knew what she'd been up to."

Ben leaned forward. "Telling the kids right now would be a mistake."

"I thought therapists were supposed to listen to their clients, not tell them what to do."

"I'm not your therapist, and you're not my client," Ben said. "You're my friend, and as such I'm free to tell you when you're being a selfish asshole."

Asa shrugged and reached for his beer, but to his surprise the glass was empty. "Where are the kids right now?" Ben asked.

"At home with the girlfriend."

"You need to improve your attitude toward her if you don't want to lose Mitchell too."

"You sound like Jillian."

"Great minds . . ." Ben's pager went off. He unclipped it from his belt and read it. "I gotta go."

"Go then," Asa said.

"I hope I didn't make you mad," he said getting up. "I don't want you doing something you'll regret."

"I know that," he said.

"If you need to talk, give me a call." He glanced at Asa's empty beer glass. "Go easy tonight. You're a cheap drunk."

After Ben left, Asa got up, thinking he would head home, but the idea of going home to his children knowing what he knew now . . . he didn't trust himself. Ben was right. He needed to keep it to himself. To fortify his resolve, he ordered a second stout and joined the group watching the game.

At some point during graduate school, he had lost interest in watching sports on TV. He regretted it though. People who watched sports seemed happier. He wondered whether or not if he had kept watching sports and gotten Mitchell to watch with him, they would've had something to "bond over."

It wasn't long before Asa ordered a third stout. The more he drank the more he enjoyed the warmth of the people in a small space, the conversations around him, the laughter. He felt buoyed, and the anger that had simmered since they'd taken Luna to Regina's office began to loosen, and his worries, for a good thirty minutes, drifted to the dark corners of the bar.

Then he looked up, and Charles Byrd stood beside his chair. "I'm so sorry, Asa."

"Thanks, Charles," Asa said.

"If there's anything I can do, please let me know."

"Thanks," Asa said, going back to his beer.

"The usual?" Roger said. Asa looked up and saw he was talking to Charles, then he watched Roger pour the beer.

"Wait a minute," Asa said. "The other night you told me you don't drink!"

An embarrassed look crossed Charles's face. "I thought if I pissed you off, you'd tell me to forget the whole thing. I'm worn out with everybody's good intentions."

Roger set the foaming glass in front of Charles, said it would be five dollars, and Charles pulled out his wallet and left a ten on the bar. Charles picked up his beer, said that he would be at the memorial service, and started to his table, but then he stopped and said, "Are you here alone?"

"I met a friend here, but he had to leave."

"I'm here with some friends from my church." Charles nodded toward a table with a couple of men and a couple of women who appeared deep in discussion. "Want to join us?"

"Another time," Asa said. As Asa watched Charles make his way over to the table, he couldn't comprehend what he'd witnessed. Charles Byrd out having a drink with friends. What had the world come to? Or rather what had he himself come to? Even Charles Byrd had more of a life than he had.

By the time Asa had finished his fourth—or was it his fifth?—stout, the cozy warm feeling had been replaced by a heightened worry and sharper anger. He walked out into the twilight, the low roar of conversation spilling into the parking lot. He sat in the car, wanting to grieve, but Betsy's betrayal made it impossible. Feeling emotionally hemmed in, he gripped the steering wheel, his knuckles white.

Someone knocked on his window. He looked up to see Charles motion him to roll down his window. "Asa, I think you've had a bit too much. Let me drive you home."

"There's no need."

"I insist." Charles opened the door and motioned for him to get in the passenger's seat.

"Really, I'm okay."

"Move over or I'll tell Melda you've been dodging my accreditation committee."

Taken aback by Charles's assertiveness, Asa did as he was told, walked around, and climbed into the passenger's seat. Charles drove them the few blocks to his house.

"How did you know where we live?" Asa asked as Charles pulled in front of the house.

"I was just here," he said.

"How many nights ago was that?"

"Three." Charles parked at the bottom of the drive and turned off the engine and the headlights.

They sat in the car and looked toward the house. Duke Power had gotten the electricity back on. Inside, lights spotlighted the kids in the big front window as if they were a storefront display, sitting around the table working on the Klee puzzle.

"I guess you know what I'm going through," Asa said.

"People said that to me a lot after Isabelle died," Charles said. "None of us knows what anyone is going through."

The men got out of the car and stood in the driveway.

"Nice night." Charles began pointing out constellations. Asa tried to follow him, but the stars started swimming around on him.

"I don't know my stars," Asa said, rubbing his eyes.

"When I was a boy my father taught me the constellations," Charles said.

"Were you close?"

"Still are. What's that over there?" Charles walked over to the tree trunk, where three or four dozen candles burned in a big circle around its base, casting the flowers and poems in a flickering yellow light.

"It'll get worse before it gets better," Charles said, still looking at the memorial.

"But it will get better. And if you ever need to talk, I promise not to mention Dunbar."

"How are you getting back?" Asa asked.

"The old-fashioned way," he said.

"Let me give you a ride," Asa said.

Charles laughed. "That would defeat the purpose, wouldn't it?"

Asa rubbed his forehead. "Maybe I have had a bit too much."

"I drank myself to sleep many a night those first weeks," Charles said. "But I didn't have kids." He looked back to the window where the children were still bent over the puzzle.

"Good night, Asa."

Asa watched Charles amble down the sidewalk, pause to study the sky a couple more times, seeming in no hurry—and, maybe he wasn't, with no one to go home to.

CHAPTER 26

• • •

Wendy, Friday Night

Wendy was startled by the crashing sound that came from outside.

"Probably bears," Mitchell said.

Wendy was always amazed to learn about just how many bears Mitchell said were in Asheville. He said they wandered the neighborhoods, raided birdfeeders, and overturned garbage cans. She'd gotten up to look out the window, hoping to see her first bear, when Dr. Flowers came in the kitchen door.

"Tripped over the recycling bin." He looked sheepish.

"I tried calling you half a dozen times," Sarah said, "You had me worried."

Dr. Flowers pulled his phone out of his pocket. "It's out of juice." He frowned toward the stereo. "Who's listening to country music?"

Luna got up from her bed and came over to greet Dr. Flowers, who absentmindedly petted her as Sarah turned down the music.

"Where's your car?" Mitchell glanced out the window.

Dr. Flowers squinted out the window as if trying to remember. "Charles parked it at the foot of the drive."

"Charles?" Sarah asked. "The professor?"

"Yeah, Charles Byrd," Dr. Flowers said. "He drove me home."

Dr. Flowers was drunk. Wendy had known it the minute he had walked in the door. The slowness, the deliberateness, the inability to focus. Her own father had had a drinking problem until one Sunday, after he delivered a nearly incoherent sermon, members of the church stayed after and confronted him. He had been sober now for thirteen years.

"We were supposed to go over the plans for the memorial service," Sarah said.

Dr. Flowers looked back to the stereo. "Who around here likes country music?"

"I want us to go over the plans for the service, Dad," Sarah said.

"I'm in no shape."

Sarah frowned at her father. "We're running out of time."

"You know what your mother wants," Dr. Flowers said. "Turns out I've never known what she wanted."

Sarah and Mitchell exchanged a look.

Dr. Flowers picked up his sleeping bag, which was tucked behind the couch. The expression on his face told Wendy the man was in shock. It was an expression she had seen on her own father's face years ago. She didn't remember much about that time. She was only four. But she did remember the look on her father's face and how much it had worried her. Her mother was dead, and her father gone, if not in body, in spirit. Who would take care of her? The answer came over the weeks and months and years that passed. In time, her father would return to himself and be there for her and support her and be a good father. But in the end, she took care of herself.

• • •

Dr. Flowers had started for the stairs when Sarah asked, "Where are you going, Dad?"

"To bed."

"I thought it wasn't safe up there."

"Your room has a hole in the ceiling. It's freezing, and the bed's broken," Mitchell said.

"I'll sleep on the mattress." He started up the stairs.

"The Lord is with you, Dr. Flowers," Wendy said. "Your wife was a wonderful woman."

Dr. Flowers stopped, turned around, and looked at Wendy as if he didn't even recognize her.

"Dad?" Sarah said in a warning tone.

Dr. Flowers turned back to his daughter. "There are things about your mother you two should know."

"Now isn't the best time," Sarah said.

"Your mother cheated on me, on you, on us."

The tarp flapped upstairs, and Wendy already wanted to protect Mitchell from whatever his father was saying.

"What do you mean?" Mitchell said.

"What I said," Dr. Flowers said.

"But how?" Mitchell asked. "With who?"

"Whom. With whom," Dr. Flowers said.

"Dad, now is definitely not the time to talk about whatever this is," Sarah said. "I think you've had a bit too much."

"I have had way too much," he said. "But that doesn't change that your mother wasn't all she was cracked up to be."

"I don't believe you." Mitchell's voice shook.

"The night the tree fell," Dr. Flowers said, "she'd just told me she was having an affair. Why do you think I was sleeping out in the studio?"

"You're lying," Mitchell said.

"Mitchell don't talk to your father like that," Wendy said, starting to put her arm around him.

Dr. Flowers turned to Wendy. "Stay out of this."

"Don't talk to Wendy like that," Mitchell said.

Wendy looked at Dr. Flowers and was about to say something when the phone rang. Nobody got up to answer it.

"I'll go on out to the studio," Wendy said, unable to keep the anger out of her voice.

"Good idea," Dr. Flowers said. "Another good idea would be for you to go back to school and let our family grieve in peace."

"Wendy *is* family," Mitchell seethed.

"What's that supposed to mean?" Dr. Flowers asked.

"Mitchell," Wendy said, "now isn't the time."

Mitchell pulled Wendy against his side. "We're getting married."

Wendy's heart fell.

Dr. Flowers guffawed.

"As soon as we both graduate," Mitchell said.

"You're children for God's sake!" Dr. Flowers said.

Wendy flinched.

"No son of mine is marrying a fundamentalist, country-music-loving right-winger."

Wendy felt Mitchell's body coil with tension, and for a minute she thought he might slug his father, and part of her wished he would. Sarah must have worried about the same thing because she stepped in between them. Even Luna came over.

"Dad, you're drunk and being awful," Sarah said.

"Our family is in shambles." Mitchell glared at their father, who seemed on the point of saying something else, but before he could, Sarah walked up to him, and in a tone she might have used with a child said, "Go to bed, Dad. Go upstairs and go to bed." She pointed up the stairs.

Dr. Flowers seemed to sink in on himself, and for a minute, Wendy thought he might collapse. Sarah firmly took his arm and led him upstairs.

"Damn him," Mitchell said under his breath, watching them go.

"He's grieving," Wendy said.

"His behavior is unforgivable," Mitchell said.

Wendy took Mitchell's hand. "Nothing's unforgivable in the eyes of God."

Mitchell turned to her as if to say something but then seemed to think better of it.

CHAPTER 27

Sarah, Friday Night

Sarah laid out a couple of blankets on the bare mattress, and her father crawled underneath them and fell asleep. She pulled off his shoes, then sat beside him and hugged her knees. Unshaven and hair disheveled, he slept with his mouth open, emitting an occasional ragged snore. She would've thought of him as a sad figure if she hadn't been so mad at him. He was in pain over their mother's death. But so was everyone else, and it was irresponsible for him to drink himself to the point of blurting upsetting things about their mother. It was bad enough they had lost their mother, but to have to deal with a mess of a father on top of it only added to the misery.

Aware she was shivering, she retrieved a blanket from her room, wrapped it around herself, and returned to sit beside her father. Ever since that angry exchange between her father and Regina at the vet's today, Sarah had been thinking back to two months ago when her mother had come to Chapel Hill, like she sometimes did, to have a girl's weekend. Sarah loved these times with her mother, but the last visit had felt different.

Her mother had taken her shopping for clothes, then they put up new curtains, and Saturday night they dressed up and walked down to the new tapas restaurant on Franklin Street. The sidewalk was crowded as it usually was on a Saturday night.

But when they walked up to the restaurant, Sarah was surprised to see Regina Hill out front. When Regina saw them, she waved and hurried over to them.

"There you are," Regina said, coming up and hugging them.

"Oh damn," her mother said under her breath.

"Betsy, did you forget to tell Sarah?" Regina said.

Her mother nodded. "I'm embarrassed to say I completely forgot."

Sarah learned that Regina was attending a veterinarian's conference in Raleigh at N.C. State. Her mother and Regina had discussed Regina joining them tonight for dinner.

Her mother turned to her. "We've been having such a great weekend it slipped my mind."

Sarah had thought of this weekend as a mother/daughter weekend. But she liked Regina and even felt a kindred connection with her. Besides, it was just for dinner.

Regina took Sarah's hand. "Sweetheart, you want your mother to yourself, don't you? I totally get it and honestly that's fine. It's a relief to get out of Asheville for a bit and have dinner somewhere where people aren't coming up to me and asking advice about their pets."

"You shouldn't have dinner alone," Sarah said.

"Are you sure? I won't linger afterward because I do have to get back to Raleigh."

They had a lively meal together. Sarah was surprised to see her mother so engaged and animated with Regina. A couple of times her mother laughed so hard she wiped tears from her eyes. Sarah couldn't remember her laughing like that with anyone except their father. She noticed from the time her mother had arrived at her apartment on Friday a new lightness she hadn't seen in her mother since before Mitchell attempted suicide. She wondered what accounted for it. Time passing? Having Mitchell doing better? Having them both off at college? Enjoying more time being alone with Dad?

After dinner and after Regina had headed back to Raleigh, Sarah and her mother walked back toward her apartment, arm in arm.

"I didn't realize you and Regina were such good friends," Sarah said.

"I've been making an effort to deepen friendships," her mother said, "Regina and I have grown close."

"That's great, Mom!" She put her arm around her mother's shoulder. She was happy she had found more time for herself. She worked so hard and did so much for everyone, it was only fair. She was, after all, a social animal. Sarah was especially glad it was Regina she'd gotten close to. It made sense that what was good for the dog would also be good for the owner.

But now here in her parents' cold dark bedroom, sitting beside her snoring dad and thinking about the testy exchange between Regina and her dad at the vet's this afternoon, Sarah realized how incredibly dense she'd been. How had she not understood what her mother had tried to tell her about Regina and her that night in Chapel Hill?

CHAPTER 28

• • •

Wendy, Friday Night

Wendy returned to working the puzzle, getting Mitchell to join her. Ever since Sarah had taken their dad upstairs, Mitchell had been looking toward the stairs. Even as they worked on the puzzle, he kept glancing at the clock over the woodstove, when he finally said, "Should I go up and check on them?"

"Maybe so." Wendy was concerned herself.

That's when Sarah came down the stairs.

"He's asleep," she said. She looked at Wendy. "He isn't a big drinker. Once in a while he drinks a bit too much, but I've never seen him like this."

"What he said about Mom cheating on him," Mitchell said. "Do you think there's anything to it?"

Sarah leaned her head on her hand, looking tired.

"What about what he said about sleeping out in the studio?" Mitchell said. "I can't remember him ever sleeping out there."

Her face empty, Sarah turned toward the woodstove, the coals glowing through the glass door. Wendy sensed her despair and how alone and responsible she must feel with one parent gone, the other flailing, and a brother she was trying to protect.

"Who would she even be having an affair with?" Mitchell asked.

Sarah kept looking at the glowing coals.

"Somebody she works with?" Mitchell asked. "Another teacher?"

As if she came to a decision, Sarah pushed herself up by her knees and said, "I'm going up to bed. Good night."

"Good night, Sarah," Wendy said.

"Good night, Sis," Mitchell said. Wendy and Mitchell watched her go up the stairs and heard her cross the floor over their heads and shut the door to her room.

Mitchell put a couple more pieces of wood in the woodstove, and they went back to working the nearly finished fish puzzle.

"Did I say something to aggravate her?" Mitchell asked.

"Your sister takes on a lot."

"I know," he said.

"I'm not sure you do," Wendy said, as she fit another piece into the puzzle.

CHAPTER 29

• • •

Sarah, Friday Night

Sarah lay on her bed staring at the wall-sized chart of the periodic table that her parents had given her when she was a freshman chem major at Chapel Hill. She found the chart elegant, soothing, and reassuring because on it everything had its place. But tonight, instead of concentrating on the elements, her mind was full of worry and confusion. She needed to talk to somebody but who? Certainly no one in her family. Next thing she knew she'd dialed a number.

"What's up?"

She disliked *What's up?* It felt abrupt, a friendlier but no less irritating version of *What do you want?* Already she was sorry she had called Josh.

"How's it going?" he said.

Sarah had to assume that he was asking about how her family was coping.

"Everybody's sad," she said. "My dad's a mess and drank too much tonight, and my brother's freaking out, and our dog has PTSD."

"And you? How are you?"

"Devastated," her voice quavered. "She was my soulmate. She knew me better than anybody."

He was quiet, and she was sure he was playing Minecraft or League of Legends. He was addicted to computer games.

"Josh?"

"That sounds tough," he said, as if he realized a response was called for.

"I needed to talk to somebody who knows me but who isn't a family member." She told him their father had said their mother was having an affair and how she hadn't believed it at first. "But the more I've realized it must be true," Sarah said, "the more confused I've become."

"Confused about?" he asked.

"About how my mother could do this to my father and my brother and to me. I can't believe she did it to me—their stable, dependable child, the one she could always count on. We were so close or so I thought." Tears began to slip down her cheeks.

Sarah heard scratching at her door. She got up from her bed and opened her door to let Luna in. Sarah sat down on the floor and leaned against her bed, and Luna lay down beside her, settling her great furry head in Sarah's lap.

"I'm sorry I'm being so melodramatic," she said. "I guess I needed to talk."

"Sure thing," he said.

"So what do you think?" she said.

"About?"

"About any of this," she said, feeling a little exasperated. "What do you think about any of it. I called to get your opinion."

He paused. "You say you're confused, but you don't sound confused to me."

"I don't?"

"You sound angry. Your mother had an affair. It made you angry. I'd be angry too."

Sarah stroked Luna's head. "It's worse that she's not here to talk it over with. If she was here, one way or another we would've talked it through." Sarah let loose a ragged sob and curled up on her floor next to Luna but still held the phone by her ear.

There was a silence.

"Still there?" she asked.

"Yup," he said.

"Thanks for listening."

"I can't believe you actually called me to talk something over," he said.

"That surprises you?" she said.

"You don't usually ask my opinion. Mostly you give your opinion."

She did not know what to say. "I'm wiped and need to go to bed," she said. "The next couple of days are going to be long." She paused. "Thank you for listening."

"No problem," he said.

As she hung up, she caught a snippet of League of Legends music. She cut out the light and crawled into bed, and Luna jumped up and lay beside her. Sarah lay there thinking over their conversation. Josh could be irritatingly inattentive, but he was right about one thing: She was angry at her mother. And, being able to name it, to see the shape and structure of it, gave her a little distance, a little breathing room.

CHAPTER 30

• • •

Asa, Middle of the Night Friday

Asa woke late in the night to the rattle of the tarp on the roof. He watched it move in as if it were breathing. Otherwise, the house was silent. He glanced at his watch: 2:30 a.m. Everybody must've gone to bed. He propped himself on his elbows and looked out the window. The tree trunk glowed in the flickering candlelight. He felt a wave of nausea, stumbled into the bathroom, and retched into the toilet. He sank onto the bathroom floor and rested his forehead on the cool edge of the toilet. He felt another wave coming on and retched into the toilet again. He slumped against the wall and pulled down a towel to mop the sweat from his face. He hadn't felt this bad since his college drinking days.

He winced remembering his behavior with his children. *Your mother cheated on me, on you, on us.* If that wasn't bad enough, he went after Wendy, calling her names and telling her to go home. He attacked this girl everyone, including himself, liked and knew was good for his son. He was a failure as a father. As a matter of fact, *failure* didn't begin to cover what a failure he was.

He pulled himself up, washed his face, and drank two glasses of water, then made his way back to the bedroom and collapsed onto the mattress.

"Oh, Betsy," he said, "you've only been gone a few days, and look at what a mess I've already made. I'm the one the tree should've fallen on."

Stop it, Asa. Yes, you have been awful the past few days. And you screwed up last night. In fact, you screwed up pretty bad, but that doesn't mean you can't do something about it. You're a better father than you give yourself credit for.

Asa wasn't so sure. He had been remembering the disaster of a talk he'd had with Mitchell when his son was in tenth grade.

As a little boy, Mitchell was sweet, affectionate, and used to climb into bed with them in the morning, snuggle against them with his worn blanket, and look out the window while telling them whatever dream he'd had. His dreams were often long magical stories about riding Crawley, his pet salamander, on adventures across the Milky Way.

Their son had always felt things deeply yet didn't know what to do with his big feelings. The older he got, the more aggravated and aggravating he became. In his teenage years, he often felt like an ill-tempered foreigner whose language they didn't speak. Which is why when Betsy told Asa one day that he needed to have "the sex talk" with Mitchell, Asa was not enthusiastic.

"Didn't I already have that talk with him?" Asa asked.

"When he was in third grade," Betsy said.

"We covered all we needed to cover then, don't you think?"

"Asa, you have to talk to him now. He's nearly a man."

"Have you had this talk with Sarah?"

"Are you kidding? Sarah and I have been talking about sex since she was five."

"I wouldn't know where to begin." Asa remembered a preschool teacher once saying that it was best to talk about sex with kids whenever they began asking about it. If they'd waited to do that with Mitchell, there would never have been a conversation.

Betsy handed Asa a book, *Sex, A Book for Teens: An Uncensored Guide to Your Body, Sex, and Safety*. The cover was the silhouette of a cow mounting another cow. Or that would have to be a bull mounting a cow, wouldn't it?

A week later, after Asa read and reread the book, preparing for this talk in the same way he would a class lecture, he was driving Mitchell to a dentist's appointment and realized he had a captive audience. "Your mother and I think it's time for you and me to discuss sex."

Mitchell laughed.

"We believe it's important you be prepared."

"You're not kidding?" Mitchell asked.

"It's a very complicated world out there these days."

"You're really not kidding," Mitchell said.

And Asa launched into his talk, reviewing what he read in the book.

"No," Mitchell said.

But Asa continued.

"No! No! No!" Mitchell shouted and rolled down the window like he was going to crawl out. Undaunted by his son's theatrics, Asa kept talking. After all, he put a couple of hours into preparing for this. If the car hadn't been moving, Mitchell probably would've jumped out, but instead he leapt over the seat and into the back.

Asa kept on, but Mitchell began to sing, "La! La! La! La! La!" and Asa could see him in the rearview mirror with his hands pressed over his ears. Asa gave up and they rode along in silence.

Having anticipated that it might go this way, Asa opened the glove compartment of the car, took out the cow book, and tossed it into the back seat. Two seconds later it came whizzing back.

"Read it," Mitchell said.

Another long silence.

Mitchell from the back. "Besides, don't you remember you all made me take those OWL classes when I was in nineth grade?"

How had Asa forgotten? They had made both their kids take the OWL (Our Whole Lives) classes at the UU church, a sort of sex ed boot camp that covered everything imaginable and more. Asa wasn't surprised he'd forgotten, but Betsy never forgot things like that.

"I didn't forget," Betsy said later when he told her what had happened. "I thought there might be things they didn't get around to in those classes that he might want to know and that you two could have a man-to-man talk. I certainly didn't mean for you to deliver the Gettysburg Address to him. Maybe if you went back and casually asked him if he had any questions."

"*Casually?* This is our son you're talking about. Trying to have a talk with Mitchell is like trying to have a conversation with a nuclear reactor. And if you think I'm going to try to talk to him again about this, you don't know me and you don't know our son."

Betsy nodded, and he could see she was thinking this over.

"Besides, after taking those classes," he said, "that boy knows more about sex than I will ever know. I should probably ask him for advice. That would really blow his circuits."

"I would give anything to see what's going on inside that head of his," she said.

Every mother's dream, thought Asa, *and every father's nightmare.*

CHAPTER 31

• • •

Asa, Saturday Morning

Early morning light filtered through the blinds. Asa sat up. The nausea had been replaced by a sick headache, and his heart pounded from the ragged remnants of a nightmare. Walking in the woods, looking for Betsy, he found her pinned to the ground by a fallen tree. Her eyes open, she smiled calmly up at him. He tried to reach for her but couldn't move. He tried calling her name but couldn't speak. Never in his life had he felt so powerless.

He crawled out of bed and went to look in the medicine cabinet, but the aspirin bottle was nowhere to be found. He splashed water on his face and brushed the sawdust, which coated everything in the bedroom, out of his hair. He walked down the hall and found Sarah and Mitchell asleep in their rooms.

No sign of Wendy. Had he run her off last night? When he glanced out the window, he was relieved to see her car in the drive. She must have slept in the studio. Why hadn't Mitchell been sleeping with her? He had to know Asa didn't care. Maybe it was against Wendy's religion, although when he was a student Asa had known plenty of religious girls who had sex. In fact, the more religious the girl, the better the sex. Or that had been the theory. That the tension between the girls' Christian beliefs and their bodily urges resulted in such an inner conflagration that to have sex with such a girl was to have sex of epic proportions. Asa had never experienced this phenomenon or anything close. The girls he dated in college were liberal, open-minded girls, not overly concerned with Jesus and even less concerned with sex, at least with him.

The more he pondered it, the more convinced he became that Wendy hadn't allowed Mitchell to stay with her out of consideration for Asa. By not letting him stay she was saying a son's place should be with his family at such a time. Wendy was kind enough or smart enough to think of Asa even if he was being an ass. Mitchell had fallen for a girl of considerable insight.

No aspirin in the downstairs bathroom either. He turned on the heat and went into the kitchen, and while measuring coffee into the filter, his eye fell on the folded AARP letter on the counter. He read it over carefully, as if it might contain some deeper message about what had gone wrong with him and Betsy. How many thousands of personal crises had this innocent form letter precipitated over the years? How many facelifts, how many religious conversions, divorces, suicides?

He poured himself a mug of coffee and was about to sit at the kitchen table when he spotted the aspirin bottle on the windowsill. When he picked it up, it dropped away, scattering pills across the floor. As he got down on his knees to pick up the pills, he felt the usual irritation with his wife. How hard was it to screw things back on? Just a millisecond of effort. Then he saw the branch through his wife's stilled heart. He sat in the middle of the kitchen floor, surrounded by pills, and wept.

After he'd taken a couple of pills and put the rest back in the bottle, he picked up his coffee, put on the fleece Sarah had given him last Christmas, and stepped outside. The morning was cold and breezy. He walked out into the yard and around the tree trunk that had been transformed into a memorial. So many flowers arranged around the foot of it with candles, some still burning. Several paperback books scattered around. Books Betsy had assigned her classes over the years like *The Handmaid's Tale*, *The Giver*, *Their Eyes Were Watching God*, *To Kill a Mockingbird*, *I Know Why the Caged Bird Sings*, *Frankenstein*, *The Color Purple*, *The Joy Luck Club*, *The Bell Jar*, and *Mrs. Dalloway*. But it was the poems and notes he couldn't get over. They covered the entire surface of the trunk from bottom to top. All handwritten, and many with drawings. They fluttered in the breeze, a living work of art.

He glanced over at Wendy's car in the drive. As he reached the foot of the drive, the woman who delivered the newspaper pulled up and was about to toss the paper through her open window when she saw him and pulled up beside him, handing him the paper.

"You and your family have been in my thoughts, Dr. Flowers," she said.

"You were the one who found her," he said.

"And I know it's none of my business," she said, "but for what it's worth it was my sense that she never suffered." Then she looked over at the memorial. "Folks thought so much of your wife."

He watched her drive down the street, sending papers spiraling onto lawns, delivering the news, good and bad, to the neighborhood.

CHAPTER 32

• • •

Asa, Fall 1992

Asa had dreaded the rehearsal reception, so he was surprised to find he didn't hate standing around drinking wine, eating finger food, and making small talk. He enjoyed catching up with old friends and family and meeting Betsy's friends and family. There was a warmth he hadn't anticipated. As nice as it was, after a while he grew weary and drifted off to a corner to rest his conversational skills.

Betsy couldn't have been livelier or more animated. She made her way around the room, hugging people and smiling and laughing. In her new dress, she looked ravishing, a word he was pretty sure he had never even thought before tonight. In pursuit of a reception dress, they'd driven all over the state of South Carolina, or at least it felt that way. Many of the dresses looked great on her, but she was never satisfied. He was especially confused when after visiting countless stores and trying on as many dresses, she insisted they return to a Belk department store in Spartanburg, the very first store where she tried on the very first dress: A wine-red satin, open-back dress that fit her like a glove.

"She looks so hot in that dress, doesn't she?" said a voice behind him.

He turned around to see a small, dark woman with wide cheeks, bright brown eyes, and glistening black hair.

"I couldn't agree more," he said, trying to remember if he had met this woman.

She held out her hand. "I'm Lily. Lily Fernandes. And no, we haven't met, although I feel like we have."

The name was familiar, but he couldn't place her.

"Betsy and I went through the grad program at USC together."

"Oh, right," he said, remembering now. "And you went on to get your PhD, didn't you?"

"Very good," she said. "I'm impressed."

"And . . ." squinting his eyes as he thought. "Weren't you teaching down in south Georgia? Valdosta State?"

"You move to the head of the class," she said. "But I'm not teaching anymore."

"What are you doing?"

"I'm a financial planner," she said. "Probably the only financial planner in the state with a PhD in gender studies."

"Better preparation than an MBA any day," he said.

She laughed.

He liked this woman but was surprised by the comfortable way she touched his arm. "Betsy's told me so much about you. I can see why she'd be attracted to you."

Asa thought maybe he heard something in her voice, something that made him a little guarded, as if she were saying some people might not see why Betsy would be attracted to him or why anyone would be attracted to him for that matter. *Cut the inner chatter*, he told himself. Still, he couldn't help himself.

"So why do you think she's attracted to me?" he asked. The truth was that he sometimes wondered this very thing.

Lily shrugged. "You're safe."

He felt a subtle tingle in his stomach. "Safe? That sounds a bit boring," he said.

"Not at all," she said, keeping her hand on his arm. "It just means that with you one gets what one sees. I sensed that about you the minute I laid eyes on you. You are authentically you. You can't be anyone but yourself. Take me for instance, that isn't true with me."

"No?"

"When it comes to relationships," she said, "I'm a shape-shifter. I never know who I'll be from one moment to the next. That's how I was with Betsy."

"You and Betsy were in a relationship?" He felt a twinge of jealousy.

"You might say that," she said.

Keeping his eyes on Lily, he took a big swallow of his wine.

"Nothing oppressively serious," she said, seeming to sense his alarm. "You know how women are. We're freer with ourselves than men are. With women, everything doesn't feel so deliberate or ponderous or cut and dried. Women are experimentalists."

"Experimentalists?"

"We're not afraid to try things out or to try people out for that matter."

"That's what you and Betsy were?" His heart began to pound. "Experimentalists?"

"For a time," she said.

"As in drugs?" he asked, hoping that was all there was to it.

"Drugs played a small part but only in their relation to enhancing the other."

"Sex," he said.

"Not to put too fine a point on it." She fixed him with a bold look. An image of Lily with Betsy flitted through his mind, and he felt shaky and aroused at the same time. Had the lights flickered? He looked around the reception, noting that the many animated conversations were melding into a general buzz.

The next thing he knew Lily gripped his hand, said it was nice to meet him, and disappeared into the crowd. And Asa, once again aware of the tingle in his stomach, finished off his wine and wondered what had just happened.

He was drifting around the room, doing his best to socialize, when Betsy appeared at his side. Her cheeks were flushed with the excitement of the evening and probably from the wine as well. He slipped his arm around her, feeling the silky material of her dress and the surprise of her bare skin on the open back. He tugged her toward him and kissed her.

"You look incredible," he said.

"So the ordeal was worth it?" she asked, smiling.

"Every single mile of it." Then he added. "I met Lily."

"Did you?" she said, cautiously.

"Your fellow experimentalist." He nodded across the room to where Lily was talking to another young woman he didn't know, but already she had her arm on the woman's shoulder.

"I saw you talking to her," Betsy said. "She's a loose cannon. You can't believe a word she says. What'd she tell you, Asa?"

"Nothing much except that you and she had sex." He raised his eyebrows at her. "Sex with drugs."

She studied him a moment, her eyes wide, then she threw her head back and laughed. "That girl's a mess."

"So then it's not true?" He felt a little relief.

"I wouldn't go as far as to say that," she said, with a vague smile. "I would say that whatever happened was before you and me."

"Still, you have to admit it's a little weird for some stranger to be telling me this on our wedding rehearsal night," he said.

"Oh, I don't know," she said, "It seems kind of perfect for the rehearsal night." And with this she kissed him deeply.

Between the wine and the kiss, his head was spinning.

"Besides, this is her modus operandi," she said. "She's a troublemaker and loves nothing more than keeping people off-balance." She glanced fondly in Lily's direction.

It was right around then that Asa's father, who Asa's mother had been gently prodding to give a toast, finally relented and began tapping his glass to quiet the crowd. His father, a kind, affectionate, enigma of a man, given to cryptic statements and famously uncomfortable at social events, raised his glass toward Betsy and Asa and shouted, "Confusion to the enemy!"

A mystified silence was followed by a sprinkle of laughter. Lily stepped up on a chair, raised her glass to the crowd, and belted out, "To the ridiculously happy couple!" which was followed by a spontaneous, joyous roar.

CHAPTER 33

Wendy, Early Morning Saturday

In a tank top and running shorts, Wendy decided to walk the last block back to the Flowerses' house to cool off. What a great old neighborhood with its trees, mossy hundred-year-old brick sidewalks, and footpaths leading to little gardens. A far cry from the neighborhood where she had grown up—a barren, treeless, sweltering subdivision whose name, Sherwood Forest, felt like irony.

The only sounds, other than the breeze in the trees, were the soft calls of mourning doves and her own breathing. Running was essential. Her mood could be lousy, and all it took was a lap around Furman Lake and the clouds parted. More reliable than prayer. She had gotten Mitchell to run with her at school. He was a natural. Fast, long, easy strides and never winded.

Last night she had been relieved to go back to the studio apartment and get away from the drama, but she hated abandoning Mitchell. No longer was he just grieving his mother but also having to rethink his parents' relationship. Wendy had been hearing her own father's voice in her head: *A relationship void of Jesus is a relationship ripe for betrayal.* On the other hand, Wendy knew plenty of Christian couples, some in her father's church, who had torrid affairs. As far as she could see, loving Jesus was no insurance against making a mess of your life.

Even so, she was unsettled by the idea of betrayal. How should she feel about Mitchell's mother? How would Wendy's father handle that? How could she, for that matter? The answer followed immediately on the heels of the question: She would love her, that's what she'd do. She would love her and her family unconditionally, like the Lord loves us all. Still . . .

When she walked up the drive, she was surprised to find Mitchell's father on the front steps. He looked pale and gaunt, his face dark with stubble. Luna sat beside him, wagging her tail as Wendy came up the steps.

"Everyone still asleep?" she asked.

"I think so," he said, in a low gravelly voice. Clearly, he'd had a long night. He moved the newspaper and his coffee cup to make room for her. Her eye fell on the folded newspaper, and she saw a picture of Mitchell's mother.

"Sarah did a good job," he said.

"Your wife was very beautiful," Wendy said.

They sat on the steps looking out at the yard and the memorial. She wished he would go ahead and say whatever he had to say and get it over with.

"Obituaries are strange animals." He glanced at the picture between them.

"Take comfort that you'll be reunited with her in heaven," she said.

Dr. Flowers didn't say anything for a moment. Finally he said, "I came looking for you this morning."

"I know it's hard having me here in the middle of all this," she said.

"I came to apologize," Asa said, sounding as if it took some effort to say it.

She followed his gaze out to the memorial.

"I've behaved horribly," he said. "I hope you know it has nothing to do with you."

Unlike the other day, he sounded sincere, and there was a softness in his face she hadn't seen before. He smiled a genuine, apologetic smile, an embarrassed smile. Mitchell sometimes gave her the same smile after one of their arguments.

"I'm glad he's found someone as considerate and loving and resilient as you," he said. "Someone who will not only ignore my rants but will act in spite of them."

Wendy was caught off guard by his words.

"Mitchell's very lucky," he said.

"I'm the lucky one," she said. "But it's not me you should be apologizing to."

Dr. Flowers scratched his beard. "He has no interest in hearing from me."

"You'd be surprised," Wendy said. The breeze scattered leaves across the walk, and she hugged her bare legs. "Mitchell says you played a big role in him becoming an artist."

"He does?" he said, looking surprised.

"He says you encouraged him to draw and paint. He says you talked to him about artists, brought him books, and took him to museums and exhibits."

"I enjoyed it as much as he did," Dr. Flowers said. "Probably more."

Another breeze made her shiver. Chill bumps had come up on her arms and legs.

Dr. Flowers took off his jacket and put it over her shoulders. "Would you like some coffee? I made a pot."

They went inside, and he poured her a cup of coffee and set cream and sugar on the kitchen table. He refilled his own cup and joined her at the table when Sarah padded into the kitchen, yawning and wiping sleep out of her eyes.

"What was all that last night?" she said to her father. "You were a mess."

He got up and poured Sarah a mug of coffee.

"I had to literally put you to bed."

"If it's any consolation I have a sick hangover," he said.

"You were awful." Then she looked at Wendy. "I'm surprised you're willing to be in the same room with the man."

Me too, thought Wendy. Except, for her, it was never about Dr. Flowers and always about Mitchell.

Floorboards squeaked overhead. Water ran through the pipes, and a couple of minutes later Mitchell came into the kitchen in his worn Birkenstocks, faded jeans, and his MoMA t-shirt Wendy had given him for Christmas.

Mitchell scratched his head and frowned at the three of them as if this scene did not compute.

"Sleep okay?" Sarah asked. "I sure didn't."

He scowled at her. Then, without a word, got the orange juice carton out of the refrigerator and poured himself a glass.

Mitchell looked at Sarah, then at his father. "What's going on?"

"What do you mean?" Sarah said.

"Sitting around here having coffee, chatting like nothing's happened?"

"Mitchell," Wendy said. "Don't." She had a bad feeling the moment he came into the kitchen.

"Dad's apologized," Sarah said.

"That makes everything okay," he said.

"Mitchell," Wendy said.

"You said awful things last night." Mitchell stood over his father. "Our mother, your wife, has died, and you're not being much of a father."

For a moment everything seemed to stop. The furnace clanked on in the basement, and the heat ducts banged. Mitchell carefully set down the unfinished glass of orange juice as if it were a bomb that might go off. Then he walked out of the house.

"Mitchell?" Sarah called out on the porch. But Mitchell kept walking.

"Should I go after him?" Wendy wanted to get out of the house herself.

"I think that's a good idea," Dr. Flowers said quietly.

"I have a better idea." Sarah turned to her father.

Dr. Flowers shook his head. "All I'd do is get him more wound up."

Sarah folded her arms and raised an eyebrow at her father.

Dr. Flowers closed his eyes. "I don't even know where he went."

"The cemetery," Wendy said. Mitchell had taken Wendy over to Riverside yesterday to show her where his mother would be buried. Mitchell had sat down beside one of the trees near the gravesite and told her how he always felt at home in the cemetery, how he and Sarah and other neighborhood kids had played there.

"What'll I say?" Dr. Flowers asked. "I've never been good at fatherly advice," he said. "You of all people know that."

"Advice is not what Mitchell needs," Sarah said.

Looking resigned, Dr. Flowers went to get his jacket, and when he came back, Luna trotted up behind him.

"Take Luna with you," Wendy said, thinking the sweet old dog would be a good ambassador.

"This is no time to walk the dog," Dr. Flowers said impatiently.

"Wendy's right," Sarah said.

Wendy stood on the porch with Sarah as they watched Dr. Flowers disappear up the sidewalk with Luna.

"Should we go with him?" Wendy worried Mitchell might fly off the handle again.

"He has to do this on his own," Sarah said.

Wendy and Sarah went back inside and microwaved some muffins someone from the UU church had dropped by yesterday.

"I'm sorry I never met your mother." Wendy looked at the paper folded to the obituary and took a bite of the muffin.

"You would've loved her," Sarah said. "Funny, kind, smart, and the best listener." Sarah began to cry, and Wendy reached over and took Sarah's hand, feeling tears well in her own eyes.

CHAPTER 34

• • •

Asa, Saturday Morning

As Asa walked through the cemetery gates with Luna, hoping to find his son, he thought about what Wendy had said about Mitchell telling her about their museum visiting days. He was surprised Mitchell remembered those days.

One summer, when the children were in middle school, they had gone to California and explored Yosemite, hiked Muir Woods, visited General Sherman in the Sequoia National Forest, waded in the surf at Big Sur, and spent several days in San Francisco walking the city, riding the trolleys, riding bikes over the Golden Gate Bridge. One of the last days in San Francisco, Sarah came down with a bug. Betsy stayed in the hotel room with her, and Asa took Mitchell to a museum they had planned to visit. The de Young Museum was itself a work of art, with a glass tower that had a 360-degree view where they watched fog drift over the park and trees push up through the clouds.

Mitchell and Asa wandered through exhibits of paintings, sculpture, pottery, and photography from all over the world. Asa was making his way through the African exhibit when he lost track of Mitchell. He walked back through the whole exhibit but didn't see him. He was beside himself by the time he found a docent and asked if she'd seen an eleven-year-old boy in a black Sequoia National Park t-shirt. She led him across the hall where Mitchell sat on a bench in front of an immense painting of snow-capped mountains towering over a deep blue lake. Asa walked up to his son, prepared to scold him for wandering off. But Mitchell, so intent on the painting, hardly noticed him.

"Oh hey, Dad." He glanced at Asa then directed his gaze back to the painting. Asa had never seen such a rapt expression on his son's face, so he sat down beside him and studied the painting with him. The painting pulsed with color, motion, and light, and the longer Asa sat there, the more he felt as if he had entered the landscape with his son. He heard the pine trees whistle in the wind and the collective trickle of a thousand little creeks flowing down the frozen mountainside. He and Mitchell had entered their own place, having the mountain to themselves.

They learned the artist was Chiura Obata, a Japanese American landscape painter. When they were about to leave near the museum's closing time, Mitchell wanted to stop by the gift shop, where with his allowance he bought a poster of the Obata painting and a textile bead bracelet made by women in India for Sarah. As they rode the train back, Mitchell yawned and leaned his head against Asa's shoulder and fell asleep. Feeling the weight of his son's head on his shoulder, Asa watched the San Francisco neighborhoods pass and knew he would remember this day as a day he was allowed a glimpse of how deeply his son saw the world.

• • •

When they arrived at the grave, Asa found Regina on her knees arranging a mason jar of sunflowers beside the foot of the grave. The grave had already been dug and covered with a tarp. Luna trotted over to see Regina, who petted her. "How are you, Girl?"

"What are you doing here?" Asa asked. Just the sight of Regina upset him.

"Same reason as you I expect." She stood up. "I know it's easier for you to make me out as the villain in all of this, but you have to understand—it wasn't all me."

"Is that supposed to make me feel better?"

"No," Regina snapped. "I wanted to see where she'll be." She looked down at Luna sniffing around the grave. "And I imagine that's what Luna wants too."

Asa realized he had to get out of Regina's presence but then heard himself say, "Can you tell Luna this is where Betsy's going to be buried?"

Regina looked a little amused. "I already did. I get the sense that she likes the idea of Betsy being nearby. She sent an image of you and her standing by the grave."

"But she's going back to Chapel Hill with Sarah."

"I reminded her of that," Regina said.

"You yourself said it was better for Luna to go back with Sarah. As you say, I'm not all that great with animals."

"I agree. She should go back with Sarah," Regina said. "I've never seen you as an animal person. And while we're at it, I've never seen you as a people person either. I never thought you were particularly good for Betsy."

"That's a shitty thing to say to someone who just lost his wife."

Regina shrugged.

He almost went on to say some cutting things himself, but the anguished look on her face stopped him. She looked like he felt, and as hard as it was to admit, he had no control over who visited his wife's grave or, for that matter, who loved her or who his wife had loved. All of it was and always would be out of his control.

"I won't be at the memorial," she said.

As he watched her walk away, he knew she had told him that so he wouldn't worry. He also realized he'd interrupted Regina's own private memorial for Betsy.

As he watched her disappear over the hill, he remembered why he'd come here in the first place. Where was Mitchell? Maybe he'd doubled-back and was already home. Asa called Sarah and asked her to call him if Mitchell had come back there.

• • •

Halfway across the cemetery Luna began pulling in a different direction.

"We need to get back to the house," Asa said, but Luna pulled so hard he had no choice but to follow. She led him across the cemetery, down a steep hill, to a remote corner of Riverside with a few worn headstones and neglected graves at the edge of an immense stand of bamboo. A creek disappeared into one side of the bamboo and reappeared on the other.

Luna began to pull harder until they stood outside the thick bamboo towering over them, darkening the entire corner of the cemetery. He was tempted to let Luna go, but what was she after? A squirrel, a rabbit, something dangerous? A copperhead? He walked with her around the edge of the bamboo, and Luna pulled him down a little path. They came out into a small circular clearing, and Asa's heart stopped when he saw his son lying face up on a bed of bright yellow bamboo leaves, his arms splayed out, his head turned limply to the side, his eyes shut.

"Oh, God," Asa said. "Please, no."

Luna jerked the leash free and ran over to Mitchell, licking his face. Mitchell sat up, petting Luna. "Hey, Girl, where'd you come from . . . ?" Then he saw Asa standing over him.

Asa put his hand to his chest with relief. "You're okay then?"

Mitchell nodded, yawning.

"You sure?" He put his hands on Mitchell's arm and legs, needing to touch him. "You haven't taken anything or done something to yourself?"

"Dad, I'm not that kid anymore," Mitchell said impatiently pulling away.

A breeze rustled the bamboo leaves, a crow cawed somewhere nearby, and Asa became aware of the hum of crickets. He felt the old awkward silence creep back between him and his son.

"I'm sorry," Asa said.

"About?"

"How I've behaved."

Mitchell looked at him as if thinking about whether to say something. "You were terrible last night. Really terrible. In fact you've been pretty shitty this whole time."

"I know," Asa said, "I know." He looked up at the shimmering bamboo then back at his son. "You're missing your mom, and I haven't been acting like much of a father."

"That's the understatement of the year," Mitchell said, wiping something out of his eye.

"I'm sorry," Asa said. "I'm really sorry." He tried to put his arm around his son, but Mitchell pulled away.

"So, is it true? What you said last night about Mom?"

"I hate that I ever brought that up," Asa said.

"Was she having an affair?"

"I don't know."

"So what was all that about last night?"

"Me drinking way too much."

"You don't usually drink too much."

Shadows flew over them, a pair of crows landed nearby, and after cocking their heads at Asa and Mitchell, began strutting around the creek's edge.

"That night of the storm," Asa said, "a few hours before the tree fell, she told me she wanted to explore another relationship."

"What did she mean?"

"She meant a relationship with someone else."

"A romantic relationship?"

Asa nodded. "That's how I understood it."

The look on his son's face made Asa wonder if he had done the right thing telling him. "We're talking about Mom. How could that be?"

"I'm not the easiest person to live with," Asa said. "I think she got sick of me and my Silas Marner ways."

"I'm confused," Mitchell said.

"When I stop and think about it, really think about it, I don't know any couples who've been married as long as your mother and I've been married who haven't had hard times along the way." This, Asa thought, was true. "It seems like a bigger deal because she died in the middle of it."

Mitchell stroked Luna's side. She laid down between them and closed her eyes.

"I'm sure your mom and I would've gotten through whatever this was," Asa said. About this, Asa wasn't so sure.

Asa's phone rang and the crows took flight, cawing as they

flew away. Asa read the screen. "I didn't call your sister back." He answered the phone. "We found him and he's okay."

They walked back through the cemetery, Luna leading the way. They heard the cry of a hawk and looked up to see it gliding alone in the empty sky high above the cemetery.

CHAPTER 35

• • •

Sarah, Saturday Night

Rain tapped at the bedroom window as Sarah lay in bed reading *Reality Is Not What It Seems: The Journey to Quantum Gravity*, when her phone pinged with a text from Josh.

JOSH: How's it going?

Sighing, she reluctantly closed her book.

SARAH: Thanks for listening last night.
JOSH: I thought I would come to the funeral tomorrow.

Sarah felt her heart lurch. She had not anticipated this. It was out of character for him to offer something like that. As she thought over a reply, her thumbs hovered over her phone.

JOSH: If you want me to.

She still didn't respond.

JOSH: You there?
SARAH: It is such a long drive. You don't need to go to all that trouble. Besides, you said you hate funerals.
JOSH: I will come if you need me to.
SARAH: A lot of people will be here, people you don't know. I'll be busy and wouldn't be able to spend time with you anyway.

JOSH: No problem.

SARAH: What does "no problem" mean in this situation, Josh?

JOSH: Whatever you need it to mean.

Sarah's thumbs once again hovered over the keyboard.

JOSH: I can feel you thinking.

SARAH: Now isn't the time to discuss it.

JOSH: What?

SARAH: I'm having second thoughts.

There was a long pause as she stared at the phone, feeling her message land. She shouldn't have done this via text. That was cowardly. Her phone pinged.

JOSH: Is this about that fellowship thing?

SARAH: That fellowship thing is important to me. But it's not just about that. It's a symptom of a bigger problem.

JOSH: If it makes you feel better, I did google the fellowship, and I admit it's pretty impressive.

SARAH: Thank you for admitting that.

JOSH: That was sarcastic?

Sarah's thumbs ached to write more, but she refrained.

JOSH: You still there?

She didn't reply.

JOSH: Sarah?

SARAH: I don't want to be with you anymore.

Sarah waited, but Josh didn't reply. He was being nice offering to come to the funeral. But that's how he operated. He'd get nice just as she'd decide she'd had enough. He had a sixth sense of how much she could tolerate. Sarah cut out her light and was lying in bed, thinking about what had just happened. A simple sentence and it was over? Just like that? Who was she kidding.

JOSH: Does this mean you don't want me to come to the funeral?

Sarah started to write something but decided to reply with an emoji of a row of thumbs up, then silenced her phone and went back to her book.

CHAPTER 36

Asa, Later Saturday Night

Asa woke in the middle of night, unable to sleep. Downstairs he put the kettle on and, while he waited for the water to boil, sat beside Luna asleep in her bed, and opened the Enneagram book that had eyed him from his bedside table for several nights. He flipped through the worn pages of the chapter on Type Fours and found passages had been highlighted.

The kettle's whistle startled him. As he made tea and sat at the table, he noticed the framed photo on the cookbook bookshelf beside him. A photograph from their wedding, not one of the staged color photos taken by the official wedding photographer, but a black and white taken by an old college friend, who took several candid shots that afternoon. This one of Betsy and him in a square dance after the ceremony. Asa had his arm around Betsy's waist as couples turned together in a star. Betsy's hair streamed out behind her, and Asa's tie flew over his shoulder. They wore big smiles as the music sped up and the dancers turned faster. Asa could still feel the centrifugal force tugging her away but he held tight.

"Betsy," he said, setting the photo in front of him on the kitchen table. "I'm not sure I can do this without you."

In the basement, the furnace clicked on, followed by the

whoosh of flame and a boom of the ducts expanding as warm air filled the kitchen.

"As far as I can tell, the kids are coping," he said. "Sarah anyway, and I think Mitchell's okay."

The icemaker clattered in the refrigerator.

Sarah came into the kitchen, yawning. She wore a flannel robe he recognized as Betsy's and a pair of Betsy's bedroom slippers. "I thought I heard you talking to somebody."

She noticed the photo on the table. She picked it up and sat down beside Asa. "I've always liked this picture. You both look happy."

"We were," Asa said.

"I didn't know you sang at it," she said.

"She told you about that?"

"A song about magic?"

"'Do You Believe in Magic?'" he said. "The Lovin' Spoonful."

"She said you sang it to her in the middle of the driveway with everybody gathered around."

"I rehearsed that song for weeks, complete with dance steps." Then he sang softly, "*Do you believe in magic in a young girl's heart? How the music can free her whenever it starts.*"

"I wish I could've been there," Sarah said.

"You didn't miss anything."

"That's not what Mom said. She said she fell in love with you all over again, watching you make a fool of yourself in front of all those people."

Luna made a whimpering sound in her sleep, and Sarah sat down on the floor, petting her so she would wake up. "Bad dream, Girl?" She got up to make herself some tea. "How did you know Mom was the person you wanted to spend the rest of your life with?"

"I'm not sure we thought in such grand terms," he said.

She sat back down at the table with the mug warming her hands. "What attracted you to her?"

"She was smart and beautiful, and we liked a lot of the same things, although I'll never understand how she could like Billy Joel. Most important, we could make each other laugh. Marriage without a sense of humor would be a very grim life sentence. Why do you ask?" As soon as he spoke, a troubling thought crossed his mind. "You and Josh aren't considering . . . ?"

"Oh, God, no. In fact, I just broke up with him. I hope."

"When?" He sat up.

She looked at her watch. "Five hours ago."

Asa nearly said, *What a relief*, then thought of a thousand reasons he shouldn't, chief among them, Betsy was no longer around to give him that don't-say-it look. He began to understand he was parenting without a guardrail.

"I'm sorry," he said.

"You're not," she said. "You hated Josh."

"It's true I didn't like how he treated you, but I didn't know him well enough to hate him," he said. "Still, do you want to talk about it?"

"That was a question Mom would've asked."

He shrugged. "I'm trying."

She took another sip of her tea, then looked up at him. "It really doesn't take a Sherlock."

"Come again?"

"To figure out it was Regina," she said. "After that scene between you two in her office. Mom was really having an affair with her?"

Asa had to tread carefully. "It sounded like not a whole lot happened, but she was clear that she planned to *explore*—her word—another relationship."

The kitchen clock scratched out the time.

She reached across the table and took his hand. "It's hard for me to imagine Mom even thinking about anybody else."

A dark little familiar form streaked across the kitchen floor and disappeared under the stove. The last time he had seen the mouse Betsy was still alive.

"I don't understand how she could've been attracted to a woman," he said. "It makes me wonder if she was ever really attracted to me."

"Dad, dad, dad." Sarah shook her head.

"I know. I'm being true to my Type-Four-ness."

"So you *did* read the book," she said. "Of course Mom was attracted to you." Sarah held the wedding photo up to him. "Exhibit A. Notice the adoring way she's looking at you. I've seen her look at you that way a hundred times. Besides, it's not uncommon for people to be attracted to both sexes."

He sat up, a tightness in his chest. "Have you ever . . .?"

"Had a sexual relationship with a woman?" she asked. "No but I might if the right person came along."

Had his sweet, open, and talkative little girl grown into a woman he didn't know? "I had no idea," he said.

"How long have you been teaching?" Sarah asked. "Haven't you noticed that nowadays young people feel different about gender and sexual orientation than you and your generation?"

"You make me sound like I'm from a different epoch."

"You sort of are," she said. "My generation doesn't compartmentalize gender and sexual orientation as either/or, black or white. For us it's a matter of shades, gradations, inclinations, and, when it comes down to it, opportunities."

She sat back in her chair, looking at the wedding photograph. "I miss her so much." Her eyes glistened.

"Me too."

"Even with all this Regina weirdness?" she asked.

The mouse streaked out from under the stove. Luna pounced, but the mouse darted behind the refrigerator. Luna poked her nose around the bottom of the refrigerator, whining and scrabbling at it.

"This morning, finding Mitchell in the cemetery lying there like that," he said, looking at his daughter. "It scared me to death."

"Now you know how it feels," Sarah snapped. "Except you don't really. How could you? Why, over all these years, have you never asked me about that afternoon?"

Asa was caught off guard by his daughter's anger, and yet part of him wasn't. He'd been dreading this question for years, but now that it was out and he met his daughter's gaze, as unforgiving as it was, he felt an unexpected relief, a calm.

"Why, Dad?"

"I knew your mom had already talked to you about it." He heard just how lame he sounded.

"Why didn't *you* talk to me about it? You and me talk. At least we used to!"

Luna came over to Sarah, nudging her.

"Those were the most frightening minutes of my life," she said.

"Sarah," he said.

"I still have flashbacks of driving him to the ER." Her jaw flexed and her eyes glistened, and Luna put her paw on Sarah's arm.

Outside a screech owl began to call so close by it sounded like it was in the room with them.

"You have never acknowledged what that afternoon cost me." His daughter's voice cracked.

He reached for her hand, but she pulled it away. "There's no excuse. Absolutely none." Then he added. "I've been a terrible father."

"Oh no you don't," she said, pointing at him angrily. "This isn't about you."

"I can't imagine what it must have been like for you," he said.

"Terrifying," she said. "Fucking terrifying."

They sat a long time listening to the owl trill farther off now.

Sarah stood. "I'm going to bed. You should too. Tomorrow's going to be a long day."

Without another word she headed back upstairs with Luna at her heels. Asa listened to his daughter's footsteps cross the floor overhead and glanced at the wedding photograph.

This is so hard, Betsy. At least they're grown now and can take care of themselves. You were here for the most important part. Still, if I want us to remain a family, I'll need to step up my game.

"Oh, and Dad?"

Asa jumped as Sarah came back into the kitchen.

"Amanda from Videolife called today about an overdue movie."

"I completely forgot," he said. "What was the movie again?"

"*Carol*."

"I don't remember that movie," he said.

Sarah handed him a DVD case. "I found it on a shelf behind the TV," she said. "I guess Mom put it there."

When he saw the picture of Cate Blanchett and another familiar actress, Asa felt a twinge, remembering a rave review he'd read of the movie, describing what it was about. But he never watched it. Had Betsy watched it by herself or with someone else?

Sarah had gone back upstairs, and Asa was studying the photo on the DVD case when the mouse darted from under the refrigerator and disappeared into the living room.

Asa went down into the basement and found their ancient Havahart trap buried underneath some camping gear. His Atlanta apartment had, in addition to roaches, mice. Betsy couldn't stand killing the mice, so she bought a Havahart trap and released the mice in a field on her drive to work. When they moved to Asheville, they had no roaches, but a mouse family or two moved in most winters. It was Asa's job to catch them, and Betsy released them in the woods behind the school where she taught.

He set up the trap in the kitchen with a piece of cheddar balanced on the metal platform inside the dusty little cage. It took a couple of tries before he could balance it with the cage doors propped open, then he set it beside the stove. Luna sniffed it a long time as if she could smell every mouse that had passed through its little doors over the life of their marriage.

CHAPTER 37

• • •

Sarah, Fall 2014

Coming back from field hockey practice at the high school, Sarah turned onto their street, and her father drove right by, not seeing her. He looked preoccupied. She hoped there hadn't been more drama in the English department. When she pulled into their driveway, she found the front door open, usually a sign that her mother was in the vicinity. Her car wasn't in the drive, and besides, she was away at an all-day conference.

"Hey Brother, I'm home," Sarah hollered up the stairs as she set her hockey stick in the corner of the foyer. No answer. Probably lost in one dystopian world or another. How her brother could read with music blasting like that, she could never understand.

She clomped up the stairs on her way to her room but stopped in Mitchell's room first. She found him lying on his bed, his hands behind his head, staring up at the ceiling. His eyes were red. He was upset about something.

He sat up. "I didn't hear you come in."

"I wonder why," she said, turning down his stereo. "Are you okay?"

"Dad and I had a fight," he said.

"What about?"

"Mrs. Norris called . . ." He bit his lip.

"Not again."

He nodded. "My grades."

"Are they bad?"

He shrugged.

"How bad?"

He shook his head.

"How bad, Mitchell?"

"She told him I might be failing." He was quick to add, "But I'm not. I mean I won't. I told him I'd get my grades back up. I always do."

She just looked at him.

"What?" he said.

She understood the grim look on her father's face when he'd passed by her a minute ago.

"We had a big fight," he said, "and he took my laptop! Can you believe it?"

"I guess he wanted to get your attention," she said, not sure she'd ever seen her brother so worked up. "I sort of don't blame him."

"Whose side are you on anyway?" He lay back down and stared up at the ceiling. "It's going to be a lot harder around here when you go off to Chapel Hill. I'll be left alone with these people."

She didn't envy her brother who would end up being the last one at home.

"You can come visit me in Chapel Hill."

"That's another thing," he said. "I'm grounded."

She noticed a few pills on the floor and knelt down to pick them up.

"Your cleats reek," he said, waving his hand in front of his nose.

Then she glanced under his bed. "It's a mess under here." She pulled out several dusty socks, a pair of underwear, and an empty Tylenol bottle.

"Yeah," Mitchell said, watching her. "After all that with Dad I had a pretty mean headache."

The weird way her brother said it made her look up at him.

"What?" he said.

She looked at the bottle in her hand. The cold dread that clamped down on her heart wasn't like anything she'd ever felt. "What have you done?" She held up the bottle.

He looked away.

She grabbed his arm. "When did you take them? I need to know."

"A minute ago, after Dad left. Just before you got here."

"The whole bottle?"

He shrugged. "Whatever was in there. Pretty many."

"All of them?"

"Yeah," he said, in that singsongy way he used when he knew he'd done something stupid yet again. "If it makes you feel any better, my stomach really hurts."

"Get up," she said, motioning him to stand up.

"Those cleats really do reek," he said.

"Shut up!" She pulled him up off his bed.

"What are you doing?" He tried to pull loose, but she kept her grip tight as she hurried with him downstairs and out to the car.

"Have you lost your mind?" He shouted. "Where are you taking me?" he asked as she slammed his passenger door shut.

With her heart pounding, she backed her car up, screeched down Montford Avenue, and raced through downtown, running half a dozen lights and causing more than a few drivers to lay on their horns.

"Sis, slow down, you're going to get us killed." He braced himself on the dashboard.

It was a blur to Sarah, the minutes from the moment she had understood what her brother had done and how little time they had, to when she swerved into the entrance of St. Joseph's Hospital ER. She led her brother inside, told the admissions nurse he swallowed an entire bottle of Tylenol, and handed her the empty bottle. The next thing Sarah knew the nurse whisked Mitchell down a hall, with him looking back at her a couple of times before they disappeared around a corner. She had a premonition that it would be the last time she saw him alive. She sank down in a chair on the edge of the waiting room, and after taking a moment to gather herself, she called her parents. Her dad didn't answer, but she left him a message. He would be in class. She was relieved when her mom answered. She'd just gotten out of her conference in Hendersonville. Half an hour later she hurried into the ER waiting room.

Sarah hugged her and in a trembling voice started to explain everything that happened when a short dark woman in a lab coat came up to them and identified herself as Dr. Sarkar. She told them that Mitchell had had his stomach pumped and been given activated charcoal and seemed to be doing fine.

"Your daughter's quick action saved your son's life," she said, "or at the very least saved him from serious liver damage." She told them she wanted to keep Mitchell overnight in the psych ward for observation, and the social worker from the unit would want to meet with the family before they left the hospital tonight.

As the doctor walked back down the hall, her mother leaned over to Sarah and whispered, "What is that horrendous smell?"

Sarah blanched. "My cleats." For the first time since they came into the ER it registered to Sarah that she was still in her field hockey clothes. "They're pretty funky."

"They need to be incinerated," her mother said scowling. "I'm pretty sure I smelled them all the way out in the parking lot."

They looked at each other wide-eyed, then laughed, causing the handful of people in the waiting room to turn in their direction.

• • •

Leaving Mitchell at the hospital to stay overnight, Asa had followed Betsy and Sarah in their cars back home. When they reached the house and went inside, Asa saw how exhausted Sarah looked.

Betsy put her arm around her. "Can I make you some supper, honey?"

"No thanks, Mom. I think I'll go to bed. Good night, y'all." With that she went upstairs.

Hearing her close her door, Asa turned to Betsy and said in a low voice, "It's a miracle she came home from practice when she did. Like someone was watching over him."

"Well, it sure wasn't you!" Betsy said.

"You're blaming me for this?" he said, surprised.

The expression on Betsy's face was one of incredulity. "How many times have we been over this? You agreed that you wouldn't engage with Mitchell when he was angry or when you were angry, because it never ends well."

Caught off guard by the intensity of his wife's anger, Asa was at a loss for words. Finally he said, "It just felt like he was testing us, and as his father, I needed to put my foot down."

She shook her head and sighed.

"What?"

She lowered her voice, glancing upstairs. "You wound him up this afternoon, our son the unknown quantity, and left him for Sarah to come home to and deal with."

Asa felt anger well up in him, but then an inexplicable calm settled over him as if Betsy was upset with someone else.

"And another thing," she said, "the way you described to the social worker how it all unfolded, you would've thought you were an innocent bystander."

"All I did was give him a consequence," he said. "Something any father would've done."

She looked at him. "How is it after all these years you still don't get it?"

And with that Betsy snapped the harness on Luna and led her out the door, down their front walk, and down the street. As he watched them disappear, Asa felt at a loss all over again. He almost went after them, but he didn't like leaving Sarah alone in the house right after he'd left Mitchell alone in the house, which had not ended well. So instead he went back inside and walked upstairs and knocked on Sarah's door. He started to open the door but decided against it. "You okay in there?" he called through the door.

"Yeah, I'm okay."

But she didn't say "Come in" like she usually did.

"Need anything?" he asked.

"I'm okay, Dad."

He found himself face-to-face with a poster of Madame Marie Curie, holding up a bottle of radium.

"I'm sorry you had to deal with Mitchell," he said through the door. "I should've been there."

"Good night." She said it flatly, like she was tired of talking. He waited, but she didn't say anything else. He went back downstairs, put the kettle on, set out two cups with tea bags, adding cream and sugar. When the kettle finally whistled, he poured the water over the tea bags. A moment later it thundered outside and then began to rain. Asa grabbed an umbrella to go after Betsy and Luna, but he'd just gotten out the front door when they came trotting up the front walk and Asa held the door for them.

"That came out of nowhere, didn't it, Girl?" Betsy said as Luna shook herself off in the foyer. Betsy sat at the table as Asa filled their cups with hot water from the kettle. She warmed her hand on her cup. "Did you talk to Sarah?"

"Just through the door. She sounded tired."

They sat across from each other, drinking their tea and not talking. Outside the rain drummed on the roof and a car passed down the street.

Asa felt a pang of desperation. He leaned over to Betsy, taking her hand. "I'm sorry," he said. "I really messed up. I could've handled that whole thing so much better. I shouldn't have reacted the way I did." He looked up at her. "Truth is I was scared, Betsy. I know that's no excuse."

She looked him in the eyes. “I was scared too.” She pulled her hand gently away. “But I can’t talk about this tonight.” With that, she picked up her cup and put it in the sink.

“Thanks for the tea,” she said and headed upstairs, leaving Asa sitting alone at the table and holding his cup between his hands, a cup that had lost its warmth.

CHAPTER 38

Wendy, Sunday Morning

Wendy's phone rang at 7:00 in the morning. It could only be one person. "Morning Dad," she said, sitting up in bed. He was up early every morning, reading his devotional. Today he would be preparing his sermon.

"I'll be praying for Mitchell and his family today." Her father had met Mitchell at Furman a couple of times and liked him. "I'll be praying for you to be there for the Flowerses in their time of need. After all, you certainly know your way around funerals."

"Thanks for calling." She yawned and glanced out the window, seeing it was overcast and drizzling. "I guess you're not going hiking." Her father almost always went on a hike on Sunday afternoons.

"It's supposed to clear up," he said. "We're planning to hike the Jones Gap Trail this afternoon with another couple from church."

Her father had been dating a woman for two years. Wendy found her to be a little too glitzy for her taste, but she grew to appreciate her. With her father dating, Wendy began to feel freer. No longer did she feel obligated to visit him as much as she had. Perhaps that was why she fell in love with Mitchell when she did.

"I have to get ready for church," he said, "I'll be thinking of you and Mitchell's family today."

"Dad, before you go," she heard herself say. "I wanted to tell you about something I'm dealing with." She paused, screwing up her nerve. "It's about school. I may have to drop out for a little while, come home and get a job."

"Why on earth would you do that?!"

With her heart pounding, she told him that the school had cut back on her scholarship money by several thousand dollars.

"I know you're not in a position to help financially, but I wanted you to know what's going on. I hope you're not disappointed in me."

Her father didn't say anything.

"I'm really sorry," she said.

"Exactly how much are we talking about?" he said.

"Nearly twenty thousand," she said.

He whistled. "Lord," he said.

"I'd move home for a year and work till I've saved up enough to finish school." She felt sick saying it, but it seemed the only way.

He didn't reply. She could practically hear him thinking it over. "Why didn't you come to me sooner?"

"I thought I could up my hours in the dining hall and the library but realized that wouldn't begin to put a dent in the increase."

"Let's get one thing straight here," he said sounding stern.

"Yes sir." She braced herself.

"The only thing that disappoints me is that you'd believe I'd be disappointed in you. Not a day goes by I don't thank the Lord for sending me such a daughter. And while the idea of having you home for a year is more appealing to me than you'll ever know, we can't have that, can we? You'd be miserable, and you'd make me miserable."

"What are you saying Dad?"

"What about we take out a loan?" he said.

"But you always said loans were . . ."

"I know what I said, but an old dog can learn new tricks. A woman in my church helped her son get a federal student loan. They're low interest, and you can pay them back over time. What about we see if we can get one of those to help cover the bill, and we'll pay it back together."

A sense of relief washed over her.

"Why don't I come over to the college next week and we can meet with the financial aid director and see if we can work out a plan. We need you good and graduated by the time the Guggenheim and the Louvre come knocking."

After he'd hung up, she hopped out of bed, made herself a cup of hot tea, and sat at the breakfast table, gathering herself. Nothing was figured out yet of course, but she already felt lighter, unaware till now just how worried she'd been.

Suddenly hungry and seeing no sign over at the Flowerses' house, she poured herself a bowl of cereal, turned on the radio, and with her mind freed, thought about Mitchell and what his family would be going through today. Her father was right. She knew her way around funerals. As the daughter of a minister, Wendy had probably attended more funerals than most people had in a lifetime. Even as a child she'd noticed everyone dealt with death in their own way. If the deceased was old, the funeral often felt more like a fond farewell. If the deceased was younger, it felt sad, and yet there were often moments of humor as well.

As she ate her cereal, she thought about the other category of funerals her father had presided over. Sudden deaths. People who'd died of a heart attack or stroke or in a car accident or something else out of the blue, like Mrs. Flowers's death. In these cases, the mourners had had no time to say good-bye. No time to ask questions. No time to get things straight. No time to apologize or forgive or confront. These deaths, her father would say, often left the bereaved trapped in their hurt or anger or resentment and, at the same time, kept them walled off from their grief. He said the only way to work through the death of a loved one was to abide in your grief. He said accepting this kind of grief, the kind of grief that turned your world upside down and made you question everything, was the closest we ever came to knowing God.

CHAPTER 39

• • •

Asa, Winter 2015

In the weeks after Mitchell's suicide attempt, Betsy had been angry and cold toward Asa and spoke little to him. Coming home from school in the evening, something Asa had always looked forward to, became onerous. The family sat down to dinner as always, but instead of their usual conversations, it was quiet and stilted. Everyone seemed shaken by what had happened. And if there was conversation, most of it was between Betsy and Sarah and sometimes Mitchell. Asa usually didn't take part. After dinner, Mitchell and Sarah would start on the dishes, but Asa, who preferred being alone to enduring the awkwardness and blame he sensed from his family, would offer to wash the dishes so that Mitchell and Sarah could join Betsy for an after-dinner walk with Luna.

With evenings at home feeling oppressive, Asa began to stay later at school to do his grading and class prep in his office. Also, once a week, he had a poetry workshop he met in the evenings to give nontraditional students, most of whom had day jobs, a chance to take his class. It had always been his favorite class. The nontraditional students were older and more mature and generally better company. They had returned to school for different reasons—some to improve their writing and some to finish degrees, while others had all the degrees they needed but came for the sheer stimulation. All of them loved the reading assignments, all came to class prepared, and all wholeheartedly took part in discussions. There was none of the painful extraction of comments often needed with the younger students. The other thing about nontraditional students was that they had more life experience and, because of it, had more to write about. It also often made them feel more like friends to Asa.

His current poetry workshop had several strong writers, and as a group, they jelled—so much so that at the end of the class period they often wanted to continue their discussions and started going out for a beer after class. They invited Asa to join them, but socializing with students took a different kind of energy, a shift in gears that he didn't always have that late in the day. Also, by that time he was ready to get home to his wife and family. But given the chilly reception he received most evenings at home, his present class, with all its laughter and animated discussion, was tempting to go out with. What made it more tempting was Eliza Bennett, a nontraditional student he'd had in classes over several semesters. In her mid-forties and divorced, she was very funny, very smart, a good poet, and, as archaic as it sounded, easy on the eyes. She often came by before class to discuss a poem or two she'd been working on, and their conversations would drift to all kinds of subjects, including her growing up on a tobacco farm up in Madison County, working as a stockbroker on Wall Street, and then finally joining the Peace Corp in El Salvador. She was a good listener, a good person to talk to.

During the week Asa found himself looking forward to the evening workshop and especially looking forward to seeing Eliza. One evening after the workshop, he was locking up his office when Eliza came by and invited him to come out with the class. He tried to beg off, but given it was Eliza doing the asking, he didn't try that hard. In fact, he was aware of his heart beating a little faster. He ended up going with the class to Three Sheets, a bar downtown, and forgot himself in the best of ways. Even after most everyone else had left, he and Eliza and one other student continued to talk for another good hour.

The whole next week his thoughts kept circling back to Eliza, flattered as he was that such an interesting woman would want to spend time with him. Against his better judgment, he joined the class at Three Sheets a second time and stayed late again, so late that he and Eliza shut the place down. It was all a little heady. It made him uncomfortable but excited at the same time. He felt younger, and the world appeared a little brighter.

By the third week, the uncomfortableness had begun to outweigh whatever excitement he felt. He didn't go out with the workshop that third night. The next night, still in no hurry to get home, he stayed late in his office to put a dent in the stack of poems his highly motivated poetry workshop had cranked out. That was one of the few drawbacks of teaching nontraditional students, not only did they write but they wrote a lot.

"Still at it?"

He looked up and saw Eliza standing in his office doorway. Now he knew who she reminded him of. Ingrid Bergman. As he gathered his wits, he couldn't remember her ever dropping by on any night other than class night.

"Mind if I come in?" she said.

"Of course not." He motioned to the chair across from his desk.

She came in and sat down, but not before closing his office door, something students didn't usually do unless they wanted to talk about something personal.

"We missed you at Three Sheets last night," she said, sitting in the chair.

"Mysteriously, the more poems I read, the higher the stack grows," he said.

"That's because you give such detailed notes," she said.

"Sorry I couldn't make it," he said.

"That's why I'm here," she said. "Thought maybe we could make up for it."

He smiled, assuming she meant next week after class. He'd have plenty of time to manufacture an excuse by then.

"Looks like you could use a break." She nodded at the stack of poems.

"You mean now?" He panicked.

"Might be nice," she said. "A reward of sorts for all your hard work."

"Just you and me?"

"If you're tired of Three Sheets, we could go back to my place." She said it so matter-of-factly it totally disarmed him.

She kept her eyes on his, and now his heart was really pounding. Ingrid Bergman or not, she was a very attractive woman. He'd always thought so. This feeling. What was it? A thrilling respite, a lifting of gloom from the otherwise past grim weeks at home? Just having her attention had made him feel twenty years younger. *You only live once*, he told himself and, deciding to throw caution to the wind, looked her in the eye and said, "I'm married."

A door slammed shut somewhere down the hall.

"I know," she said, "You wear a wedding ring."

He fingered the simple gold band Betsy had slipped onto his finger in her parents' garden that November afternoon decades ago, a ring he'd worn for decades and that felt no less part of his hand than his fingers.

"I was hoping it was camouflage," she said.

He smiled.

"You can't blame a girl for trying," she said.

"I'm worried I misled you," he said. "I find you very attractive. But as corny as it may sound, I love my wife." Although at present, he wasn't at all sure how his wife felt about him.

"It doesn't sound corny," she said.

"I'm not cut out for subterfuge," he said.

"Some of us aren't," she said.

She slid a few paperclipped sheets out of her backpack and handed them to him. "In that case, I'll chuck a few more poems onto your pile and let you get back to work." There wasn't a hint of anger or resentment in her tone.

"I look forward to reading them." As her footsteps faded down the hall, he slid the poems into his satchel, cut out his office light, and headed home to whatever awaited him.

• • •

Asa found Betsy in the kitchen sipping on a glass of wine and reading, or rather rereading, *Brown Girl Dreaming*, a novel in poems that she assigned her classes each year, and one Asa had read a few times himself, set as it was in his hometown. Luna got up from her bed and greeted him. He petted her and then took down a wineglass and poured himself a glass from the bottle on the kitchen counter.

"What smells so good?" he asked. He spotted a dish wrapped in tinfoil sitting on the stovetop. He went over and inspected it. "I can't remember the last time you made quiche."

"Me either," she said, looking up from her book. "And I didn't make this one."

"Sarah?" Occasionally Sarah would be inspired to make a nice dinner for the family.

"When I came home today," Betsy said, "there was a big mess in the kitchen, and Mitchell was in the middle of it, all mittened up and sliding this beautiful quiche out of the oven."

"Mitchell cooked dinner?" Asa got a fork out of the silverware drawer and took a bite. He looked at Betsy. "It's good."

She nodded to the wooden bowl on the counter. "There's also a spinach salad."

"What gives?"

"You know what I think?" she said, looking at him over her reading glasses.

"He's feeling better," he said.

She nodded.

Ever since he was a small boy Mitchell's level of creativity had been a reliable emotional barometer. When Mitchell was making things, whether drawing or painting or shaping clay or making up board games or designing his own potholders or lanyards or weavings, it reflected their son's engagement with the world, his happiness. Even though he wasn't a big cook, he went about cooking like he might any other art, immersing himself in the process, making a big mess and rendering something delicious. Asa had recognized this in his son very early on because Asa himself experienced the same feeling whenever his writing was going well.

"You've been getting home late." Betsy set her book on the table.

"It's been easier to do my schoolwork at my office," he said, hoping to change the subject. "Where is everybody?"

"Upstairs in their rooms doing homework."

Upstairs safe in their rooms, Asa thought.

"You have that poetry class on Thursday nights," Betsy said. "But it seems like you've been getting back later than you usually do."

He told her that the class was such a good class and their discussions so animated that they'd been continuing their discussions at Three Sheets and that they invited him to come along.

"That was nice of them," she said.

"I thought it might be fun."

"And was it?"

He told her he enjoyed talking to the students outside of class and that he enjoyed one student in particular, a woman he'd taught in a number of classes.

"A woman?" She looked at him as if she'd heard something in his voice.

"In fact, she came by my office tonight, asking if I'd like to go out for a drink."

"By yourselves?"

"I told her I couldn't go. I told her I was married."

She took another sip of her wine. "I'm glad you finally got around to telling her."

"She knows I'm married," he said. "I talk about you and the kids a lot in my classes. No one could take a class with me and not know I'm married."

"Should I be worried about this student?" she asked.

"She's been a pleasant distraction. I was just flattered by her attention."

She looked at him, biting her lip. "What's going on, Asa?"

"It was just nice to know she enjoyed my company." And then he added, "Not everybody seems to these days."

She shook her head in such a way that he knew she was pissed. *Good job, Asa. You already had her angry with this whole Mitchell nightmare.*

"I haven't been great company lately," she said, "I know."

"I don't blame you," he said. "I really screwed up with Mitchell."

"Yes, you did," she said, "but I don't think it's fair of me to hang on to my resentment. I wasn't around that afternoon. You were alone with him. Something needed to be done, and so you acted. You did what you thought was best, and the more I think about it, the more I wonder if I wouldn't have taken his laptop too, or worse."

"I doubt it," he said.

"Mitchell can be infuriating."

Asa wasn't sure he'd ever heard her say that. "You're not mad at me?" he asked.

The kettle whistled, and he got up and turned it off.

"I have to admit that I'm a little ticked that you've been flirting with this woman," she said. Then tears came to her eyes.

"It didn't mean anything, Betsy," he said. "I swear."

She waved her hand as if she wasn't even thinking about it anymore. "Just the idea of losing one of our children . . ." Her face crumbled, and he sat down on the couch beside her, putting his arm around her and pulling her against him.

"It scared me too," he said, and it had, frightening him to his core. And they sat there listening to the stove tick with heat.

CHAPTER 40

Asa, Sunday Afternoon

Half an hour before the memorial service, the minister had family members gather in the church basement where the Sunday school classes met. Asa hadn't been here since the kids had attended classes. The place smelled like finger paint and Play Doh.

Besides Sarah and Mitchell and Wendy, Asa's sister and her three college-age boys had come and brought Asa's dad with them. His father used a cane now. Asa hadn't seen him in a while and was struck by how frail he appeared.

He took Asa's hand, in his still-vigorous grip. "I wish I could say something wise or at the very least consoling. When your mother died, there was nothing for it except time. I miss her like crazy."

When Betsy's mother arrived, she'd been so agitated all she could do was hug the children and hug him. Finally, she said, "The first time she brought you to visit I knew you were the one. I'd never seen her look at anyone the way she looked at you."

Her words surprised Asa. Never had she spoken to him in such a way.

"It's a balm to know I'll be joining her in Heaven." She took his hand. "And I hope, if you get right with the Lord, you'll be able to join us."

Ever since Asa and Betsy had first married, Betsy's mother had been concerned for the status of Asa's soul. He'd never understood the logistics of being saved. For one thing he didn't see why Betsy's mother wasn't worried about her own daughter's soul since Betsy was Buddhist, openly declared she wasn't Christian, and adamantly did not believe in Jesus.

"Once saved always saved," Betsy explained in a conversation they'd had early in their marriage.

"You're kidding."

"It's a Baptist thing," she said.

"Even though you're no longer a Christian, you can waltz into Heaven no questions asked because when you were a teenage, stoned Jesus freak you got saved?"

"Bingo," she said.

"What about me?" he asked.

"You, my friend, are going to burn in hell."

"That sucks," he said.

"It's never too late," she said.

"To be saved?"

"Another Baptist thing," she said.

"I think I prefer hellfire and damnation to spending eternity with your mother."

"Hmm," Betsy said rubbing her chin. "You may have a point."

• • •

In his white ministerial robe, Mark Ward gripped the lectern as he addressed the congregation. The sanctuary was so packed an overflow crowd had backed out into the assembly hall, listening to the service over the intercom. Asa sat on the front row with Sarah, Mitchell, Wendy, and Betsy's mother. When the family had first filed upstairs into the sanctuary, Asa was floored by the size of the crowd.

Many mourners he knew, many he didn't. Betsy's connections had gone far and wide. He recognized her teacher friends. Some of those he knew better than others. The school superintendent, a tall, imposing woman who had guided the school system through treacherous waters, had come. Community leaders. Two pews of his colleagues from the lit department, including Charles and Jillian and of course Melda.

Ben sat with Linda right behind the family. Behind Ben sat Jack and Norma Hodges. A few rows off to the side sat Henry and his wife, Clare.

As the minister spoke, Asa watched his children. Sarah, smiling and teary-eyed, met Mark's eyes. Mitchell kept his gaze to the floor but had held Wendy's hand ever since they'd walked into the sanctuary. The presence of so many people come to pay their respects amplified everything Asa felt—his loss, his children's loss, his confusion about Betsy, the betrayal. His chest began to ache in such a searing way, he wondered if he was having a heart attack.

"Dad?" Sarah leaned over and whispered to him, "You okay? You're as white as a ghost."

Asa looked into his daughter's swollen eyes, saw his job, and took her hand. "I'm fine, Honey. Are you okay?" She leaned against his shoulder.

Asa put his arm around her and looked beside her where Mitchell sat in remote mode, but Wendy kept him grounded, his hand in her lap.

As Mark talked about all Betsy had done as a teacher, a church member, a mother, and a wife, the pain in Asa's chest faded, opening to a deeper devastation, a devastation he and his family would have no choice but to somehow live with.

Mark asked anyone who wanted to say a few words to come up and light a candle. Asa had always liked this part of the memorials. A good dozen people came down to the front and lined up. The first in line turned out to be none other than Quentin. Why did this not surprise Asa? With a studied grave expression, Quentin lit a candle and placed it in the big circular candleholder in front of the altar. He stepped up to the podium, looked out over the sanctuary, then gripped the podium like a preacher and even rocked back on his heels as he said, "Dear friends, Betsy meant so much to so many of us students. For us, she was a committed teacher, a trusted mentor, and a dear friend, and our hearts go out to Dr. Flowers and his family for their terrible loss." Then he seemed to be done, and Asa thought, *Hallelujah*. But in the way of all things Quentin, the boy seemed to think better of it, stepped back up to the mic, and said, "There's no doubt in my mind as I'm sure there's no doubt in the mind of anyone here who knew her, that above all else Betsy was and always will be the real thing."

Asa noticed people cutting their eyes at each other. Perhaps they were wondering what Asa himself was wondering. What exactly was the real thing? Had Quentin just compared his wife to Coca-Cola? As Quentin returned to his seat, Asa thought what a Herculean effort this boy was making to worm a better grade out of him when all he'd ever had to do was the work.

With Quentin back in his seat, Asa relaxed, and the testimonials continued as people lit candles and said kind and touching things about his wife. He wasn't sure how much time had passed when he looked up and saw Regina join the line of the few left to speak, her expression grim yet determined. She'd said she wasn't coming. Maybe his rudeness at the cemetery had pissed her off. Asa's heart pounded. What was she going to say for the whole world to hear? He started to get up to talk to her. But a firm hand on his shoulder kept him in his seat. Ben leaned forward and whispered, "You'll only make it worse."

The line of speakers in front of Regina dwindled from four, to three, to two, to finally just one. Heather Greene, his wife's close teacher friend, lit a candle and talked about how she'd never known a teacher to love her students more. She talked about the day, a day Asa and a lot of people in the community would never forget, when a student strung out on OxyContin pulled a gun from his knapsack in the middle of class and held it to his head. She told how Betsy had never flinched, how she calmly dismissed the class and then sat with the boy, talking to him in the kindest, gentlest voice for twenty minutes, until he gave her the gun.

"That was the sort of teacher she was, the sort of person," Heather Greene said and then returned to her seat. There was a long silence as the story settled on the mourners.

Then it was Regina's turn. She took a candle, but when she tried to hold it to the flame, she shook so badly the minster had to steady her hand. When it was finally lit, she stared at the candle so long people began to whisper. The minister started to step up, but Regina seemed to recover herself. She looked out over the sanctuary. "I think I was the last person to talk to Betsy. My phone rang, and it was her. We sometimes talked at night. Anyway, it must've been only minutes before the tree fell."

The sanctuary grew so quiet Asa could hear his heart slamming against his rib cage. Why hadn't she said anything to him about having talked to Betsy that very night?

Regina went on to say that they'd been friends for years, ever since she began to care for Luna, their family dog. "Betsy loved animals," she said, "and connected with them, and because of that, Betsy and I connected, and I saw sides of her a lot of people probably never did." She looked straight at Asa.

"What is she doing?" Asa whispered to Sarah.

"That last night when my phone rang, those last minutes I had with her," Regina said, "she talked about her favorite subject—her children, who she loved so much and was so proud of." She smiled at Sarah and Mitchell.

"And the last thing we talked about was marriage."

Asa thought that was a strange way to put it, making it sound like marriage was a condition.

And here, Regina lost her smile, and her voice went flat. She said that Betsy had often said that Asa had been a supportive partner and a good father to their children. And that there was no one she would rather spend her life with. Regina delivered this in a tone that could only be described as reluctant, as if what she said had caused her real physical pain to speak.

When she finished, instead of going back to her seat, Regina walked up the aisle and disappeared through the doorway. Asa went after her and caught her heading back to her car.

"Regina."

She didn't stop, so he called again. "Regina!"

She whirled around, palming tears from her eyes. "What?"

"What you said in there, is that true?" he asked. "Did she really say those things?"

She shook her head, which Asa saw wasn't denial but disbelief. "Aren't you going to leave me a shred of anything, Asa?" She glared at him with contempt, then turned and hurried out to the street.

Asa was watching her drive away when Ben came out of the church. "You just walked out of your wife's memorial service. Get back in there. Your family needs you."

Asa hurried inside and joined his family on the front pew.

"We have to read, Dad," Sarah whispered.

"Read?" Asa asked.

"The poems Mom wanted read," she said. "I gave you a copy the other day."

"You did?"

Without missing a beat, she handed him a manilla folder. "Like we talked about the other night. I'll read first. Mitchell reads second, and Dad, you read last."

"We talked about it?" Asa said.

"You were drunk," Mitchell whispered.

Mark got up. "Now we'll hear a few of Betsy's favorite poems."

Sarah went up to the podium and read "'Hope' is the thing with feathers," Betsy's favorite Emily Dickinson poem, and then Mitchell read a funny Billy Collins poem. Asa was amazed how well his son read, pausing at all the right places, letting laughter in, milking the crowd.

Then Sarah nudged Asa.

Asa went to the podium, opened the manila folder, pulled out a single sheet, and as soon as he read the title was undone. He looked up at Sarah, thinking there'd been a mistake. She nodded for him to continue. He raised his eyes to the sea of faces. He cleared his throat. "The title of this poem is 'All Our Belonging,' something I wrote in our early days.

"Books pulled off their shelves, prints askew—our
favorite, Chagall's
Flying Lovers half crumpled on the couch, and your cherished vase—
a wedding present—shoved off the mantel, shards
scattered.
We'd been robbed.

In the living room a half-eaten pear placed carefully
in the middle of the floor, a taunt, a weird still-life
signature.
Your jewelry box spilled onto our bed. Earrings,
bracelets, and rings
spread out on your grandmother's crazy quilt. As you
inventoried . . ."

Suddenly all Asa could see was the branch through his wife's heart, and his own words went swimming across the page. He was lost. He had never felt so lost. He looked up helplessly at all the people waiting. Then Sarah was beside him, and Mitchell on the other side, and flanked by his children, Asa found his voice:

". . . As you inventoried,
I did reconnaissance. Frenetic paw prints circled the
kitchen sink.
I reached for my yellowed Boy Scout handbook, its
faded chart
of animal prints. Rocky. The name we gave to the
raccoon we glimpsed
sometimes in the woods beside the old house. I leaned
over

to pick up the pear and found scat beneath the couch. In bed that night
you said Rocky's visit was a blessing, a reminder of our belonging.
'You mean belongings,' I said, and you answered 'Belonging, singular
but plural. Apart but together. What we have. In each other.'

I stared out the window at what was left of the moon. You went on
to sleep. I put my hand on the flat of your back, feeling you
breathe until I couldn't keep my eyes open and followed you
into our own little patch of woods, where, it turns out, we're all we ever need."

They returned to their seats, Mitchell holding Asa's arm as they stepped down, as if he sensed how unsteady his father felt.

Mark asked the congregation to stand and sing "Simple Gifts," one of Betsy's favorites. Asa stood between his children, joining in the congregation's raised voices. As they sang, the sanctuary lightened and darkened, lightened and darkened. Through the skylight, rain clouds were breaking up.

CHAPTER 41

Sarah, Sunday Afternoon

As the sanctuary emptied, Sarah was surprised to see Josh in coat and tie coming toward her. "Wow, your mother must've been famous. That was quite a crowd." He hugged her.

Sarah pulled away. "I thought I was pretty clear last night."

"I know I shouldn't have come," he said in the same singsong tone as "my bad."

"I don't have time for you right now," she said. "The family's going over to the graveside in a little bit."

"I brought you something," he said.

"You do know I'm coming back to Chapel Hill tomorrow?" she said. "Couldn't it have waited?"

"This morning I remembered that I forgot to bring in your mail while you were gone. I went over to your place and found the mailbox crammed with flyers and junk mail mostly, but I did find this." He reached inside his coat, took out an envelope, and handed it to her with a bit of a flourish. "I thought you might want this today of all days."

She looked at the envelope and with a pang recognized her mother's neat, even handwriting, the handwriting of a schoolteacher. It was addressed to Sarah.

"She mailed it on Tuesday." He pointed to the postmark.

The last day they talked, she thought. The last day she was alive.

"It might not be anything, but I felt like getting out of Chapel Hill, and with today being the funeral and all, I thought you might like to have something from your mother."

"You drove all the way over here to deliver this?"

"And to see how you were."

"That was very thoughtful." She pressed his hand and looked him in the eye. She didn't know what she was feeling. "Thank you. I wish I had more time right now, but I don't."

"That's okay," he said. "I think I'll head back. Weather seems to be improving. See you at school." He leaned over and kissed her cheek.

As she watched him walk away, she thought maybe she was wrong about him, maybe she should give him a second chance. He had good qualities. She sat down in the empty sanctuary and carefully opened the envelope, then slid out the card. It was a watercolor of a squirrel holding a cup of tea, and the steam from the tea formed a heart above the squirrel's head. Sarah remembered when her mother had bought this card at a little store downtown. In fact, she had liked it so much, she bought several.

Betsy opened the card:

My Dear Sweet Physics Girl,

I'm still buzzing with your news and had to write even though we just talked. To say I'm proud of you doesn't begin to cover it. You've worked so hard for so long. You deserve this fellowship. Do you know that? You need to know that. Sometimes I'm not sure you do.

Sarah looked up from reading and blinked away a tear.

You talk about how few women physics students there are, and how at times you feel isolated and unsupported in the department. Yet you've just received this prestigious honor. You don't let them stop you. You don't let them hold you back. I've always loved that about you.

Which brings me to Josh. Don't waste another minute on that boy. When I was your age, I knew boys like Josh, insecure boys not comfortable with their girlfriends' successes. I realized soon enough I didn't have time for that nonsense, and neither do you. To quote your favorite book when you were a little girl, "Oh the places you'll go!"

Including Copenhagen!

Be thinking if you want pecan or pumpkin pie for Thanksgiving? Heck, we'll have both to celebrate!

Love,
Mom

Someone cleared their throat and Sarah looked up to see Josh standing over her.

"I thought you'd gone," she said, closing the card.

"I started wondering what was in her note. Not that it's any of my business. I just wondered if whatever it said was good for you to get today?"

"Yes," she said, emphatically. "It was very good to get now. Thank you so much for bringing it. That was a long way for you to drive."

He nodded and just stood there, clearly expecting something more. This was the thing about Josh whenever he did anything nice for her. He expected thanks in triplicate so that by the time he extracted enough thanks to satisfy his ego, whatever kind thing he'd done had been wrung of all its kindness.

He started to leave but then turned around. "I could stay if it would help."

"It wouldn't," Sarah said, losing patience. Then said in a softer tone, "Thank you for the offer, but I need to get over to the cemetery. I'll see you back in Chapel Hill."

So, with shoulders slumped, he walked out, leaving her alone in the sanctuary, where she sat transfixed for a few moments, watching the bare trees sway in the great windows overhead.

CHAPTER 42

Asa, Sunday Afternoon

After the memorial service, the sky cleared to a deep blue, but the temperature plunged, so the mourners, not being dressed for it, headed for the warmth of their cars. The private graveside ceremony, intended for family only, was cut short. It was too cold and the grave itself too difficult to access for Asa's father, so the only mourners present were Asa, Sarah, Mitchell, Wendy, and Betsy's mother.

How strange to think of Betsy inside the simple pine casket. The funeral tent over the casket flapped in the cold breeze. He hoped Betsy was wearing a coat. Mark gave a eulogy they couldn't hear. Their minister had never been the best at projecting, and being outdoors on a windy day, his words scattered across the cemetery.

Asa's thoughts went back to a balmy summer night twenty-five years ago. It had been around midnight when he and Betsy had climbed the locked gate, carrying a blanket and a bottle of champagne, then made their way to the beautiful little spot they'd chosen for their gravesites. Asa worried they might get caught. Betsy, who never met a rule she wouldn't break, insisted that the gravesite was so secluded no one would see them, not to mention that it was the middle of the night, and no one was around anyway.

"I can think of better places to celebrate," he said.

"Don't be such a stick in the mud," she said.

"I come from a long line of sticks in the mud," he said. "It's in my DNA."

They spread the blanket out on the grass, then Asa popped the cork on the champagne. He looked around to see if anyone could've heard. Betsy was right, not a soul anywhere. The little hill and the trees made it feel as private as a room. He handed her the opened bottle, which she raised and said, "To a long and happy life," then took a swig, wiped her mouth with her sleeve, and handed the bottle back. They passed the bottle back and forth, taking swigs and discussing their disbelief that earlier in the day, they'd actually bought a house.

"It feels so grown up," she said.

"So domestic," he said.

"You make it sound like a bad thing," she said.

"Not at all," he said. "Domestic is a good thing. Domestic is sweet and homey. Domestic is another word for nothing left to lose."

"I don't think that's how the song goes," she said.

"I'm already a little tipsy." He kissed her.

"You're such a lightweight." She kissed him back.

He began unbuttoning her blouse when the voice of God spoke, "What's going on here?"

"Shit!" Betsy clutched her blouse closed.

A middle-aged man in a security guard uniform stood over them, shining a flashlight.

"It's all right, sir," said Asa. "We're part owners."

"Owners?"

"Of the cemetery," Betsy said. "We've purchased a double plot, big enough for the both of us."

"And we're celebrating," Asa said.

"Also, we closed on a house today," Betsy said.

The security guard aimed his flashlight away from them, so it wasn't in their eyes. "I have to say, that's a new one. I guess congratulations are in order then." Then he added. "You are the most mature late-night trespassers I've encountered. Mostly it's high schoolers. How'd you get in?"

"Climbed," Asa said.

"I understand why you two feel you have some stake now in Riverside Cemetery, since you've made this investment," he said. "However, it's not a timeshare. To spend the night here, you have to meet one basic criteria, and I can safely report, neither of you meets that."

He aimed his flashlight on the half-empty champagne bottle. "Also, it's illegal to consume alcoholic beverages in the cemetery."

The guard tapped his flashlight against his hip like he was thinking. "Let's do this," he said. "I'm going to finish my rounds, and I'd appreciate it if y'all packed up in the next little bit and went home to your newly purchased abode where all the activities you've undertaken here can be freely pursued without legal consequence."

"Of course, sir," Asa said.

"I'm assuming since you climbed in you can climb out?"

"Absolutely, sir," Asa said.

They watched the man's flashlight disappear across the cemetery, reflecting off the headstones. Asa started packing up, but when he looked over at Betsy, his wife had taken off her blouse and her bra and was stepping out of her jeans.

"What are you doing?" he said. "You heard the guy. He wants us to leave."

"He has to say that," she said, "because that's his job, but note he didn't confiscate the champagne."

"Maybe he forgot it."

"Or maybe he wanted us to stay here and finish it."

She sat down on the blanket and raised the champagne bottle to her lips. "Take off your clothes."

"What if he comes back?"

"Take off your clothes."

He looked across the dark cemetery and could now barely see the guard's flashlight on the far side. Against his better judgment, Asa took off his shirt and sat down beside his wife who handed him the bottle. He took a long swig.

"Now the pants," she said, taking a drink from the bottle.

"You know how nervous this makes me?" He slid out of his pants.

She handed him the champagne bottle, and he took a big swallow.

He handed the bottle back to her. "We're going to be thrown in the clink."

"He won't come back. He said as much."

"I didn't hear him say anything along those lines."

She was right; he didn't come back, and as they finished off the bottle, Asa felt a warming wooziness all through his body. He kissed Betsy, then ran his hands over her smooth shoulders and breasts. After they made love, they wrapped up in the blanket and lay listening to the raucous song of the crickets and the katydids.

"I wonder what it's like to be dead," Betsy asked.

"What brought that up?"

"Well, we are in the middle of a cemetery."

"I subscribe to the School of Uncle Cleve."

"Uncle Cleve?"

"My great-great uncle," he said. "When I was a little boy, he used to tell me death was nothing to be afraid of, that it was like going to sleep and never waking up."

A warm breeze blew through the big pine tree over them, and a screech owl tittered somewhere above.

"Do you believe in The Hereafter?" she asked.

"Why are you getting all theological on me?" He leaned on his elbow.

"I realized that I don't know what my husband believes."

"What do you believe?" he asked.

"I believe in The Hereafter or some sort of hereafter," she said. "Not a place really and not some kind of permanent family reunion either."

"Talk about Hell," he said.

"More of a spiritual thing," she said, "a kind of convening of essences."

"Like at the end of *Ghost* when Patrick Swayze walks off into the ether?"

"No, not like *Ghost*." Then she paused. "Maybe a little like *Ghost*, like *Ghost* without the schmaltzy music and the melodrama."

"Hey, I liked that movie," he said.

"More like *Ghost* if Martin Scorsese made it," she said. "Or maybe Spielberg or even Woody Allen . . ."

* * *

A frigid wind blew the flowers off the coffin and Asa started to go after them, but then a tent stake snapped loose and another and the next thing they knew the whole tent was tumbling across the cemetery as if it had taken on a life of its own.

As they watched the funeral director and his assistant scramble after the tent, Betsy's mother said, "My daughter was always big on dramatic exits."

CHAPTER 43

Wendy, Sunday Night

After the reception Mitchell and Sarah washed dishes while Wendy and Norma put food away. Jack and Ben carried the folding chairs down into the basement. Wendy wasn't sure how many had come, but it had been wall-to-wall people, and more spilling onto the front porch and into the yard. Mrs. Flowers had been loved, and the turnout must've warmed Mitchell's and Sarah's hearts. Mitchell actually mingled, shook hands, and even hugged people.

After Ben and the Hodges had gone home, Wendy sat at the kitchen table with Mitchell's family, sipping hot tea and listening to the crackle of the fire in the woodstove Dr. Flowers had stoked. Everyone looked exhausted from the long day. After a little while Wendy said good night and went out to the studio.

Trying to linger in her last night alone before returning to Furman, Wendy put on her long t-shirt and sat up for a little while listening to the radio. Mitchell would be coming over any minute. He would want to spend the night, and even though she was tired, she would let him, because who could deny such a boy on the night of his mother's funeral? Unable to keep her eyes open, she went on to bed. She had just fallen asleep when the buzz of her phone woke her.

A text from Mitchell: "Thank you for everything you did today. Thank you for getting me through this. See you in the morning."

This surprised her. How grown up of him. Or maybe he was just tired. Either way she was relieved to be able to go to bed.

"See you in the morning," she wrote.

A long moment passed, and she assumed he'd gone to bed, but then her phone buzzed again. "I love you," he'd written.

She typed out "I love you and God does too," let her finger hover over the send button, then pressed it.

CHAPTER 44

Asa, Monday Afternoon

Asa and Sarah helped Wendy and Mitchell load up Wendy's car with leftover reception food.

"Thank you for having me," Wendy said. "I hope I didn't get underfoot."

Asa took the girl's hands in his, then looking into her green eyes, said, "Thank you."

Then Mitchell gave Asa a perfunctory hug, the first hug his son had given him since Asa's drunken disaster of a night when he'd gone after Wendy.

"Good-bye, Girl." Mitchell knelt beside Luna and buried his nose in her fur, petting her. "You're taking her back to school with you?" Mitchell looked at his sister.

"Dad thinks she'll be happier with me," Sarah said. "I'm dubious."

After they saw Mitchell and Wendy off, Sarah and Asa packed up her car. As they loaded Luna's bed and her bag of dry food, her food and water bowls into Sarah's Volvo, Luna stood watching, looking confused. When it was time to leave, Sarah called Luna to the car and patted the seat for her to jump up. Luna didn't budge.

"Come on, Girl," Sarah said.

"Come on, Luna," Asa said in a stern voice.

"She doesn't want to go, Dad."

Asa gently led her by her collar to the car, helped her into the passenger seat where she always sat, and closed the door.

Sarah hugged Asa. "It's all so sad," she said.

He wiped a tear on her cheek with his thumb. "Are you okay to drive back?"

She nodded and reminded him she would be back at Thanksgiving. Asa stood in the driveway until Sarah's Volvo disappeared around the corner. He turned around, facing the house. How exposed it looked, how vulnerable without the tree.

"Everybody gone?" A gravelly voice called from the next yard. It was Jack Hodges, who'd been raking leaves.

"The kids had to get back to school," Asa called back.

"They've grown up, haven't they?" Jack leaned on the rake. "Was that Mitchell's girlfriend?"

"Wendy," Asa said.

Jack nodded, looking like he wanted to say something more but didn't know what.

"I'll let you get back to it," Asa said.

"I guess they aren't going to rake themselves. Now that'd be a trick, wouldn't it?"

Asa started back to the house.

"Asa?" Jack called. "If you need anything, Norma and I are here. We mean that. We really do. From the bottom of our hearts. If you need anything at all."

As he started inside, he noticed the mailbox wedged full of what he knew would be sympathy cards. He carried them inside and set them on the kitchen table but didn't open them. He noticed at the back of the notes, where the mail deliverer always placed junk mail, the position of least importance, a letter from AARP. Addressed to him, it was an offer for term life insurance.

He boiled water and made himself a cup of tea. He sat there, listening to the rhythmic strokes of his neighbor raking. So this was what people talked about: Not till the funeral was over and family and friends had returned to their own lives did grief, seeing it had you all to itself, pull up a chair and make itself at home.

He stared at the cup of tea in front of him. Had he made that? He picked it up and took a sip. It was cold. Just how long had he been sitting here?

CHAPTER 45

• • •

Sarah, Monday Afternoon

Sarah had driven a few miles out of town when Luna, sitting in the passenger's seat, began to whine. "It's all right, Girl," Sarah reached over and petted her. "You'll like Chapel Hill." A lot of Sarah's friends had dogs.

They drove for several more miles and were outside of Black Mountain when Luna began to whine and scratch frantically at her window. Sarah wondered if Luna had figured out that they weren't just running an errand.

"Calm down, Girl. It's going to be all right. We'll be back here in a few weeks." Luna continued to scratch at the window, then jumped into the back seat, scratching frantically at the rear windows.

"It's okay, Girl," Sarah said.

Luna started to retch, not a good sign with Luna, who was easily carsick.

"Do I need to pull over?"

Luna retched again as Sarah took the exit that wound down to Highway 9, a two-lane highway. Sarah pulled off to the side of the road, opened the car door, and was reaching for Luna's leash when Luna jumped out, ran into the grass, and threw up. Sarah noticed dark clouds up ahead, an afternoon storm.

When it seemed Luna was finished, Sarah held the car door

open and called for her to get back in. "Okay, Girl, we have a long way to go still."

Luna looked at Sarah as if she was thinking something over. Sarah walked toward her with the leash, but Luna trotted away, along the side of the road, away from the car and back toward Asheville.

"Luna!" Sarah shouted, but Luna didn't so much as glance back. If anything, she seemed to pick up her pace. Worried Luna might get hit, Sarah, still carrying the leash, ran after her.

Luckily the road wasn't busy, but it was narrow and every now and then a car or two would pass going sixty-five miles an hour, coming within a couple of feet of Luna. Sarah shouted for Luna, but either she didn't hear her over the traffic or she ignored her. At one point a long tractor trailer passed within a foot of them, its air horn blasting. This caused Luna to run faster, and Sarah tripped on a bottle on the side of the road and stumbled, falling hard on her hands and knees in the gravel. When she picked herself up, Luna was nowhere in sight. Lightning flashed in the distance, followed by thunder.

Sarah kept running in the direction Luna had headed and hollered her name every now and then. Every bend she came around, Sarah worried she would find Luna hit. Once Sarah had run for several minutes with no sign of the dog anywhere and thunder rumbling louder, she started to turn around.

That's when she saw an old Chevrolet van parked on the edge of a field, its flashers blinking. As she came up to the van, she noticed that a Confederate flag covered the rear window and a rear bumper sticker read *I'll give up my gun when they pry it from my cold dead fingers*. There were other decals of skulls, antlers, and guns of all sorts. One big decal said, *Armed Redneck Inside!*

Not having a great feeling about this van, she started to turn around but then heard Luna's bark. Cautiously, she walked around to the side of the van, where she found a long-haired man in a camo t-shirt and overalls sitting in the open side door, holding Luna by her collar.

"Luna!" Sarah hurried over and hugged her neck. She looked at the man. "Thank you so much for catching her."

"You're lucky I seen her when I did or she might've got hit after that asshole blasted his horn and scared us all to Kingdom Come."

"Thank you so much," Sarah said, putting Luna's leash on her.

The man seemed to be studying Luna. "She got wolf in her?"

"She was found wandering a field with a few other starving puppies, no mother in sight."

"I'm confident she's got wolf in her," he said. "I once had a dog that was part wolf. Wound up nearly killing a fellow, who I have to say had it coming."

Sarah became aware of a set of yellow eyes watching her from the depths of the van. A chill went up her spine. She cleared her throat and smiled. "We better get going," she said. "Thanks again!"

"You need a ride back to your Volvo?"

Sarah got a very uneasy feeling. Her car was nearly a mile back down the road. How did he know she was driving a Volvo?

A bolt of lightning tore across the sky, the thunder shook the ground. The man indicated her skinned-up hands.

"You're bleeding," he said.

"It's nothing." She wanted to get Luna and herself the hell out of there.

The man went inside his van, and Sarah considered running

for it, but before she could, he came back with a box of wipes. "Here, clean yourself up. I'll hold onto her." He took Luna's leash so Sarah could wipe the dried blood from her hands and arms.

It was about that time that, with Sarah's heart slamming against her ribs, a large dark form emerged from inside the van. A cat, she realized as it sauntered into the light of day, but not just any cat. This was without a doubt the biggest, fattest, roughest looking cat she had ever laid eyes on.

"This is Claude," he said. "He's been my traveling companion for God knows how long." He looked toward the cat as if it had spoken. "Twelve years, you say?"

Smelling of fish, Claude rubbed his immense girth against Sarah's legs, while Luna, who had never met a cat she wouldn't chase, did not make a move or emit a sound or do the least little thing that somehow might attract Claude's attention.

Sarah looked closer at Claude's face. "Is he missing an eye?" She had already noticed he had a big chunk missing out of one ear.

"Lost it in a fight a few years back," the man said. "But you should've seen the other cat, what was left of it anyways."

Lightning crackled and a few drops of rain started to fall.

"We have to get back home," Sarah said. "Thank you again for catching Luna." Not waiting for him to answer, she and Luna headed back toward the road as the rain fell harder. But it wasn't any time before the van pulled up next to her.

"It's not safe for y'all to walk this highway," he said, speaking to her through his open window. "Especially in this rain. Folks can't see you."

As if to underscore his point, a truck carrying caged chickens looking miserable in the rain, passed within a whisper of them, blasting his horn.

"I'll drive y'all back to your car."

"I appreciate it, but we can walk."

"Listen here, I'm no psychopath, and even if I was, which let me underscore I am not, do you think your Luna here wouldn't rip out my throat before I could touch a hair on your head? That's the thing about dogs with wolf in 'em. You have no idea what they'll do till they do it. Y'all get in the van before you end up on a buzzard's plate."

Sarah didn't have any confidence that Luna would protect her in such a situation, but she believed this man believed that. It was coming down in sheets and wasn't far back to the car. A short ride. She started to climb into the passenger's seat.

"That's Claude's seat," he said. "He likes to ride shotgun."

Sarah and Luna sat in the back seat, as the man ran around and slid the van door shut then got back in the driver's seat. The rain came down so hard the world blurred, so they sat there, the rain drumming on the roof of the van. She glanced furtively around the inside of the van, not a gun or a knife or an angry bumper sticker anywhere in sight. Instead, the walls were covered in beautiful color photos. Nature scenes from all over the country it seemed. "Who took these?" she asked.

"Claude and I like to visit national parks." He pulled out onto the highway. "All in all, I think we seen thirty-six." He turned his head toward the cat as if the cat had spoken. "Claude says thirty-eight."

"Wow!" Sarah said, looking at the cat.

"In the spring we went out to Utah." The man pointed to a

group of pictures. "We saw Zion and Bryce Canyon and Arches." There were jaw-dropping photos of twisting canyons, delicate arches, sheer mountains and ridges, spires and buttes, all of it cast in red otherworldly rock.

"Claude thought Arches was a little overrated, but he can be particular."

The more she looked at the photos, the more remarkable she realized they were. These were nearly *National Geographic* quality. She became suspicious that he hadn't taken them at all. That was until she started noticing in the foreground of almost every one of them a one-eyed cat scowling in the general direction of the camera.

Sarah had just begun to take in what amounted to a tiny gallery inside the van when the rain abruptly stopped and the clouds parted. The man drove them down the road to the Volvo.

"Thank you again," Sarah said, feeling no small relief as she and Luna climbed out of the van. "Good-bye, Claude." She reached over to pet the cat, but Claude hissed, baring his sizeable teeth, and Sarah jerked her hand back.

The man looked at Claude and nodded. "Claude apologizes and says he's not in a good place right now."

After Sarah got Luna in the car and pulled away, she double-checked now and then to make sure the Chevrolet van wasn't in her rearview mirror.

• • •

Asa heard the old Volvo's clattery engine in the distance and hurried outside to see Sarah pull into the drive. Sarah had barely gotten out of the car when Luna jumped out, ran up the front walk, and sat down right beside him.

"You're wet, Girl," he said petting Luna. Sarah looked pretty soaked herself, her hair hanging down and her clothes clinging to her. "What on earth happened?"

"We got rained on," she said, "Let me change out of these, and maybe you can towel off Luna."

Asa dried Luna, and then made them a pot of tea. When Sarah came back down in dry clothes, they sat at the breakfast table and drank tea and ate homemade oatmeal cookies a neighbor had brought over.

Sarah took a sip of her tea. "We've had an adventure." She told him about Luna's escape, about her own tumble on the shoulder of the road, and about the redneck Ansel Adams who saved the day.

"I'm not sure how wise it was to get in his van," Asa said.

"The whole thing felt like I had stepped into some eerie Gothic story." She sighed. "Anyway, the long and short of it is Luna has made it abundantly clear that she has no intention of leaving this house, the house she's known all her life, nor does she intend to leave you, the man who brought her home from the shelter that day fifteen years ago."

Asa knelt down beside Luna and petted her, looking into the old dog's tired eyes. Then he stood back up, assessing his daughter.

"Are you still driving back to Chapel Hill this afternoon?"

"I thought I would," she said, "since I'm packed and everything's in the car, and I've got class tomorrow."

"You better get on the road. I don't want you getting back late."

"It's okay if Luna stays?" Sarah asked.

"Luna and I will deal," he said.

After Sarah left, Asa carried Luna's bed into the kitchen where it always had been, with Luna following right behind him. The moment Asa set it down Luna curled up in it as if to say, *I'm not going anywhere.*

Asa sat down beside her on the floor, petting her a long time. "Okay, Girl, we can miss her together."

CHAPTER 46

• • •

Asa, a Month After the Memorial

Asa walked Luna down the street heading out on what had become their nightly walk. He passed Jack and Norma's house and could see the couple through their side kitchen window, eating supper at their little nook in the semidark, their faces bathed in blue light. Fifty years they had been married. He and Betsy had gone over one evening last spring for a sweet little anniversary celebration with the neighbors.

Asa and Luna continued through the neighborhood. The night lit up by a full moon, or at least appeared full. What would he do without Betsy to tell him whether a moon was full?

He had been thinking about the Enneagram book, something he read about Fours holding onto their hurt and negative feelings. He thought about what Regina said at the memorial, what Betsy told her that last night on the phone, right before the tree fell. That couldn't have been easy for Regina to say before the crowd of mourners. He flashed back to last spring when he and Betsy had gone on one of their weekend getaways.

They had gone to Bryson City, a small town two hours west of Asheville, at the foot of the Great Smoky Mountains. When they arrived at the Airbnb, a cabin tucked back in a wooded meadow a few miles outside of town, they had just climbed out of the car when dogs began to bark nearby, a lot of dogs.

Through a screen of pine trees, they could make out a large dog kennel with what must've been a good dozen or more dogs in it. The dogs looked healthy and well cared for, but as Asa and Betsy returned to the car to get their bags, the barking didn't let up.

"They'll stop after a while," Betsy said.

After looking around, Asa found a key under a brick that, judging from the number of roly-poly bugs that had taken up residence underneath it, hadn't been moved in some time. After Asa unlocked the front door, he couldn't budge it. It seemed swollen shut. With some pushing and shoving, it finally popped open. They peered into the cabin, dark as a cave. Asa flipped a switch, and an overhead fluorescent light buzzed and flickered on, revealing a sad little kitchen, its windows covered in heavy floral curtains, giving the place a funereal vibe. The place reeked of air freshener. Asa managed to pull back some of the curtains, allowing enough daylight to reveal cobwebs.

He picked up his bag and started to walk out.

"Where are you going?" Betsy asked.

"We can't stay here."

"I showed you pictures weeks ago," she said, "and you said it looked okay."

"Those pictures were taken twenty years ago, and I recall there weren't any inside. And the description hadn't included anything about being cheek to jowl with a *One Hundred and One Dalmatians*."

"It's only two nights," she said, "and most of the time we'll be out hiking." Betsy had a high tolerance for sketchy accommodations, but her tolerance had gotten higher since they began paying for Mitchell's college.

"Besides," she said, "we've already paid for it."

"How much?"

"Two hundred and fifty dollars for two nights, a good deal in the tourist season."

The dogs began barking louder than before, and some howled.

"Really?" he said.

She pulled out a chair and sat at the kitchen table, wiping away mouse droppings with the back of her hand. "I'm so tired of this," she said. "We make plans, you say a place looks fine, and then we get there and you freak out. A place is either too hot, too stuffy, too noisy, smelly, too whatever."

"I admit I can be picky," he said.

"You're not just picky, you're high maintenance," she said.

"Come on, Betsy," he said. "Look around." He swatted at a cobweb floating directly over his head. "Miss Havisham wouldn't put up with this."

She glared at him. "What do you want to do?"

He felt irritated with her for being unreasonable and irritated with himself for not being sure if maybe she was right. He did have a history of bugging out of places.

"I know it's not very nice," she said. "But can't we just make the best of it?"

"I'm not staying here," he said. "It's depressing."

She shook her head. "I go to so much trouble to find a nice place for us to stay, to find a place you're willing to stay, and nine times out of ten you do this."

"That's an exaggeration," he said.

"It's infuriating," she said.

"Maybe we should just go home." He regretted it as soon as he said it.

"Maybe so," she snapped.

They climbed into the car, which got the dogs barking again, and Asa drove them back to the main road. Betsy sat in the passenger's seat, arms crossed, staring out the window.

Asa felt anger, like an unwelcome passenger, sitting between them, and he knew he would have to get past it if he was going to salvage the weekend. "I apologize," he finally said. "I know you put a lot of thought into these plans, and I know I'm not an easy person even in the best of circumstances. However, I think, in this case, Airbnb has hit a new low. Dickens couldn't do that place justice."

They drove a little farther in silence.

After a few more minutes Asa said, "Call the woman and see if we can get our money back."

"Why would she give us our money back?" she said not looking at him.

"Maybe she's nice."

Betsy looked at him skeptically. "Are you kidding? Nobody's nice." After they had gone a little farther, she got out her phone and called the woman in California who owned the cabin. Betsy started out in a polite tone, saying that the accommodations weren't exactly what they had been looking for, and they would be most appreciative if she could possibly see her way to a refund.

"I'm sorry, but we don't do refunds," Asa heard the woman say.

"I see," Betsy said, as if she actually did see.

"I'm sorry," the woman said.

Betsy paused, then said, "Given the general state of the premises, including the layer of dust blanketing every surface, cobwebs worthy of Doctor Zhivago, and enough mouse droppings to sicken the entire East Coast with hantavirus, you might see your way to a refund."

There was a silence as if his wife's words were registering.

Finally the tinny voice over Betsy's phone said, "Sorry."

Betsy's bit her lip. "Did I mention the multihued mold flourishing in the shower stall or the incessant din of the dogs barking their heads off?"

Trying to keep his eye on the road, he sensed his wife losing patience. "Let me put it this way," her voice now full of fury. "If you don't refund our money, we will post a review that will not only make your head spin, it'll have the folks at Airbnb banning you from operating for the rest of your natural-born days. Also, we've taken upon ourselves to document your accommodations with photographs. Refund our money or say good-bye to the sweet little racket you have going, luring suckers like us out here to the sticks and ripping them off..."

Betsy looked at her screen. "She hung up on me."

"I can't think why," he said.

Then she looked out the window and said quietly, "Bitch."

They rode along a couple of miles, then he said, "I take it she's not giving us our money back?"

Betsy shook her head, but then she turned to him. "But boy did that feel good."

"I'm not sure I've ever seen you quite like that," he said. "Did you actually take pictures?" He hadn't seen her take out her phone there.

"I threw that in," she said, "to keep her worried."

A few more miles down the road he said, "So I guess we're headed home?"

She looked mystified. "Why would you think that?"

His stomach dropped. "You don't mean we're going back to that hellhole?"

"God, no," she said. "But I'll be damned if I'm going to let some scammer woman out in California ruin our weekend. Let's find some other place to stay."

Asa felt the mood in the car lighten. Seeing they were about to pass Bryson City, he veered off the highway and down into the little mountain town, a few blocks of stores and craft shops and cafés and restaurants. "Maybe there's somewhere here?"

He parked in an empty lot off Main Street, and she made a few calls and almost immediately found a place two blocks away. When they pulled up to the building, they saw it was an old motel but when they looked closer realized that it had been totally renovated with modern woodwork and iron sculpture. Inside, they found an open airy space. Two floors connected with a spiral staircase, high ceilings, and big windows flooding the rooms with light. The kitchen appeared brand new. There was a living room and a cozy breakfast nook.

"Can we afford this place?" he asked.

"Would you believe me if I told you, it's half as much as the place we just left?"

They went upstairs to check out the master bedroom with its four-post king-sized bed and big bathroom with a jacuzzi.

"I can't get over this place," Asa said.

But Betsy, who had plopped down on the bed, appeared to be feeling the mattress, pressing down on it and frowning. "Uh oh," she said.

"What is it?" he asked, feeling that old dread.

She pressed down on the mattress. "I don't know if we can stay here."

"What?" he asked. He felt around on the bed where she was pressing. "I don't feel anything."

But she kept feeling the spot. "I think there might be a pea under the mattress."

Then he got the joke. "You know yourself that place was vile. I mean and all that you said to that woman."

"It was awful," she said. "Truly."

"And you have to admit we're in a much better place now."

"I'm glad we didn't stay there," she said. She got up and looked out the window.

"But?" he said.

"Let's go for a walk."

They went on a short two-mile walk along the winding Tuckasegee River, and the walk seemed to clear the air between them. They came back, took showers, and dressed. Betsy slipped on a dress he recognized as one he bought her a couple of years ago at a thrift shop. The red print cotton dress reminded him of something she might've worn when they were first together. A little old-timey but fit her in such a way that it showed her figure. They walked down to the little Italian café Betsy had read about and had a wonderful dinner, splitting a bottle of Chianti.

It was a nice evening, the nicest they had had in a long time. Toward the end of dinner, Asa noticed a distracted look in Betsy's eye. The whole evening he had weighed the pros and cons of splitting the bottle of Chianti with her. It was a balancing act. Alcohol made his wife more amorous, but if she drank too much she could easily slip into her argumentative mode.

It wasn't long after he had noticed the change in his wife that she said, "About our fight this afternoon," and his heart sank. He should've known. This would take some time and could significantly diminish chances of lovemaking.

"I'm sorry," he said, hoping to nip it in the bud.

"What are you sorry about?" she asked.

He cleared his throat.

She narrowed her eyes at him. "You don't know what you're sorry about."

"I'm sorry about everything," he said.

"The thing about this afternoon and the thing about whenever we go to a new place, we hardly get to our destination before you announce we can't stay there. Your negativity wears me out," she said, "rejecting things outright before we've even had a chance to discuss them."

"I apologize, and I will try not to be so negative," he said.

"The truth is," she said—and he thought, *Oh God, there goes our night*—"in the end I think it can, at times, be a good thing."

He looked up. A good thing? What was a good thing? What had he missed?

"I've learned from you that it's not always bad to be picky," she said.

"You have?"

"I tend to accept what I'm presented without question, so I'm often dissatisfied, maybe even resentful. We would still be in that cabin if you hadn't insisted we leave. I would've let that woman get away with tricking us without so much as a peep. We certainly wouldn't have ended up in the place we are now, having a lovely dinner." She put her hand over his. "I've learned from you that sometimes we need to be a pain to get what we want."

"So I should be less negative, and you should be more of a pain."

When the waiter, a young guy, cleared their dishes, he asked, "Would you'uns like any dessert? We have a chocolate torte that's to die for." He spoke in a mountain accent Asa could've listened to all night.

Asa looked at his wife, who didn't get dessert very much anymore. "What do you think?"

"Sounds tempting," she said.

• • •

As Asa walked Luna down Montford Avenue, past the elaborate old homes, several already outlined with Christmas lights, he knew that Regina had told the truth at the funeral, even if it was begrudgingly, that Betsy had loved him. And in that same moment, he knew in a way he hadn't until now that she was gone. She had loved him, and she was gone.

He passed by the old elementary school building that he had always felt fondly toward. Both their children had attended there. He passed the convenience store when a familiar figure stepped out of the shadows. An elderly man had been panhandling here for as long as Asa could remember.

"How we doing tonight?" the man said. With his white beard and long hair and hat, he always reminded Asa of Walt Whitman.

"All right." Asa pulled out his wallet and handed the man a couple of dollar bills. Betsy had always made it a point to have money ready to give the man whenever they went on a walk. Sometimes she even dropped off canned goods or other food with him. She'd pieced together that the old man, like a lot of the people who hung around the convenience store, was probably a casualty of Montford's gentrification. A lot of people had been priced out of their homes due to the rising taxes or had been forced out by landlords who could now charge higher rent.

"Where's the missus?" the man asked. "Haven't seen her in a bit."

Asa looked into the man's rheumy eyes. "She's out of town."

"While the cat's away." The man laughed a phlegmy laugh. "You better behave yourself. She's one great lady. You don't want to lose her."

"No, I don't," Asa said.

"Have a good night," the man said.

Asa walked a couple more blocks, then turned around, and as he and Luna headed home, he noticed the moon had slid behind a bank of clouds, making them luminous.

Acknowledgments

I am grateful to novelist Abigail DeWitt, who has inspired and encouraged me through many of my novels, and to writer Sam Hodges, who's been reading and supporting my writing since undergrad days when he liked a story I wrote about fondu. Both Sam and Abigail tirelessly read and reread revisions of *The Marriage Bed*, helping me find my way through.

Eric Nelson, a poet and teacher, helped in many ways, including fleshing out my main character, Asa Flowers. Eric revised my heavy-handed attempt at a poem that appears later in the novel. Novelist Jessica Keener lifted my spirits, offered help, and gave me encouragement when I most needed it. Kathy Sheldon has given feedback and encouragement on all my novels, including *The Marriage Bed*. Sherrie Crow was an early reader of *The Marriage Bed*.

I couldn't be more indebted to my indefatigable agent, Joelle Delbourgo, who believed in *The Marriage Bed* and found it such a good home at Blair. My thorough and thoughtful and kind editor Robin Miura has helped make *The Marriage Bed* a much stronger novel. Publisher Lynn York has given me much appreciated encouragement and support.

I'm forever indebted to my wife, Connie, my first reader and my last reader, whose instincts in portraying the complexities of the human heart have helped me explore my characters in deeper ways. I would not be who I am without Connie, and neither would my books.

And I so appreciate the love and understanding my children, Max and Ruth, have shown me. In teaching me what it means to be a father, they have led me to the central theme of my writing—what it means to be a family.